**"Do you have any** [ ] **I found that child today?"**

Primed to go on the attack, Lane was caught off balance by Matt's salvo.

"Found?" she repeated. "How could I possibly know where you found her? Look, I enjoy having Cheyenne here at the market, but that doesn't give you the right to expect me to be responsible for her when she's not here."

"My mistake," Matt said icily. "I thought responsibility came with the territory."

"Territory?"

"With motherhood."

Her voice breaking in a falsetto, Lane squeaked, "You're telling me you're not Annie's father?"

"I'll grant the possibility you don't know who Cheyenne's father *is*," Matt said, outraged, "but you damn well know it's not me!"

## ABOUT THE AUTHOR

Jenny Loring lives in California's Sacramento
Valley with her husband, Roger, an attorney,
and has three grown children. She lived on a
farm as a child and thought that would make
an ideal setting for *Cheyenne Summer*. She had
"a ready-made hero" in former playboy Matt
Cheney, who was introduced in the closing
chapters of *Interlude*. "He seemed to be a
favorite with readers, who wanted to know
how he fared in his unlikely new position as
CEO of Cheney, McCrae. I must say, I was
curious myself. The only way I could find out
was to write him into *Cheyenne Summer*. To my
satisfaction, he fit right into the role of hero."

## Books by Jenny Loring

### HARLEQUIN SUPERROMANCE

74—A STRANGER'S KISS
129—THE RIGHT WOMAN
202—SCENES FROM A BALCONY
280—THE WHOLE TRUTH
388—INTERLUDE

# Cheyenne Summer

## JENNY LORING

# Harlequin Books

TORONTO • NEW YORK • LONDON
AMSTERDAM • PARIS • SYDNEY • HAMBURG
STOCKHOLM • ATHENS • TOKYO • MILAN
MADRID • WARSAW • BUDAPEST • AUCKLAND

Published August 1992

ISBN 0-373-70510-7

CHEYENNE SUMMER

Printed in U.S.A.

# PROLOGUE

IN THE GRAY of early dawn the man stopped rowing and let the boat ride on the rise and fall of its own wake, his muscles aching from the unaccustomed pull of the oars. His sensual mouth under cover of grizzled beard was drawn in a savage line. Red-rimmed eyes, windows of resentment, were heavy lidded from lack of sleep.

Looking up, he saw the ghostly outline of a large structure in the near distance, and a spurt of adrenaline brought new energy to his tired body.

He'd been drinking Scotch in a Manhattan bar around midnight, trying to figure out how he could still get his hands on all that money when the idea hit him. Within the hour he was headed out the Long Island Expressway in the van. Ten bucks to an all-night patrolman in Seahampton had bought him directions to what the cop called Fairchild Cottage on Pocket Cove. What the cop hadn't told him was that it was hidden on three sides by a high stone fence that had a gatehouse and a guarded gate. The only way to get a good look at the house without getting caught was to come in by water. It had taken him an hour to find a boat.

As he leaned on the oars, waiting for daylight, his gaze strayed, darting nervously into the shadows around him, then following the broad landscaped slope up from the water's edge to the huge three-story, three-winged building gradually taking shape at the crest as the darkness lifted.

The first rays of the morning sun touched its balconies. The man swore viciously. So this was the "cottage" she'd walked out on when she took off with him eight years ago!

A searing rage flared deep in his gut at the thought of the years wasted because she'd never let on she was the heiress to the goddamned mint and had an old man ready to cough up a hundred grand to get her back. If he'd known then, he'd have turned her over to Fairchild early on and pocketed the money instead of marrying her and having the kid. With that kind of bread, he could have bought the best promoter in the business to put Wolf and His Pack on the map. By now the band would have had its first Grammy.

Damn her! She always was a closemouthed bitch! Like the way she'd kept quiet about being pregnant until her belly got so big he'd have had to be blind not to see. He'd given her a belt in the chops, for all the good it did him. It was too late then for an abortion.

She'd written "Marigold Luna" on the marriage license application and let him think the name she went by was her real one. "Fairchild" hadn't meant diddly to him. How was he supposed to know her old man used hundred-dollar bills for toilet paper? He still wouldn't know Frances Fairchild was her given name if it hadn't been for her picture in *People* magazine. That article about all the missing teenage girls who'd run away from rich homes in the past ten years. More than seven years she'd been gone, and all that time her old man had had an offer out for a hundred grand to get her back. God, if he'd only known.

With that kind of money, you'd think even with the way she'd changed her looks and her name someone would have spotted her that first year when she was singing with the band. He would have caught on himself if he'd read the papers. Or maybe not. Those were the peyote years. Most of the time he'd been bombed out of his skull.

She'd taken the kid and been long gone before he saw the magazine, so the first thing he'd had to do was track her down. By the time he caught up with her she'd died and the kid was gone.

It looked as if he'd blown it. Then, last night in the bar, it had come to him about the kid.

The layout before him spelled money. Some of it by rights should be his. Hadn't he let the silly broad tag along with him all over the country? Hadn't he kept the guys from coming on to her and let her sing with the band? Fairchild was lucky his daughter hadn't run off with some dude that took advantage of her. The old man owed him, goddamn it!

He'd hop a plane to California this afternoon and make the Craddock dame tell him what she'd done with the kid. He'd get a photocopy of the death certificate to prove to Fairchild his daughter was dead and a birth certificate to show that the kid had been hers. If Fairchild had been offering that kind of bread for his daughter, it stood to reason he'd still pay out once he knew she'd left him a grandchild.

Turning the boat, he started across Gull Cove, staying near the shore, where he'd be hidden from early risers by foliage along the bank. A mile or so on his way he pulled into the shallows close to land, stepped out into the marshy water and set the stolen boat adrift.

Sinking to his knees in mud, he waded to the bank and scrambled up a low, wooded rise to the road. By the time he reached his van he'd made his plans.

First the Craddock woman, then the birth certificate and then the kid.

# CHAPTER ONE

*Cheyenne, Cheyenne, hop on my pony.*
*There's room here for two dear and*
*a-a-a-fter the cer-e-mo-ny...*

THE CLEAR, FLUTY child's voice floated on the Long Island breeze as Elaine Fielding stepped from her pickup at Fielding's Farm Market outside Seahampton that May morning. She stopped to listen, cocking her head.

*We'll both ride on....*

Looking about, Lane moved slowly away from her parking spot along the east side of the rustic wooden building. After a few steps she homed in on the old apple tree that overhung the enclosed multipurpose unit she called "the office," her eyes probing the cloud of pink and white blossoms that hid the tree branches. For a moment she saw nothing else.

The song stopped and a small voice called out, "If it's me you're looking for, I'm up here."

Shifting her focus, Lane found herself looking up at a pair of round, solemn blue eyes that seemed to be suspended among the blossoms like the Cheshire cat's grin. Her own eyes adjusted to the dappled light and saw a heart-shaped face as pink and white as the cloud of petals around it, fringed with flaxen bangs.

What in the world was a little girl doing in her apple tree?

"Well, hello!" Lane said. "Who are you?"

"Cheyenne." Then, as if in answer to something she saw in Lane's upturned face, she said, "*Cheyenne*. Like Cheyenne in the song, but you can call me Annie if you..." The word broke off on a shrill, rising squeal. The next second the face was gone.

Lane shook her head as if to banish an apparition, ready to doubt the whole improbable scene but for a thrashing about in the tree branches that sent showers of petals down around her.

In a moment a small towheaded, pigtailed girl dropped to the ground in front of her. She was dressed in a blue denim coverall and a Big Bird T-shirt and was clawing frantically at one arm. The look on her face threw Lane into mild panic. *Please, Lord, don't let her cry!*

"Are you hurt?" she asked cautiously.

The child let her hands drop, stuffing them in her coverall pockets. After a moment she pulled out one hand and held up her arm to show an angry red welt near the elbow.

"A bee bit me," she said in a shaky voice.

"Ooh! You poor kid," Lane murmured. "Didn't anyone ever tell you to stay out of trees in full bloom?"

There was no answer. Lane said, "What were you doing up there...uh...Chey...Annie?"

There was a moment's hesitation. Then, "You know Rodney."

It was a statement, not a question. Lane blinked. She had a feeling somehow she'd missed a play.

"You mean the Rodney who worked for me? Is he a friend of yours?"

The small nose wrinkled in distaste. "I hate him."

"Come to think of it, at the moment I'm not that wild about Rodney myself," Lane agreed wryly. "He walked out on his job without saying anything. He's not your brother, I hope."

Cheyenne gave her a withering look and shook her head. "He lives on the same street as me."

Lane knew the neighborhood—a scattering of ramshackle houses with unkempt lawns on the edge of town a mile or so from the market. For one so young, Annie seemed a long way from home.

"What's Rodney got to do with your being in my apple tree?"

The blue eyes shifted uneasily. There was a moment's hesitation before they met Lane's squarely again.

"I was waiting for you to come," Cheyenne said, her voice suddenly shy. "I'd do better than Rodney."

"I should certainly hope so," Lane agreed with a startled laugh. *Oh, my! The moppet was after Rodney's job.*

Involuntarily, she backed off a step. She hadn't had anything to do with children since she was a child herself. Keeping the Fielding farm interests afloat was hairy enough without the complication of a small girl underfoot.

"Honey, if you're asking for Rodney's job, I'm afraid you're too young," she said gently.

"I'm *seven!*"

"And a very capable seven, I'm sure, but not old enough. Rodney was twelve, and you can see the job was too much for him."

"Oh, *Rodney!*" Her tone disposed of Rodney. The relentless gaze didn't waver.

"Granted you'd be better than Rodney, but you'd need to be a *lot* better," Lane found herself arguing weakly. "You'd have to get all the dirt off the potatoes and wash the carrots and green onions and beets and tie them in bunches and..."

Cheyenne's shoulders lifted in a small, accepting shrug. "That's not so hard," she said.

Lane tried again. "You have to count them to make sure you put the right number in each bunch. I bet you don't know how to count." The words were no sooner out than she regretted them. Would she have talked this way if the applicant had been an adult? The fact that she was a child was no reason for putting her down.

Undaunted, Cheyenne protested in an outraged voice. "I can *too* count! I can count to a hundred." Her brow furrowed in thought under the pale feathering of bangs. "I prob'ly could count to a thousand, maybe. To a trillion, even, if I had to, I bet. One, two, three—"

Hastily, Lane interrupted. "I believe you. I believe you."

Cheyenne stopped counting. Their eyes locked in a measuring silence. Lane cast around for a way to proceed, blaming her bungling on her lack of experience with children.

The little girl was the first to speak. "I'd do better than your crummy old Rodney," she said plaintively, her voice seeming to run down as she ducked her head and brought her arm up to her mouth to suck on the bee-stung welt.

Lane braced herself to deliver a definitive "No," but the word stuck in her throat. *Not while the poor kid's hurting,* she told herself.

"Come on, Annie," she said aloud, laying a hand on the wiry little shoulder. "Let's go put baking soda on that bee sting and see if we can find some cookies and milk."

The shoulders resisted. The eyes turned up to Lane as Cheyenne waited for an answer. Lane felt a grudging admiration for the small, stubborn will that wouldn't quit. Something about it reminded her of herself.

By way of a peace offering, she said, "You can have any kind of cookie you like. Let's take care of that sting."

She nudged Cheyenne toward an enclosure at one end of the marketplace, making a stop along the way at Mrs. Brandon's bakery stall, a recent addition to the market. Even the fiery welt on the child's arm seemed momentarily forgotten as Cheyenne took in the temptations of the cookie display.

With a bag of cookies clutched tightly in one hand, Cheyenne followed Lane to her office—a room that held, in addition to the furnishings and equipment needed to run a small business, an oversize refrigerator, a counter and sink, a first-aid cupboard, a pullman-size stove and sundry other amenities not normally found together within the same four walls.

After the bee sting had been coated with a slathering of baking soda worked into a paste with water, Lane took a carton of milk from the refrigerator and poured a glass for Cheyenne. A thirsty gulp left a white mustache on the youngster's upper lip. With a quick dart of her pink tongue she licked it off and gazed up at Lane expectantly.

"Look, Cheyenne, let's get this straight once and for all," Lane said firmly and, she hoped, kindly. "I just can't give you a job. And by the way, aren't you supposed to be in school?"

"They won't let me start until next fall," the child said in an aggrieved voice. "I moved here too late. School lets out pretty soon for the summer."

"Oh," Lane said, and was relieved when an interruption from outside the screen door saved her from further argument.

"Hey, Miss Lane," a voice called. "There's a guy out here wants to sell you a load of onions. He says they're Vidalias. You want to take a look?"

"Be right there," Lane called back. Hardening herself against the disappointment she saw in the blue eyes still trained on hers, she said awkwardly, "When you're finished with the cookies, honey, you may as well run along home. If you can't eat them all, take them with you. They're all yours."

BY THE TIME Lane had determined that the onions were indeed the mild, sweet variety grown only in Georgia and completed a transaction with the seller, half an hour had passed.

When she returned to her office, she was taken aback to find the little girl curled into a ball on the cot in the corner, fast asleep, her mouth covering the sting on her arm. Closing the door behind her quietly so as not to disturb the sleeping child, Lane stepped out into the marketplace feeling strangely unsettled. There was something infinitely appealing about the small, stubborn character. It made her think of her own long-ago campaign to leave the beleaguered household of her parents for the gentle environs of her uncle's farm. She must have been about Cheyenne's age.

She knew then that it wasn't in her to let such tenacity go unrewarded, and began to compile a mental list of chores within the capabilities of a seven-year-old girl.

ON THE DUNE SIDE of the highway a mile or so west of the market, Matthew Cheney stood knee-deep in salt grass, his head tipped back to catch the full force of the Atlantic breeze on his face. After a minute he sighed and turned to tramp reluctantly back through the grass toward the big, old house where he'd spent the summers of his childhood. He took the graveled driveway that ran alongside the house to a parking area that fanned out in back.

God, what he'd give to spend the whole day just hanging out on the beach again! But those years were gone forever, he reminded himself sardonically, looking back on that time of careless pleasures in the unforgotten past—a time of sleek boats, fast ski slopes and expensive cars, of new women and old wine; a time when he'd seized whatever the moment had to offer and to hell with anything that stood in his way.

A humorless chuckle broke in his throat as it struck him that he—Matt Cheney, infamous philanderer—could not recall the last time he'd had any kind of relationship with a woman, even a platonic one. It had gotten so he couldn't take a day off to check out the Seahampton house for Cora Meigs without feeling he was letting somebody down.

Still, it was a yearly chore he had to perform. After all, he'd been the one who'd talked his mother's old friend into spending her summers at the unused family beach house she loved so well. He wasn't about to let the woman who'd been like his second mother move into a house that had been closed for six months without first making sure she wouldn't walk into a nest of problems. This time he'd found ants and mice, a cracked window and a rusty lock to be replaced.

Crunching through the gravel at the back of the house, Matt bypassed the late-model Taurus he'd driven out from Manhattan and walked to the garage beyond. He unlocked the door and slid it open to gaze fondly upon a faded blue 1955 Chevrolet station wagon. He ran a loving hand over scarred chrome around the bumper.

It was the first car he'd ever owned. When his dad wouldn't let him use the family car the year he was sixteen, he'd spent the summer picking beans for a truck gardener near Wainscott and taken the nineteen-year-old Nomad parked in the barn as payment. He'd spent all his spare time that summer and most of the next getting the old car in shape to move out of the barn under its own power. Using an auto mechanics manual from a used-book store and spare parts from wrecking yards for miles around, he'd finally got the old buggy roadworthy the next year. He'd been running it off and on ever since.

Slowly he circled the car, nudging the tires with his toe as he passed. Leaving the car door open, he got in behind the wheel and tried the starter, neither surprised nor disappointed when the engine's only response was a protesting groan. He got out, took a set of jumper cables from the trunk and moved the Taurus close enough to couple it with the Chevy. In a matter of seconds the ancient engine took hold with a wheezy roar.

A minute later he was on the road to see to a variety of errands he intended to take care of before he returned to Manhattan later in the day. By the time he'd lined up a housecleaning service and an exterminator and driven several miles out into the countryside to track down a handyman recommended by the caretaker of the Seahampton property, it was nearly noon.

As he headed back on the Montauk highway east of Seahampton, a hand-printed sign caught Matt's eye: Season's First Strawberries—Fielding's Farm Market, One Mile, and he remembered that Cora loved Seahampton strawberries. He'd surprise her and drop off a couple of baskets at her apartment when he got back to the city this afternoon.

He pulled off in front of the market, a rectangular wooden building to the right of the highway, from which extended an open arena roofed over with rustic shakes. At center front was a U-shaped counter with a cash register on either side. Bins and tables and stalls were placed in rows, laden with fresh produce. A lone woman was buying a loaf of bread at a bakery counter.

As he stepped out of the Nomad, his gaze was drawn to a figure on a stepladder struggling with a wide, unwieldy roll of paper. Beaming in on two long legs and a pair of round, firm, patently feminine buttocks snugly encased in faded blue denim jeans, his eyes widened with pleasure. An admiring breath just short of a whistle escaped his lips. He stood rooted to the spot, his gaze taking in the slim waist and moving up the pink-shirted back to a slender neck and a mane of sorrel hair that fell loosely to an inch or so above her shoulders.

Transfixed, he watched the young woman lean far out to hold one end of what appeared to be a banner in place at the edge of the roof while the other hand aimed an industrial stapler at the top corner of the paper.

*Good God, she's going to fall,* Matt thought with a quick intake of breath, at once aware of the precariousness of the woman's position as the ladder began to sway.

"Watch out!" he yelled, springing forward to catch the ladder, but catching instead 115 pounds of warm, vibrant, delicious-smelling woman. The main force of her body caught him squarely in the chest, knocking the wind out of him. For a moment her arms clung to his neck. Supporting her full weight, he took a step backward in a last-ditch effort to regain his balance and went down flat on his back, the young woman sprawled on top of him.

She disentangled her arms, pulled herself to her knees and looked down on him with concerned eyes. Matt made no effort to move.

"I liked it better the other way," he said cajolingly. "How about coming back?" The echo in the audacious come-on of that other Matt Cheney—the one he'd imagined he'd put aside—was like hearing the voice of an old and somewhat disreputable but sorely missed friend.

The woman looked at him with amusement and sprang lightly to her feet. She was tall and lithe, the fair skin of her face and arms a pale, golden tan, lightly dusted with freckles. Her face crinkled with laughter that deepened tiny laugh lines around gray-green eyes.

"Nice recovery," she said in a sweet, slightly husky voice. "I must say I'm relieved. I was all ready to worry about you. Thanks for cushioning my fall." She smiled and wrinkled her nose. A small crescent-shaped dimple played at one corner of her mouth.

Looking up at the woman from where he lay, Matt knew there was something special about her—something more than the enchanting trill-like break in her voice and the hint of humor in her eyes. She reached out to give him a hand up, and Matt scrambled to his feet, wishing he'd been a little more circumspect.

"I'm Elaine Fielding, but everyone calls me Lane," she said, giving him a soft, firm handshake and another crescent-touched smile.

"My name's Matt Cheney." He wanted to add, "Feel free to throw yourself on top of me anytime," but stopped himself just in time.

"The banner says strawberries, but I don't see any," he said instead. "Are you putting it up, or taking it down?"

"The berries are in the cool room. The banner's for the weekend traffic that'll start rolling in tomorrow if the weather stays nice," Lane said. "There's very little midweek business until after Memorial Day, and the berries keep better when they're not on display. I'll be glad to get them for you, though."

But Matt was in no hurry to complete the transaction. He couldn't get enough of the low, bluesy voice. To keep her talking he said, "Nice market you've got. Are you open year-round?"

"We've only been open a couple of weeks. There's not much homegrown produce ready yet, so most of what you see is shipped in," she said. "The first local strawberries should get us off to a good start with the weekenders, and next week the cherries will be ripe. By the time the summer people start coming there'll be peas and beans and squash—all kinds of good stuff for the rest of the season."

"How late in the year do you run?"

"Not as late as last year, I promise you," she said with a rueful grin. "We stayed open into November. The last week in October we sold our entire pumpkin crop and literally barrels of apple cider. The day after Halloween you could have rolled a bowling ball down any aisle and not hit a soul."

"Then this is only your second year?"

"For the market, yes," she said. She bent and began reeling in the roll of paper still in a heap on the ground, smoothing out wrinkles as she retrieved it. "My family has farmed here since the early 1900s. My uncle grew vegetables and sold them in Manhattan most of his life. Lately it's taken so many middlemen to get the produce to the buyer that the profit margin's almost at the vanishing point. The market is an experiment in letting the customers come to us.''

Matt's eyes took in the marketplace. ''Your uncle thinks he can do better selling directly to the consumer?'' he asked skeptically.

Her face clouded. He had a feeling he'd gone too far.

After a moment she said, ''My uncle died three years ago as the result of a farm accident the year before.''

''*You* started the market?''

''Well, I . . .'' She hesitated, plainly weighing whether she wanted to tell him more. ''I was with a business management firm in Manhattan when things began to collapse out here. Someone had to come up with a way to turn enough profit to keep the farm operating. The alternative was to sell the land for condominiums, which would have broken my Aunt Mercy's heart. So far the market's keeping the farm and me afloat and lets my aunt live near her grandchildren in California without having to be financially dependent on her son.''

''What about you?''

She gave him a shaky grin. ''I always wanted to see if I could start a business of my own. If I can swing it, I hope eventually to be able to buy out my aunt.'' As he watched her gathering the banner that lay in folds on the ground, Matt recalled why he was there.

''The strawberries,'' he reminded her hastily.

The young woman straightened, embarrassed. ''I'm sorry,'' she said. ''You come in looking for berries and what you get is a history of Fielding's Market. I can't believe I told all that to a complete stranger.''

''No harm done,'' Matt assured her. ''If the choice is mine, I would like to hear more.''

Clearly flustered, she made no attempt to answer but said instead, ''Wait a minute. I'll get the strawberries from the cool room." She turned abruptly and made her way between the bins and tables, disappearing through a door at the back.

As he waited for her return, Matt gradually became aware of an eerie feeling that he was being watched. Turning slowly, he noticed for the first time a small connecting building that opened into the marketplace a few yards behind him. Through the screen of its only door, two wide, solemn blue eyes surveyed him with unguarded suspicion from a small face framed by pigtailed hair the color of ripe corn.

"Well, look who's here," he ventured softly, moving closer to see better through the screen. But the child withdrew into the depths of the room and disappeared. At the same time, Lane Fielding reappeared from the back room with a full crate of strawberries in her arms.

"Here, let me get that," Matt called out, hurrying to relieve her of her burden.

"Thanks. I believe I can manage."

Reaching her, Matt laid a hand on the berry crate, bringing her to a stop. The sweet, delicious scent of the sun-ripened strawberries wafted up to him, but it was no more delicious than the sensuous sparkle of amusement in her eyes. She was laughing at him. He wondered why.

"If you insist," she murmured demurely and relinquished the strawberries. It was only when the crate was in his hands, and he found it weighed so little it could have been carried by the child behind the screen, that he saw the humor in the situation.

"I overreacted?" he asked with a sheepish grin.

"Never mind. I liked it. Do come back when I have a fifty-pound sack of potatoes to move," she said, leading the way to the front, where he set the crate down next to the cash register. "How many berries do you want?"

Matt hesitated. For a foolish moment he wondered how Cora would react if he deposited a crate of strawberries on her kitchen counter. He decided against it.

"I can only use a couple of baskets," he said apologetically.

Moving to the cash register to complete the sale, Lane paused to call out to a craggy old fellow in bib overalls who appeared at the doorway to the cool room, "Would you mind waiting a minute, Angus? I need you to hold the ladder for me."

Turning back, she gave Matt a smile that seemed candled by some inner glow as she handed over his purchase. "I hope you'll enjoy the strawberries. Do come again."

With no further excuse to linger, Matt took his two baskets of berries to the car and drove back to the house at the beach, where he locked the Chevy in the garage and headed back to Manhattan in the Taurus. But the brief encounter stayed with him. He had only to let his mind wander from the road to find his thoughts engaged with the blithe spirit of Lane Fielding and the small, unfriendly countenance of the child behind the screen.

Were they mother and daughter? And if so, was Lane Fielding a single mother or a married one? *Happily* married? he wondered. She wasn't wearing a wedding band, but nowadays that didn't necessarily mean anything.

Nearing the turnoff that would take him to the expressway, with the rich green landscape of Long Island's south-fork countryside rolling away on either side, Matt braced himself against the inexorable pull of the city and the family brokerage firm that held him there. He was seized by an unexpected urge to turn around and go back to the Seahampton house where he'd spent some of the best days of his young life.

Let Cliff Harris and the rest of the board look after the company for a while. After all, they were the ones who'd pressured him to take charge three years ago when he'd caught Evan Langley with his hand in the cookie jar after his father's death. They'd been nagging him to take a vacation for the past two years. Maybe it was about time he did.

# CHAPTER TWO

IT WAS AFTER ten o'clock when Lane left the field and headed the pickup back to the market, loaded with fresh corn for the July 4th weekend. A few minutes later she turned off the highway and eased into the shade of the apple tree at the far end of the open-front building. Craning her neck to see through the bug-specked windshield, she scanned the cluster of stalls in search of Cheyenne.

The bench that had become the little girl's workplace since the May morning she'd dropped out of the tree to make herself a fixture at the market was empty. Lane felt a renewal of the uneasiness that had disturbed her when she'd come upon the child curled up on the bench sound asleep the day before.

She hadn't thought much about it the first time or two she'd found her sleeping, even after she'd questioned her and Annie said she sometimes had nightmares and couldn't go back to sleep. Didn't all kids have nightmares?

Except she soon found that in Cheyenne's case the dreams, though they had their differences, were remarkably alike, and one thing never changed. The fright figure was always a mercilessly pursuing wolf.

What did it mean—this recurring dream? Was Lane missing a clue to something sinister going on in the child's home life?

Despite a growing concern, she'd had no luck prying even the most basic personal information out of the little girl. At the mere mention of anything to do with home or mother, the small, stubborn chin would begin to quiver. From some inner well of unshed tears Cheyenne's china-blue eyes would fill, and Lane would put off questioning for a better time.

But yesterday, as she looked down on the sleeping child, Lane had suddenly wondered what she would do if Cheyenne got hurt or sick while she was in her care. She'd be obliged to notify somebody. But whom?

Reluctantly, she'd left the child asleep. The next time she'd thought to look, Cheyenne was gone.

The sight of a workman arranging a display of neatly bunched carrots, radishes and green onions on a tiered table as she stepped out of the truck relieved her mind. Cheyenne had been here while Lane was out picking corn. She might have known her girl wouldn't pull a Rodney on her and quit without a word.

Tossing her broad-brimmed straw hat into the pickup, Lane ran her fingers through her moist, hat-flattened hair and set it free. Rolling up the sleeves of her oversize blue chambray shirt, she cast a jaundiced eye at the fluorescent sign: First Fresh Corn of the Season.

She'd hung the sign early that morning on the advice of a greenhorn farmhand, only to find that ears ripe enough for market were few and far between. Served her right, she thought crossly. Next time she'd do her own checking and save herself a lot of hard work.

But a glance around the marketplace improved her humor. There was an unusual number of morning customers brought in by the promise of corn, and if she knew shoppers, once they got what they'd come for, most of them would stay on and buy fifteen or twenty dollars' worth of produce they would otherwise have bought at the supermarket.

Her gaze came full circle and fell on the spare figure of Angus Bairn hobbling through the entrance from the back. She watched with concern as he made his labored way across the market toward her.

Angus had been Uncle Charlie's field foreman and right-hand man for as long as Lane could remember. After the tractor rolled over on Uncle Charlie, Aunt Mercy had left the running of the farm to Angus, spending her own time and energy in fruitless efforts to break through the wall of silence the accident had built around her brain-damaged husband. Within the limits of his own expertise, Angus had carried on valiantly, but he lacked the business skills and acumen of Lane's uncle.

Lane's mind harked back to that morning in her Manhattan office a year after the accident and the phone call from her aunt that had brought her first inkling that all was not well at the farm. Aunt Mercy's distraught voice echoed back to her. Their son, Howard, had flown in to see her at the behest of a real estate developer who'd made an offer to buy the farm. Howard was pressuring her to sell and move to a condominium near him and his family in California.

"I gather you don't take to the idea," Lane said, surprised at the anguish in her aunt's voice.

"There's nothing I'd like better than to live where I could watch my grandchildren grow up, but selling the farm to a developer would be like selling Charlie, Lane," her aunt said. "We gave Charlie's father our word when he signed the property over to us that we'd never sell the family land for any purpose but farming."

"Then tell Howard to forget the developers and start looking for a buyer who wants to farm."

"Howard says no one but the developers are buying farmland these days," Aunt Mercy told her glumly. "If we sell, he says we'll have enough money to take care of us for the rest of our lives, and if we don't sell, the farm will go broke."

Through Lane's mind had scrolled an instant replay of all Uncle Charlie and Aunt Mercy had given her over the years: love, comfort, moral support, a shoulder to cry on, a haven. A home. Money when she needed it. But for them, she could never have gotten through college when her own parents failed her. Her aunt and uncle had been busy people who always took time to listen to a lonely child. As surely as if she had signed a promissory note, Lane knew her debt to them was long overdue. Into the phone she said, "Hold tight, Aunt Mercy. I'll be there as soon as I take care of a few things here."

It had meant giving up her upper-five-figure salary and a low rung on the corporate ladder of a top-ranking business management firm in exchange for bare living costs that first year at the farm. A quick study of the books had made it clear her cousin Howard's determination to sell came from an understandable fear that the farm was nearing bankruptcy.

After Uncle Charlie's funeral Lane had poured her savings into the farm operation and started a roadside vegetable stand that had grown into the busy produce market she looked out on now. Her main goal had been to squeeze enough out of the failing farm for her aunt to spend her remaining years near her grandchildren in California without being financially dependent on Howard. Lane crossed her fingers. *So far, so good.*

From where Lane stood beside the pickup, she saw Angus pause along the way to cast an appraising eye on a bin of new potatoes and pluck out a couple that didn't meet his exacting standards. Much of the credit for the high quality of their produce belonged to him, she thought appreciatively. How could she have managed without him if he'd taken offense and quit when she arrived to take over the management of the business from him?

She smiled to herself, remembering the prickly old voice, thick with emotion as he put the keys to the office in her hand.

"We need ye here, lass," he had told her. "Now I can get back to the land."

Now a slight unevenness in the old fellow's walk as he approached told her his arthritic knee was acting up again. The seamed face, seasoned to the color of saddle leather, framed in a shock of straw-colored hair laced with white, wore a look of reproach.

He greeted her dourly. "Mornin', lass. What took ye so long?"

"Sorry, boss," Lane said cheerfully. "Finding the ripe ones today was slow going."

Bairn cast a critical eye over the load. "Your Uncle Charlie always said if ye speed the season ye get nothin' for yer labors but half-filled cobs."

"Or a lot of hard work. Maybe someday I'll learn to consult you first," she said. "I wish I'd gotten back sooner. I wanted to talk to Cheyenne. Looks like she's come and gone."

"Hasn't been here," Angus said.

"But the vegetables..."

"Bunched 'em myself."

Lane furrowed her brow. "You don't suppose she's deserted us?" she asked, suddenly anxious.

"Couldn't say. We better get this corn unloaded. It won't be fit to eat if it sits out here in the sun all morning.'' Placing his forefingers between his front teeth, Angus blasted a whistle that brought a boy on the run.

"Fetch me a wheelbarrow, son," the old fellow said.

Alerted to the corn by his whistle, marketers began to converge around the pickup. Before the boy could leave, Angus changed his orders.

"Forget the wheelbarrow. Just bring some bundles of paper bags."

"How much for the corn?" a customer called out.

Without hesitation, Angus replied, "Ten cents apiece, twelve for a dollar."

Lane glanced at him and gave a cluck of annoyance. Darn! With the season just beginning, it was worth twice that much. No wonder they'd gone into the red while Angus was in charge. About to intervene, she held back. It was one thing to override Angus when the two of them were alone and could argue the point unheard. To do so in public would be a put-down not worth the cost to the old man's pride.

Her attention pricked up again as Angus talked on. "If some of these ears be a wee underripe, remember it's the first of the season. Don't hold it against us if we have overstepped a mite to get it to you for the Fourth."

Lane suppressed an astonished gasp. She didn't need to be in public relations to know bad-mouthing the product wasn't the way to make a sale. Furthermore, she'd worked too hard to make sure every ear was market ready to let his words go unchallenged.

"Angus! That's not so. I picked that corn. I *promise* there's not a green one in the lot," she protested sotto voce. Her pitchman darted her a resisting glance as people began to call out orders. Grabbing a sack, Angus reached into the truck bed for corn and said over his shoulder to Lane, "Run get me some change, lass."

By the time Lane got back with the change box, Angus was already doing a brisk business from out of his pocket. Tossing an armload of bags on top of the load, she swung one long leg over the side of the pickup and hoisted herself lightly into the truck bed, where she started bagging the corn and handing the full bags down to Angus.

Pausing for a quick survey of the morning shoppers, she found herself again half looking for the remembered face of her onetime strawberry customer, Matt Cheney, though she couldn't have said why. That May morning when he'd stopped to buy berries, he had been on his way back to the city. There was no reason to suppose she would ever see him again, and yet she kept almost hoping she would.

Knee-deep in corn, she sacked the silk-tasseled ears mechanically, her mind returning to the missing Cheyenne. She didn't know the child's last name, let alone where she lived. How was she going to check up on her if she didn't come? Suddenly she remembered a single fact she *did* know: Cheyenne lived somewhere in the neighborhood of the ill-favored Rodney.

For a moment she fancied herself canvassing the cluster of ramshackle cottages for a clue to the youngster's whereabouts: "Excuse me, do you happen to know a little blue-eyed, towheaded, seven-year-old girl who calls herself Annie but whose name is really Cheyenne?"

Her mind on the improbable scenario, Lane picked up an ear of corn and fumbled beside her absently for a bag to drop it in. When her hand came up empty, she looked down and saw her supply of sacks had run out.

At the same time, the crotchety voice of Angus brought her back to the moment.

"Look sharp, lass. Where's them eight ears I'm waiting for?"

ON THE DUNE SIDE of the highway a mile or so away, Matthew Cheney trod glumly down the path that led to the beach, oblivious to the clear blue day around him and the sounds and smells of the sea.

What was it Cora had just said?

"I never thought I'd live to see the playboy of the Western world turn himself into Jack-a-dull-boy!"

He grinned in spite of himself.

Leaving the path, he made his own shortcut through salt grass to reach the head of the breakwater where it joined the dune. There he came to a stop and gazed absently out to the sea.

He couldn't believe he had just let Cora Meigs shoo him out of his own house the same way he'd let her finagle him into a vacation he didn't have time for.

Cora had been with the family too long to have forgotten that vacations were not a tradition with the male Cheneys. As far as Matt knew, his father had never taken one in his working life and wouldn't have countenanced such weakness in either of his sons.

The thought of his father reawakened old feelings of inadequacy Matt had covered with a what-the-hell attitude in other years. He turned and looked back at the big, old two-story shingle-sided house where he'd spent the happiest summers of his childhood. Through the kitchen window he could see the round, solid figure of Cora in a flowered apron, her gray head bent over breakfast dishes at the sink. For a moment he hesitated.

He should be back at the house, reviewing the Jordan portfolio before the Exchange opened for the day in the city, he thought uneasily. When stocks started moving on

Wall Street, the computer and fax he'd had hooked up to keep in touch with his office allowed no time for dallying on the beach.

But try and explain that to Cora! She'd already made up her mind he was giving too much of himself to his work and had made it her mission to save him from himself. He'd long ago learned that Cora with a mission had the tenacity of a pit bull.

Locked into the already-lost debate with her, he watched a fishing boat on the horizon without seeing it. Damn! Cora took advantage of the fact she'd been his mother's best and lifelong friend. He was of half a mind to go back to the house and put his foot down.

But even as he shaped the thought, Matt knew he wasn't about to do any such thing with Cora Meigs. He'd just go on doing what he'd done as a kid—figure out a way to circumvent her.

The truth was, he and his brother, Birch, were the kids she'd never had. It was something he'd always known— even before their mother was killed in the car crash when he was eight, and Cora, widowed and alone, had come in the guise of housekeeper to live with them. It was Cora who had tempered Matthew's furies, bound his wounds and stroked his ego. Long after he left home for school— even after he went to work for the family firm and moved into a place of his own—she'd been the buffer between him and his father.

And beyond saving a night to take her to the Tavern on the Green for an annual birthday dinner with candles, balloons and the works, what had he ever done for her? If anyone had earned a right to meddle in his affairs, it was Cora.

From his vantage point at the top of the dune a flash of color on the periphery of his vision made Matt glance across the broad drift of sand below him to the water's edge, where a small, solitary figure in a red sweatshirt chased a receding breaker back to sea.

Should such a small child be here at the beach alone? Matt wondered. It was early. The sun worshipers would soon be along, but for the moment the only other creature he could see was a very large dog who seemed bent on impeding the child's game.

Curiously, Matt watched the child turn and splash back up the beach, pursued by an incoming wave; watched her turn again and run to meet another. Above the low rumble of the tide and the screech of wheeling gulls, he heard the excited bark of the dog as it lumbered across the sand in a clumsy bid to join the child's ongoing play.

"Barkis!" Matt exclaimed aloud in pleased recognition. It was the town dog who belonged to no one and to everyone—a big, shaggy vagabond mutt that had adopted his brother for a while during that awful summer the muggers had attacked Birch in Central Park and left him temporarily blind. Birch would say the kid was in good hands. He watched the child once more dart away from an incoming breaker, the animal in joyous pursuit.

Then, unexpectedly, the wave caught up with the child. He saw the small figure disappear under a wall of water and reflexively took off running. He saw her come up struggling against the ebbing flow, saw the big dog seize a mouthful of blue denim in an attempt to drag its wearer to safety.

Drawing near, he saw a water-soaked pigtail of flaxen hair and a small, delicate, very wet face. Too small and too young to be playing in the surf alone, he thought, angry at whoever should be looking out for the girl.

Barkis held the wiry body pinned gently to the ground while the youngster bucked and fought to get out from under, filling the air with great gulping sobs and an astonishing string of street expletives, aimed at her captor.

At the sight of Matt, the animal hoisted his huge frame off the child and stood wagging his great wet duster of a tail, clearly relinquishing custody to the man. Freed, the little girl lay where Barkis had landed her, struggling now to quell her sobs.

"Don't be afraid. He's your friend," Matt said quietly. "He means well. He just doesn't know much about drawing-room manners."

Still she didn't speak. His mission accomplished, the dog turned and loped off across the sand.

"Are you all right?" Matt asked with rising alarm as the child shivered convulsively.

Bending, he scooped her into his arms. She made a sturdy effort to fight him off, but he pulled her firmly against him and rose to his feet.

"Take it easy, little girl," he said seriously. "Nobody's going to hurt you. I'm going to get you warmed up and dried out and see that you get back safely to wherever you belong. Let's don't make a big deal out of it. Okay?"

When he felt the small, wet body give tentative permission to be carried, he started back across the beach to the dunes and the house, wondering where such a very small girl had learned such a low-down bunch of cuss words.

"Good heavens! What have we here?" Cora Meigs exclaimed when Matt arrived at the kitchen door a few minutes later, his arms full of dripping child.

"The sea washed up a mermaid for you," Matt told her, trying to retain his grip on the little girl as she wriggled to get down.

"Gracious!" Cora exclaimed. "I must say she's *wet* enough to be a mermaid."

"I'm not either a mermaid," the child cried out indignantly, her teeth chattering like a party clacker as she slipped out of Matt's grasp and glared up at them. Sliding down his front, she planted her feet on the floor. "I'm a girl. I've got legs. See!"

"Of course you're not a mermaid," Cora said soothingly. She turned to Matt and said, "Enough of your foolishness. Can't you see the poor tyke is chilled to the bone? Get a blanket out of the linen closet and we'll wrap her up. She can't go home like this."

The blanket did little but soak up what water hadn't already dripped on the floor. If anything, the child's shivering became more acute.

"We'd better call her parents," Cora said. "Tell me your name, honey, and your telephone number. I'll call your mother and let her know where you are." The little girl stared up at them, plainly too miserable to speak, her body shaking so violently now she seemed almost to be having a seizure.

"This'll have to wait," Cora said firmly. "The child has got to be warmed up before we do anything else. Go run a tub of warm water for her, Matthew. I'll get her out of these wet clothes and put them in the dryer."

"Now, wait a minute, Cora. Do you really think that's such a good idea? People can be pretty touchy about…"

"Go!" Cora interrupted. "Time to worry about what people think later. She can't be left to go on like this."

Looking down at the little girl, Matt saw her lips were blue and her face so pale it appeared bloodless. He was stirred by alarm. Cora was right, he thought. Demurring no further, he went to turn on the water in the bathtub and adjust the temperature. Leaving the faucet to run, he came out to find Cora and the shivering child waiting outside the door.

"You think you can undress yourself and turn off the water when the tub's full, honey?" Cora asked, and was answered with a nod. "Throw your wet clothes out in the hallway when you're ready to get in the tub, and I'll put them in the dryer. By the time you're warmed up, they'll be ready to put back on."

The blue lips parted in a shivering wail. "I c-c-can't. I h-h-haven't got time. I'm s'posed to b-be at the market."

"Well you can't go anywhere until we get you into some dry clothes," said Cora in her reasonable, no-nonsense voice.

Relieved to have Cora take over, Matt went directly to the room upstairs he'd taken for his office. A glance at his watch told him the stock exchange would open on Wall Street in a few minutes. He settled down in the high-backed leather chair at his desk and turned on the computer, calling up the program that would bring the on-going sales to the screen. While he waited, he picked up a file from the stack of portfolios he'd brought along from the city to review.

It was an endless job he'd set himself. Each portfolio was a reminder that someone had entrusted his financial security to him. An awesome responsibility, he thought now. It made him wonder if the responsibility was what had made his father bury himself so deeply in the business that he hadn't had time for anything else.

In the downstairs bathroom a clear child's voice began to sing. "'Cheyenne, Cheyenne, hop on my pony....'"

For a moment he'd forgotten the kid. Drawing the portfolio toward him, he tried to refocus his attention on his client's affairs.

The child's voice came through to him again, distracting him from his work. The words on the page before him blurred. He got up and closed the door to his room, hoping to shut out the intrusive sound.

In all fairness, the kid was just doing her thing, but the situation confirmed what he'd learned long ago as his father's child, he thought grimly. There was no place in the life of the head of the family business for kids. Or a wife. He'd seen too much of what his mother had endured to wish it on anyone else.

But none of that had entered his mind when he went to work for his father right out of grad school. He was already hooked. Had been since the first time Birch, unbeknownst to their father, had sneaked Matt into the visitors' gallery of the stock exchange, explained the changing figures on the screen that circled the arena high above the busy floor and left him with a pencil and paper to work out what it was all about.

After that, all he'd thought of was getting through college and grad school to take his place in "the loop" at Cheney, McCrae.

He might have known the "position" his dad had waiting for him would be little better than that of errand boy. He hadn't expected to start very high on the ladder, but he hadn't worked his tail off earning an M.B.A. for the privilege of fetching cheese danishes for the top brass, either.

And Birch, who'd never made any secret of how much he disliked working in the brokerage firm, had said acidly, "Once he's made you humble, he'll get off your case and give you a job where you can learn something. Get it over with, bro. You want to be ready to step into my shoes when I take off."

But had he listened? No. He'd set off to outrun everybody in the fast lane and show the old man he couldn't care less. Long before Birch left the firm to team up with Julia and devote himself to the two loves of his life—his wife and his photography—Matt had earned a lasting reputation as a playboy. And by the time Birch pulled out, Matt had managed to blow it with his father for all time.

He'd had a hell of a lot to make up for after his dad got sick and Cliff Harris started turning over a few clients to him. He'd brought in a few new ones himself. And then he'd lucked out and stumbled on the file that put the screw on Evan Langley and sent him to prison.

And none too soon, he thought now, looking back. If the company hadn't gotten a handle on what Langley was up to under the cover of the Cheney, McCrae name, before the Securities and Exchange Commission had found out, it could have cost the family firm its venerated reputation—the foundation of their business.

It was the only reason he could figure for the board of directors' decision to let the family maverick step into his father's shoes when the time came. A thank-you for saving the firm that could be voted away anytime the board decided he wasn't shaping up.

On the computer screen before him Matt noticed the Exchange was now open, stock shares already beginning to move. He snapped guiltily to attention.

The market started off sluggishly, offering little to hold his attention, yet in a minute it grabbed him. Once again he fell under the old spell.

Absorbed, he neglected to answer the light knock at his door. After a moment the voice of Cora Meigs broke through his shell of concentration.

"Matthew? You are in there, aren't you?"

Matt got to his feet, and with a last reluctant glance at the video display, went to open the door.

"Come have a cup of coffee," Cora said. "Our guest is warm and dry and downstairs at the kitchen table drinking cocoa until the dryer gets done with her clothes."

"Not right now, Cora," Matt said impatiently. "I'm watching the market."

"Stop it, Matt. You're beginning to sound like your father," Cora said. "You're going to stop in a few minutes, anyhow. The clothes are about dry and you'll have to take her home."

Matt drew a deep breath. He might as well quit and get it over with. He obviously wasn't going to get settled into anything as long as the child was here. "Did you find out where she lives?" he asked, turning back to shut down the computer as Cora started for the stairs.

"Not yet, but her name's Annie. I haven't had time to ask a lot of questions. It's been all I could do to convince her you're not the bogeyman. I'm not sure how well I've succeeded," she said over her shoulder, not waiting for Matt, who followed her downstairs a moment later.

Looking into the kitchen, he came to a surprised halt. At the far side of the table sat the little girl he'd seen at the produce market some weeks before. Soaking wet she'd looked different. A vision of Lane Fielding rose to his mind.

He'd been about to see if he couldn't persuade Cora to act as chauffeur, but it suddenly seemed like a good idea to do the job himself.

# CHAPTER THREE

"So your name's Annie," Matt said, picking up the mug of coffee Cora had poured for him.

Seeing no welcome in the child's eyes, he perched on a stool at the counter some steps away from where she sat and surveyed her, trying not to appear to do so. If he'd seen her as now when he scooped her out of the waves, the sea-sodden hair hanging in a neat pigtail down her back and dried to the color of flax, he would have recognized her, even with the big eyes, frosty with suspicion, squinched into two tight little pockets. Her small frame was almost lost in the folds of one of his cotton flannel shirts that Cora had borrowed to serve the little girl as a bathrobe.

"I'll take you home as soon as you're dressed," he said, but the child pretended not to hear, turning her eyes to Cora, who was entering the kitchen from the laundry room, Annie's dried clothes over one arm.

"*You* take me," Annie said to her.

"I can't, love. I've got a cake in the oven," Cora said. "Besides, Matt needs to get out of the house."

From across the table, Annie turned suspicious eyes on Matt and looked away. Her eyes downcast, her shoulders slumped, she sat in brooding silence. Finally she slipped out of her chair and went to take her clothes from Cora. Hugging the garments to her chest, she headed for the bathroom, banging the door shut behind her.

Cora said in a low voice, "I'm afraid Annie holds men in low esteem."

"Well, that's good to know. I thought it was just me."

Pouring herself a cup of coffee, Cora said, "You haven't told me what happened."

As Matt completed a brisk account of his part in Annie's morning escapade, he felt a growing irritation toward Elaine Fielding. Damn the woman! If she was the person charged with overseeing this little girl's welfare, she was sure as hell casual about it.

"Doesn't she seem pretty young to be...?" Cora began in a dubious tone and stilled her words as the child came into the kitchen fully dressed.

"You don't have to take me," Annie announced. "Lane's gonna wonder what's happened to me, but I been thinking. I can get there just about as fast on my bike."

"You've got a bicycle out there on the beach?" Matt asked in exasperation. "You'll be lucky if somebody hasn't run off with it."

"It's hid good."

Matt started for the door. "Come on. We'd better go see if the bike's still there."

Annie let out a yell and ran after him, protesting at the top of her lungs. "No! I'll get it! You stay here. That's my hiding place. I'm not gonna take you there."

Matt continued out the door and reached the beach in a few minutes, the sullen little girl right behind him.

"All right, Annie," he said amiably. "Where's the bike?"

She shook her head and compressed her lips into an unyielding, colorless line. She gazed up at him, her eyes resentful.

"Come on, Annie. I haven't got all day. Quit horsing around. Show me what you did with the bicycle."

The lips pulled tighter and he got another negative shake of her head for his pains. His patience was nearing its limits. He tried another approach.

"Tell you what. I'll turn my back and close my eyes and *you* go get the bike."

His words unlocked her lips. "What do you think I am? A stupid baby? You'd peek," she said scornfully. "Go home. I'll get my bike when you're gone."

For a moment he was tempted to do as she said. But having accepted the responsibility of taking the child safely back where she belonged, he was determined to see things through.

With a snort of exasperation, Matt took off on his own to find the hidden bike, Annie tagging along behind.

The strip of beach had been his backyard in the summers when he was growing up. He'd explored and memorized the shoreline practically down to the last grain of sand. In spite of its restless, ever-changing nature, he knew all its nooks and crannies, which ones were likely to be gone, where new ones might appear.

In a few minutes he homed in on what to the casual eye looked to be no more than a pile of driftwood backed up against the breakwater, half-hidden by clumps of reed-like grass and sand. The sea had cut deeply beneath the driftwood to create a space large enough to hold two boys and a fair amount of plunder. Dubbed "the pirate's cave" by Matt and Birch, it had been *their* hiding place when they were kids.

Glowering, Annie watched Matt pull out the bike and set it upright on solid ground—a standard girl's bicycle that had seen hard usage and been built for an older, much taller girl. Inasmuch as he hadn't intended to let her go pedaling off on her own anyhow, he was not sorry to see that one tire on the bike was flat. It saved having to argue the point.

Later, after Matt had stowed the bicycle in the back of the old Chevy wagon, and Annie climbed into the front seat beside him, he sensed a change of attitude. The air of mistrust was lost in a sudden burst of chatter at the sight of the car.

"Where'd you get this car?" she asked. "At a junkyard?" The question was asked uncritically, and Matt gave the straight answer called for.

"Not all in one piece or all at one time," he said. "Or even all from the same junkyard."

Annie looked impressed. "You mean you gathered up pieces and put them together yourself, like a puzzle?"

Matt grinned. "Something like that."

As if catching a second wind, the old car wheezed into action at the first touch of the starter. They were out in the road and on their way when Matt remembered he still hadn't found where her home was.

Annie settled back on the seat with a satisfied sigh. "It's sure a neat car," she said. It seemed a propitious moment to approach the subject foremost in his mind.

"By the way, if I'm to take you home, maybe you'd better tell me where you live," he said.

Annie shot bolt upright. "Nobody's *at* where I live. I'm s'posed to be at the market." As if it were his fault, she added, "Lane's gonna be real mad."

"Is Lane your mother?" Matt's curiosity got the best of him.

When his question was met with silence, he turned his eyes from the road to find the little girl staring at him uncertainly. As if yielding to some thought process in her head, her face changed decisively under his glance. He had to strain to hear her mumbled "Uh-huh" as she nodded and lowered her eyes.

So he was right. Suddenly the morning lost its color. Her mother was Elaine Fielding, and Annie was what you could call a latchkey kid. A kid with no place to go but an empty house or her mother's place of work. A mother so wrapped up in her own shaky business she didn't think twice about leaving her child to fend for herself.

So what the hell did it matter to him that the lovely Lane Fielding didn't measure up? Unless Annie came from a single-parent household—which offered complications of its own—there was a husband somewhere in the picture.

His eyes on the road, Matt considered what he should say to Annie's mother when he arrived at the market. He was torn between a strong instinct that said how Elaine Fielding took care of her daughter was no concern of his, and a voice of conscience that wondered if there was anyone else to speak up for the child. The bottom line was, the kid could have drowned. The woman should pay more attention to her daughter.

Approaching the center of Seahampton, he turned off the main road on Quogue Street, looking for a service station he'd gone to as a boy to repair his tires and use the air hose. He wondered if it was still there.

Annie, slumped low in the seat beside him, straightened, bristling again with suspicion.

"Hey, where you taking me? This isn't the way!" she cried.

"Relax. I'm going to get your tire fixed."

"We can't. I don't have time. Lane'll..." She stopped. "What time *is* it?"

"A little after eleven," he said. From her place beside him, Annie let out a wail.

Matt heaved a sigh of waning patience. "Okay. Okay. If you insist. I'll take you straight to the market." He slowed to make a U-turn. "Your mother can take care of the bike."

All expression washed from the child's face. Her eyes stricken, she shook her head and slumped back in her seat.

"Maybe we better get the tire fixed," she said dully.

Plainly her mother was not a viable option.

THE FIRST STAMPEDE for Lane's freshly picked corn made heavy inroads in the supply at Fielding's Farm Market. As the morning moved on, the rush eased off to a more normal level of trade. At the same time, the rest of the market teemed with shoppers laying in supplies of garden-fresh green goods for the holiday ahead.

When she saw a cluster of people waiting to be checked out, Lane quit sacking corn and jumped down from the pickup to help at the cash register, where she could see she was needed more.

There was no room in her head now for anything but the business at hand. On such a boom day her wits were obliged to carry on a kind of juggling act. While a part of her mind kept track of and added up sales, the remainder threw out an ongoing stream of directions, information and advice to tourists and weekend vacationers. She struggled to recall names of last year's summer customers, exchanged small talk with others she scarcely knew and carried on a losing battle to discourage friends and acquaintances from lingering to impart family news while the checkout line backed up.

In the late morning the merry-go-round slowed down long enough for Lane to notice her mouth was as dry as ashes after her early shift in the corn patch. Turning to take advantage of the lull to go for a drink, she was stopped by a voice she knew almost as well as she knew her own.

"Lane, darlin'! No need to ask *you* how's business."

"Roz!" Lane felt a rush of affection at the sight of Rosalyn Kramer, a friend since school days whom she hadn't seen in months.

"Look at us! You'd think we still called each other every morning to decide what to wear," Lane said with amusement. "How come when you put on a pair of washed-out jeans and a cotton shirt you look like you stepped out of a fashion window, and I . . . ?"

"Look like you've been in a corn patch, which I'll bet money you have," Roz finished for her with a glance at the dwindling stock of corn in the pickup.

"True," Lane admitted. "It's also true that with the right belt or the right scarf or a few *faux bijoux* you could make one of those triple-armholed hospital gowns look like it came from a couturier."

Roz touched a long, heavy silver-and-tourmaline necklace that dangled over her bosom, and grinned.

"I guess it doesn't hurt to have New York's top rich-ladies' store give its head honcho in Accessories a discount to die for," Lane said. "I was just going to get a drink. Will you join me?"

SETTLING DOWN beside Roz on the office couch a few minutes later, after a long thirsty swallow of iced tea, Lane marveled as always at how she and Roz could pick up right where they'd left off, though they sometimes didn't see each other for months. All through high school, except for the summers when Lane was needed to help out on the farm, they'd practically lived in each other's pockets. They'd gone to different colleges, then run into each other again in New York and leased an apartment together for nearly three years until Lane left her job there to come to the farm.

"So tell me what you've been up to," Lane said, kicking off her sneakers and flexing her toes a moment before curling her feet under her.

Roz's witty, self-effacing account of her most recent shopping foray to Hong Kong led to talk of other mutual interests until sounds from outside gradually began to encroach upon their visit. When she could no longer ignore the noise, Lane swung her feet to the floor and slipped them into her sneakers.

"I wish we could visit all afternoon, but I'd better go," she said regretfully. She tied her laces and got to her feet, complaining, "Since your folks moved, you never come to Seahampton anymore. No chance you could spend the weekend at my place now that you're here, I suppose?"

There was an uncomfortable moment of silence and then Roz said, "Would that I could, Laney. I can't wait to see what you've done to the old farmhouse since you moved in, but..." She hesitated, her cheeks flushing, and hurried on. "I'm sorry. I...I'm sort of involved this time. Got a new fella...I think. Ask me again—soon." It didn't sound like the usual forthright Roz, but one of the reasons for their long friendship was the fact that they refrained from prying into each other's affairs.

Holding the screen door open for her, Lane said, "It's an open invitation. You know *that!* Come..."

She broke off in midsentence. Aware that Roz was looking at her quizzically, she couldn't drag her attention away from an outdated Chevrolet station wagon, scarred by time, that was pulling into the marketplace. Wordlessly, she watched the car come to a stop. The driver turned off the motor and stepped out.

"Someone you know?" asked Roz.

"Not really," Lane murmured, thinking of her first encounter with this tall, rangy man with the heavy thatch of unruly wheaten hair.

*Matthew Cheney.* The name came to her so clearly she imagined for a moment that she'd spoken it aloud. Her gaze followed him to the back of the car as he opened the trunk, moving with a wonderful lazy grace. His features were arranged in an oddly attractive off-balance fashion that struck her as an agreeable change from traditionally symmetrical good looks.

"I've seen that man somewhere before," Roz said from beside her as Cheney lifted a bike out of the trunk and wheeled it through the gravel to the front.

Watching the man move around to the door on the passenger side, Lane barely heard her. For the first time she saw a small figure inside struggling with an unyielding handle. A sound of surprise broke from her throat as a towheaded child slid out of the car and landed on the ground feetfirst.

*"Cheyenne!"*

A feeling of incredible relief distracted Lane's attention from the man. Forgetting Roz beside her, she ran to meet the little girl, who had grabbed the bike away from the man and was pushing it stubbornly through the gravel, disregarding his effort to help.

"Annie! I was worried about you," Lane said as the child approached. "What happened to you?"

Cheyenne brought the bike to a stop beside Lane and looked up at her for a second, then her eyes shifted uneasily. She ducked her head and began to edge the bike forward.

"I...had to do something with...my dad," she mumbled, finishing in a rushed whisper.

Glancing across the lot, Lane thought for a moment Cheney was about to follow and braced herself for the meeting. Then, in the face of the child's determination to manage the bike herself, she saw him give a what-the-hell kind of shrug. Acknowledging Lane with a cool nod, he turned back to the car and in the next second took off, gravel spinning out from beneath his wheels.

With her own childhood as a yardstick, Lane measured and fit the pieces together. Before the car was out of the marketplace, she had put a label on Matthew Cheney. Divorced Father With Visitation Rights. Worse, a reluctant one! Any father who would dump his child on one of his visiting days wasn't all that eager to spend a lot of time with her, she concluded disapprovingly.

In a sudden rush of aching tenderness, Lane reached out to the little girl. Seeing her, Annie dropped the bike in the gravel and came running into the curve of her arms.

Her face buried in Lane's midriff, Annie said, "I'm sorry. I thought you'd be mad."

"It's all right, honey. I understand," Lane said gently, letting her go with a final protective hug. Who knew better than Lane Fielding the terrible need to hang on to every precious moment given her by a sometimes father? she thought.

A small movement beside her reminded Lane that Roz hadn't a clue as to what was going on.

"I'm sorry, Roz. Let me introduce you to my new assistant," Lane said, her tone lending the words importance. "Roz, this is Cheyenne, but we call her Annie. Annie, this is my old friend, Roz."

"Hi, Annie," said Roz.

Muttering an embarrassed "Hi," Annie hung her head and scuffed her feet along the ground.

Resting lightly on the pale, silken head, Lane's hand slipped to the child's shoulder and turned her toward the office door with a gentle nudge.

"There's sandwich stuff in the fridge," she said. "Go fix yourself something to eat. When you're through, come back and I'll have a job for you. We can certainly use you today."

"Where did she come from?" Roz asked curiously when Annie disappeared inside.

"Oddly enough, out of my apple tree," Lane told her, and described Cheyenne's coming; her determined campaign to make herself a fixture at the market, at the same time disclosing next to nothing about where she came from or who she was.

"I suspect her parents are divorced and that the bastard doesn't give the ex-wife and child any more than enough to get by on," she concluded, a new edge to her voice.

When she saw Roz waiting, expecting more, Lane felt suddenly defensive. "I honestly don't know that much about her, Roz. I've been really busy setting the market up for the summer. No time...lots of interruptions. And besides, I haven't wanted to ask too many questions. I wouldn't want her to think I was putting her down."

After a moment, still adjusting to the conclusion she'd reached but a moment before, Lane said tonelessly, "That man who dropped her off just now is her father. All I know about him is his name, Matthew Cheney." She proceeded to give a tight-lipped account of their meeting at the market in May.

"Matt Cheney. I knew I'd seen that face before," Roz said musingly. "He was one of the Ivy League types who used to hang out at the marina all summer when we were in high school. The ones our folks were always afraid were going to seduce us or worse. With good reason, no doubt. Surely you remember.''

"No. My virginity was never at stake. I was at home picking beans,'' Lane reminded her dryly.

"You didn't miss a thing, believe me,'' Roz assured her. "We all had a crush on Matt Cheney.''

Lane's eyebrows went up in surprise.

"Don't get excited. It was from afar!'' Roz said, laughing. "He was an 'older man'—must have been all of twenty-five. Besides having a sailboat that we all drooled over, he was a real hunk.''

"You might at least have told me about him.''

"Nothing personal, sweetie. He never gave any of us the time of day. Besides, that was the summer Chip Skinner was hanging around. If I'd told you I had a crush on a man who didn't know I was alive, you'd have thought I was fickle,'' Roz said. "Anyhow, Matt Cheney went in for beautiful, sexy-looking women and had them in abundant supply. God, how I envied them.''

*AND I ENVIED YOU,* Lane thought sheepishly a few minutes later as she watched her friend drive away. Envied her the crushes Roz had engaged in so lightheartedly all the time some self-protective instinct within Lane made her start backpedaling at the first flutter of her own cowardly heart.

What if she had spent her summers hanging out at the marina with Roz as a teenager? she wondered later as she sat at her desk in the office waiting for the computer to play through its start-up game. Would that same cautious instinct have warned her against the Ivy League charms of Matt Cheney? Would she have seen in him the makings of a womanizer...a failed husband...an uncaring parent?

Unexpectedly, a ghost of a shiver whispered across Lane's shoulders at the too-apt description of her own father, who had abandoned wedlock and all pretense at fathering the year Lane was five years old. Remembered recriminations from parental quarrels echoed unexpectedly in her mind. In conditioned response, she felt a queasiness in her stomach.

She'd felt certain for years that the ever-widening breach between her parents was all her fault, until a wise and worldly therapist helped her to understand she'd never been to blame. But now, at last, she could forget. When her mother remarried and moved to Santa Barbara, Lane had stowed all the unpleasantness of her past in what she'd dubbed "the dumpster" of her psyche, along with other emotional baggage she could do without and hoped eventually would biodegrade. *Like Perry Sloane.*

She reached for one of the invoices she'd set out to work on, but her mind reeled back unwilling to the first and only love affair she'd ever had. After tiptoeing cautiously through the dangerous years to maturity, she'd thrown caution to the winds at twenty-five and let herself fall in love.

What a heady time that had been for her, she thought sardonically. She'd just been promoted to her position as a junior executive of the company and was engaged to marry her boss. Heady, indeed. Right up to the moment she had asked her fiancé for a leave of absence to answer Aunt Mercy's call for help.

Like an old war wound, the pain and humiliation he'd put her through that night was with her again. *Damn him!* she muttered under her breath, suddenly on fire with a new spurt of outrage as she recalled how she'd all but bared her soul when she asked him for the leave. In order to make him understand how deeply indebted she was to her aunt and uncle and how important it was to her to be there when they needed her, she'd told him things she'd never told anyone before or since. And Perry Sloane—the man she'd loved and trusted and made love with—had answered her with an unequivocal no.

"Why don't you suggest your uncle and aunt become clients of the firm? That way you could act as their business consultant and the company would get its standard fee for your services."

Turning from the computer screen, Lane stared out the window, not seeing the crop of green apples that hung heavy on the branch outside almost within reach.

It had hurt. Damn it, it had really hurt. For a long time she'd had a sick feeling in the pit of her stomach and had wondered if that was what they meant when they talked about a broken heart. Even now, after three years, she could still feel the scars.

But as she turned again to the computer, she was suddenly surprised to realize that for the first time she'd been able to look back on her interlude with Perry Sloane without hurting. It still made her mad, but it didn't hurt. Moreover, somehow it didn't seem all that important anymore.

Her fingers touched the keys and began to move. Under her bemused gaze she watched her own personal "words to live by" take shape on the computer screen: DON'T CARE TOO MUCH, AND YOU WON'T GET HURT.

THE "VACATION" he'd envisioned here at Seahampton just wasn't working out, Matt acknowledged gloomily ten days later as he tramped alone through the dune grass toward the beach. He'd expected to get as much done here as he would in his Wall Street office and at the same time breathe in the smells of the sea through his open window and rest his eyes on the ocean across the dunes. With a telephone for conference calls, a computer to keep him abreast of the market and a fax machine for documentary exchange, he couldn't see any reason why it wouldn't work. Except it didn't.

Like today, for instance. Just as the stock market opened, Cora came to the door to say the rug cleaners were there to shampoo his office carpet.

The only time he'd gotten anything done since he'd come here was during the three days he'd gone into the city, and even there the staff was as bad as Cora when it came to getting on his case about taking a vacation. About the tenth time one of his colleagues pointed out how smoothly things were running without him, it began to get on his nerves. It had been almost a relief to come back here.

A muffled bark came from somewhere nearby and brought Matt to a stop. Raising his head to listen, he saw that he was only a few yards away from his boyhood hiding place, recently usurped by Annie.

Ducking to see under the shelf of driftwood half-hidden by clumps of grass, he looked into the enormous blue eyes of Elaine Fielding's small daughter, her eyes frozen with terror, both hands clasped tightly around Barkis's muzzle.

"Annie, it's me," he said gently. "It's all right. I'm not going to hurt—"

"Be quiet! He'll hear you," the little girl whispered.

Matt blinked in surprise but remained squatted, peering in at her, wondering what to do.

"What are you hiding from, Annie?" he asked.

"Shh! He'll hear you."

"Who'll hear me?" Matt asked quietly.

"Wolf!"

In astonishment, Matt raised his head and looked around, his mind actually set for a moment on seeing some large, ferocious creature bristling with fur. He couldn't remember if he'd ever actually seen a wolf, even at a zoo, but he was damn sure there wasn't one in sight.

Feeling unreasonably annoyed, he was about to tell the exasperating child that he was in no mood for games when a closer study of her eyes assured him that to Annie it was no game. Fact or fantasy, Annie believed in the wolf.

"I swear there's nothing here but you and me and Barkis," Matt assured her, "and if you don't let go of the dog's muzzle and let him breathe, there won't be anyone here but you and me!"

"I saw him! He's lookin' for me. I saw him comin' across the dune."

"Well, there's nothing there now. Just a couple of women and some little kids way down the beach," Matt said.

"I saw him!" Annie repeated stubbornly.

In spite of a certain admiration for her tenacity, Matt found his patience wearing thin.

"I'm sure you did," he lied, "but he's gone now, and you'd better head for home. Get out and I'll pull the bicycle out for you."

She gazed at him dubiously for a moment before she crawled out from her shelter. Barkis came bounding out behind her and took off down the beach, clearly glad to be relieved of a responsibility that was becoming arduous.

Matt set up the bicycle, but Annie hung back, her eyes darting fearfully up and down the beach and across the dunes. He pushed the bike through the loose sand to the hard-packed path. Annie followed as closely as a shadow. He steadied the bike and waited for her to take the handlebars and get on.

"Wolf's hid someplace. He's waiting to get me," she said doggedly, and Matt saw a look of the gallows on her face that he could not turn away from.

"Nobody's going to get you," he said. "Come on. I'll take you back to the market myself."

# CHAPTER FOUR

WHAT WAS KEEPING Cheyenne this time? Lane wondered a little anxiously as she stepped out of her office shortly before ten that morning and saw the child still hadn't come. The arrival of the old Chevy wagon turning into the marketplace with Matt Cheney at the wheel answered her question a moment later. Beside him she saw the tip of Annie's pale blond head rising above the seat.

Lane gave a grunt of disapproval. *Ah-so! Visiting day again.* She started, tight-lipped, across the gravel to where the car had come to a stop, her mind set on having words with the feckless father, who was getting out of the car. He took a few steps to the rear and lifted Annie's bicycle out of the back.

The door opened on the passenger side and Cheyenne got out, her spirits evidently at rock bottom. Her eyes darted around uneasily before coming to rest on Lane.

The guy might at least give the child his undivided attention when he exercised his visiting rights, Lane thought. Today Annie was in disarray. He hadn't even bothered to get her clean and tidy, as she normally was. Unruly wisps of hair escaped around her face, and her T-shirt and jeans were rumpled and smeared with dirt.

It was a subdued little girl who came to meet Lane.

"I didn't mean to be late again," she said in a small voice.

Lane gave her a reassuring pat on the shoulder. "It's all right, honey." Then, not wishing to discuss Cheyenne in the child's presence, she said, "Angus'll be glad to see you. He hates to bunch vegetables. You run on and help him now."

There was something in the uneasy way Annie glanced around her before she lit out to join Angus at the workbench that struck Lane as not right. Stiffening her resolve to tell Matt Cheney a few things about the responsibilities of fatherhood, she turned to face him as he came around from behind the car, pushing Annie's battered bike through the loose gravel. Face-to-face with him, Lane was taken aback to see his jaw set in a militant line. His eyes met hers with an unfriendly look that matched what she felt herself.

"Do you have any idea where I found that child this morning?" Cheney demanded before she could speak.

Primed to go on attack, Lane was caught off balance, momentarily disarmed.

"*Found?*" she repeated, instinctively backing off a step, but with no thought of retreat.

"Yes, found. You seem surprised."

He made it sound like an accusation, she thought indignantly. He was the child's father! He shouldn't have to *find* her. He should know where she was.

"How could I possibly know where you found her?" she said in the controlled tone one would use on an obtuse child.

Cheney brought the bike to a stop a few steps away from her.

"At the beach," he said. "A good three miles from here. And not for the first time, either." Glaring at Lane, he moved a step nearer. Lane stood her ground and glared back. "In case she neglected to mention it, I'd fished her out of the breakers the other time I brought her back.''

Shocked by the disclosure, for a moment Lane couldn't speak. Then a flood of anger engulfed her.

''Well, bully for you,'' she said scathingly, but before she could pour out the indictment that festered in her mind, Cheney was again on the attack.

''Never mind the smart talk,'' he said coldly. ''Need I remind you there are worse dangers than drowning for a little girl left to run all over the countryside alone? She's too young to be wandering around public beaches by herself. Somebody should be looking out for her.''

Now livid with rage, Lane could hold back no longer. ''At least we have one thing we agree on. I can't wait to hear what you plan to do about it.''

''Plan to... My God, woman, that's not the question! The problem is yours. It's high time you address it.''

She stared at him aghast. Struggling to hold her temper, she took care answering.

''Look, Mr. Cheney, I resent your implication that I'm somehow to blame for all this. I enjoy having Cheyenne here at the market, and I can't deny she's a great help, but that doesn't give you a right to expect me to be responsible for her when she's out from under my eyes.''

Cheney pushed the bike forward with the clear intention of leaving. For a moment she thought he wasn't going to reply. Then he stopped and turned back to face her. Mad as she was, she wasn't prepared for the look of contempt he gave her.

''My mistake,'' he said. ''I thought responsibility came with the territory.''

''Territory?''

''With motherhood,'' he said over his shoulder and pushed on.

Lane's thoughts were running in circles. Too confused to speak, she followed Cheney mutely with her eyes as he stepped out of her path and steered the bike off course to go around her.

Her voice breaking in a falsetto squeak, Lane cried after him, "Wait a minute.... What you just said... You're telling me you're not Annie's father?"

Cheney came to an abrupt halt a few yards away and turned his head to stare at her as if she'd spoken in a foreign tongue.

Seconds passed. There was no sign of thaw in his face. The cold was there in his voice when he spoke.

"Ms. Fielding, I won't venture to guess what you hope to gain with this maneuver. Whatever it is, you may as well forget it. You know I'm not her father. Except for a glimpse the day I stopped at your market for strawberries, I'd never seen the child until I pulled her out of the water a couple of weeks ago."

Gradual understanding dawned on Lane. At the same time a wonderful, lighthearted feeling warmed her.

"Oh, my," she murmured softly, her face breaking into a smile. If he believed she was Annie's mother, certainly he wasn't her father.

With no clear idea how to say what she was thinking, she tried to explain. "I honestly thought..." She broke off uncomfortably as she suddenly realized that when Annie excused her lateness by saying she was doing something with her dad, Lane should have probed further.

Feeling guilty and bent on making amends, she moved to close the new distance that lay between them.

"Well, you *did* bring her here twice," she said defensively, hurrying a bit to catch up. "Can't you see how I might assume you were a divorced parent looking for relief from the pressures of visitation rights?'' She laughed self-consciously. ''I even imagined I could see a resemblance between Annie and you. I felt a bit put upon.''

''*Put upon,* Ms. Fielding?''

The bike plowed on through the gravel a few more steps and came to a stop.

''Will you kindly tell me what this is all about?'' he demanded in a voice of outrage. ''I'll grant the possibility you don't know who Cheyenne's father *is,* but you damn well know it's not me.''

''You seem to think I'm Annie's mother, but I'm not. When you kept bringing her back and she said she had to do something with her father, I naturally assumed....'' said Lane, trying to be reasonable. ''Obviously I'm not the only one to jump to conclusions, Mr. Cheney.''

''Try again, Ms. Fielding,'' Matt said grimly, giving no sign he was about to unbend. ''I assure you, I didn't jump to any conclusion. The information came to me on the highest authority.''

Lane's eyes widened.

''Cheyenne,'' he said in answer to her unasked question.

''Cheyenne told you I was her *mother?*''

''Well, she didn't come out and volunteer it in so many words, but when I asked if you were her mother, she admitted it.''

Lane stopped a moment in dismay. When Cheney started to move doggedly on, she reached out and caught his arm to stop him and said, ''And who do you think gave me the idea you were her father?''

''Cheyenne? I don't believe it!''

But, watching, she saw a corner of his mouth lift slowly in a puzzled smile and she knew he did.

"Well, I'll..." he said at last. "It looks as if we've both been had. Why do you suppose she lied?"

With her heart harking back to the lonely days of her own childhood, Lane didn't answer at once.

"If you're a little kid, like Annie, and know no one's much interested in you, sometimes a pretty fantasy helps get you through a lousy day," she began, but her voice caught with a sudden caring for the child, and it was a moment before she could finish. "I don't think Annie thought of it as lying." She looked up, and finding Matt's eyes upon her, gave him an uncertain smile.

Together they started back toward the office, Cheney pushing the bike and then balancing it on its kickstand out of the way of cars.

After a moment he said dryly, "You have to give her credit for a fertile imagination. When I found her this morning she had me ready to believe she was hiding from a wolf. I almost think she believed it herself."

"Not really," Lane assured him, relieved to see the rancor gone from his face. "It's a dream she keeps having. She makes it seem very real. I'm not surprised you misunderstood."

"This was no dream. She'd hidden herself from a real, live, honest-to-God wolf. She swore it was lurking out there on the beach, waiting to grab her," he declared. "I couldn't get her out of her hiding place until I'd convinced her the wolf was gone."

"Oh, Lord, you don't suppose she can't tell the difference between the dream and reality anymore?" Lane said, suddenly anxious.

Was it possible Annie was withdrawing into a world of her own making? Lane wondered and knew she couldn't postpone the inevitable. She had to make a serious effort to find out who—if anyone—was in charge of the child's life. If Cheyenne needed help, Lane was determined to see that she got it.

Raising her eyes, she saw that Matt Cheney was gazing at her curiously.

"Granting you're not Annie's mother," he said, "would you mind telling me just where you fit into the picture?"

So once again Lane unfolded the tale of the child in the apple tree—told so many times now, it rolled off her tongue almost without thought. The resolute quality she'd seen in Matt's face earlier was tempered now with humor and understanding. *I could like this man,* she thought uneasily, not sure it was what she wanted.

By the slightly bias tilt to the septum, she knew his nose had been broken at some long-ago stage in his life and left to mend on its own. Baseball? Hockey? Some garden variety of adolescent hell-raising? Whatever. She found it attractive. The same for the cowlick that sprang untamed from the heavy head of wheat-colored hair. As for the rest of his body, it was tall and easy moving and smoothly muscled where muscles belonged.

*Sexy?* Yes, definitely sexy.

Every instinct warned that here was a man who could hurt her if she let him get too close. The last man Lane wanted in her life was one her friend Roz classified as a *hunk.* Her own tried-and-true aphorism flashed before her mind. *Don't care too much, and you won't get hurt.*

Abridging her account of Cheyenne's arrival, she brought her story to a hasty close.

"That was in May. She's been coming here every day since," she said. "Now, if you'll excuse me, I'd like to talk to Cheyenne."

Matt watched her turn away, mystified. She seemed suddenly remote. He'd be damned if he knew why.

"Wait a minute, Lane," he said. It was purely a delaying action. He had nothing on tap to say when she paused and turned her head to look back at him.

His mind was a blank. *Quick. An idea...a-a-ah!* "Since you're not her mother, and I'm not her father, just who the devil does she belong to?"

"That's exactly what I intend to find out," she said, her voice cool. "Now if you'll excuse me...?" She walked away, leaving Matt feeling as if a door had been politely closed in his face.

He watched her departure regretfully, even as he took a purely masculine pleasure in the lovely feminine body in motion. Seconds passed before he drew a rueful breath and turned back to his car, feeling strangely left out and a little foolish.

What in the world had he said that had suddenly gotten her dander up? he wondered, exasperated. She was like a sail in a shifting wind. He hesitated, of half a mind to go back and find out why. But what did it matter? Until he could look at the directors around the boardroom table and know he was running the family business as well as his father had, he had no time to explore the moods of Lane Fielding or any other woman.

Not now, anyhow, he thought as he got in and started the car. Maybe never if he was to follow his father's example. It was a mystery where the man had found time to court and marry his mother. He hadn't even left his desk to take her to the hospital when she gave birth to their two sons. That had been left to Cora Meigs.

Matt gave a last glance around the market, his eyes lingering on the slender young woman walking toward the office now with Cheyenne. He hoped for a glimpse of her face, but her head was bent toward the little girl, the face lost to him behind a fall of tawny hair. Reluctantly he pulled his thoughts away from Lane Fielding and the enigma of Annie. He'd wasted too much time already. The child was obviously in good hands. Future interruptions from that source were highly unlikely, he thought, but found little satisfaction in the prospect.

Turning back toward the ocean road that led to the summer house, he wondered if the carpet in his office was dry enough for him to get back to work.

AT THE MARKET OFFICE, Lane opened the refrigerator and brought out a pitcher of iced tea and a canned soft drink, under Annie's solemn gaze. Pouring tea over ice for herself, she motioned the child to a place on the couch beside her. "I thought you said you weren't going back to the beach alone anymore, Annie."

The blue eyes were suddenly cloudy.

"I had to. I lost Marigold's ring out of my pocket that other day," Annie said defensively. "It could have fell out when I put my bike into the hiding place, so I had to go back and see, but I didn't find it." To Lane's consternation, she looked as if she was about to cry.

"Who is Marigold?" Lane was only trying to divert a deluge. She was unprepared for the shock that came.

"My mother," Annie answered in a voice so low Lane had to strain to hear.

Lane caught her breath. After a moment she said, "Annie, if you already have a mother, why did you tell Mr. Cheney—"

As startling as an unexpected crack of a pistol, a scatological four-letter word exploded from Annie's flower-like lips and cut Lane short.

"*Chey-enne!*" Lane gasped.

"He *told!*" Clearly, the child considered herself betrayed. Recovering, she said morosely, "I didn't mean to say... You can wash my mouth out with soap if you want to."

Inwardly amused, Lane asked, "Would that help you to remember not to say it again?"

"I guess. Marigold used to do it."

"Let's leave that to Marigold then," Lane said. Holding back what might be construed as a conspiratorial grin, she continued sternly, "Let's get back on track, Annie. Why did you let me think Mr. Cheney was your father?"

Annie hung her head and looked at Lane through pale blond lashes. "I didn't want you to be mad at me for being late."

Feeling she was on her way up a dead-end street, Lane backtracked. "You still haven't said why you told Mr. Cheney I'm your *mother*. Do you think that's quite fair to Marigold?"

There was a sudden stillness. At last Annie said, "Marigold died."

The keening of loss and sorrow and loneliness in the still, small voice brought a sudden lump to Lane's throat. In spite of herself she reached out and laid a tentative hand on Annie's narrow shoulders, half expecting to be turned away. When she felt no resistance she surprised herself by drawing the child into her arms and giving her a quick, comforting hug.

She had intended to let her go, but the nearly weightless little body clung. Lane tightened her arms and held the child, rocking her lightly, wondering at herself as she did. She'd never been a spontaneous toucher. Nor did she welcome this too-poignant reminder of all the hugging it had taken from her aunt and uncle to make up for what she'd never gotten at home. Yet there was no way she could deny the little girl's need.

After a minute she gently detached herself from Cheyenne's arms and stood up, bringing the child to her feet in front of her, tipping her head to look down at the heart-shaped face.

"I wish I could bring Marigold back to you, Annie," Lane said slowly, "but some things just can't *be.* Any more than I can be your mother. I can be your friend for as long as you want me to be, but I can't be your mother. Telling people that I am doesn't make it true."

Half expecting a burst of tears, she was disconcerted to see that Cheyenne wasn't buying it; was, in fact, preparing to argue. The moment Lane stopped talking, she began.

"Well, but it'd be true if you're *adopted!*"

"Except you're not adopted, honey."

"Not me. *You!*" Annie said triumphantly. "You're my *adopted* mother. I adopted you."

"Annie...now...wait a minute." Lane couldn't go on, her voice shut off by an uncharacteristic wave of pathos in recognition of the ultimate tribute she'd just been paid by the remarkable child. She was tempted for a moment to let the matter stand. Surely it would work itself out. But the realist within said no. With Annie she dared not take any such chance.

"I'm afraid that's not exactly how it works, sweetie," she said when she was back in balance and had found her voice. "Kids don't adopt parents. Parents adopt kids. And they don't just *say* they want to adopt. It takes months, sometimes years, and lots of people—lawyers, judges, social workers—and they have to go to court. Adopting is no small thing."

Cheyenne listened, her face growing longer with each new barrier the words raised. At the end she put her arms around Lane's waist and pressed her head against her in quiet defeat. Lane ran her hands helplessly over the small shoulders.

After a moment Annie raised her head. "You could be my *pretend* mother."

Lane experienced a moment of helpless panic. How could she say no to those unwavering blue eyes gazing up at her, bright with hope?

Yet quite apart from her own unwillingness to become any more involved, she knew instinctively that she must stand firm. She dared not risk damaging the child's psyche for the rest of her life by letting Annie pretend she was the mother she had lost.

Unexpectedly, a compromise came to mind. "Not even your *pretend* mother, love," she said briskly. "But if you want, I can be like a big sister."

Cheyenne wiggled away, her eyes unforgiving. Lane let her go.

After a moment Annie asked in a tone that said it didn't really matter, "What would that make me?"

"My *little* sister, I suppose, unless you'd rather be something else."

"It's all right," Annie said in a lackluster tone. After a moment of silence, she said plaintively, "I don't see what's so good about a big sister."

Hitting on the one thing she guessed the child missed most, Lane said, "Well, a big sister's very good when you need a hug, for one thing." She watched Annie mull the words in her mind, heard her sigh, saw a flicker of a smile at the corner of her mouth.

"Yeah," Cheyenne said slowly. "That might be pretty neat."

Pretty neat, but not exactly what the child had in mind when she started out, Lane thought sadly. With a sense of frustration she realized she'd learned little more about

Cheyenne than she'd known before except that her mother's name was Marigold and that Marigold was dead.

Stalling for time, she said, "How about sealing our sisterhood with a hug?" She was not prepared when the little girl threw herself into a bear hug that knocked the wind out of them both, nearly sending them into a heap on the floor.

"All right, Your Sistership," Lane said when she felt the intense pressure of the child's arms begin to relax. "As your big sister, there are still a few things I need to know."

Annie looked up at her in innocent surprise. "What d'ya mean?"

"Things like where do you live?"

"I already told you. On the same street as Rodney."

"Yes, I know, but who do you live *with?* Your father?"

At the change that came over the little girl's face, Lane wished her question had gone unasked. A strange mixture of emotions—resentment, anger, fear—drove out the satisfaction she had seen there the moment before.

"My father's not Wolf!" Annie cried out.

"Of course he's not a wolf," Lane said, bewildered as much by the sudden change that had come over the child as by what she had said.

"My *real* father's gone someplace," Annie said in a defensive tone. "My real father's a hunk. That's what Marigold said. She said even if I'd never get to see him, to always remember he was a special man. And never let anyone ever say my daddy is Wolf."

Lane's regret at having gotten them into what was so clearly a subject of pain outweighed the rampant curiosity aroused in her by the child's cryptic words.

"I'm sure your father was special. You are a special child," she said quietly. "What I really wanted to know was who you live with." She wouldn't be surprised to hear Annie say she lived by herself, she thought, and said aloud, "You *do* live with somebody, don't you?"

"Yeah," Cheyenne said glumly, her face still clouded from the recent storm. "With Edra."

"Edra who?"

The child thought a moment and then shrugged. "Just Edra. She's not home much."

"Tell you what, Annie, we'll put your bike in the pickup and I'll give you a ride home," Lane said. "It's time Edra and I got acquainted."

"That'd be okay, but Edra won't be there. She works from eight to four."

*At last we're getting somewhere!* Lane said to herself. Aloud she said, "Okay, honey. Let's fix a sandwich and find something to do around here until four. I'll give you a ride home then."

FOLLOWING Annie's directions, Lane pulled the pickup to a stop in front of a small, well-kept two-story house in a run-down neighborhood about four-thirty that afternoon.

As she reached to lend a hand to Annie, who was struggling impatiently to free herself from the seat belt, a road-weary blue Volkswagen turned off the uncurbed street and came to a stop a few feet in front of the pickup.

"There's Edra," Annie announced.

Lane raised her eyes to see a trimly built, coffee-skinned woman in her late sixties step out of the small car. Leaving the pickup, Lane walked to meet her, trusting Cheyenne to scramble down from her seat and follow. Beneath gray-streaked hair, Lane saw a warm, strong face and dark, intelligent eyes.

Drawing near, Lane held out her hand. "My name's Elaine Fielding. I must ask you to forgive me for dropping in on you unannounced this way."

"And I'm Edra Hardy," the other woman said with a smile, taking Lane's hand in a firm, friendly grasp. "I'm pleased that you came. Thanks to Annie, you're no stranger to me, you know. Please come inside and I'll fix us something to drink."

She led the way into a pleasant, comfortably furnished living room in which the most expensive item was a twenty-inch TV. There Annie turned inquiring eyes upon the woman.

"It's almost time for *Sesame Street.* Is it all right if I turn it on?" Annie asked.

"If Miss Fielding won't mind having iced tea in the kitchen," the woman said amiably. "I'll fix a glass of lemonade for you. You can come and get it."

In the cheerful, gingham-curtained kitchen, Lane sat at a painted wooden table and watched the other woman take glasses from a cupboard and fix their drinks.

"I thought by the time children reached Cheyenne's age they'd outgrown *Sesame Street,*" she said after a moment of silence.

"I don't guess children ever really outgrow it," Edra replied. "When it comes to Annie, she's just started seeing it for the first time, so it's all fresh as sunup to her."

"Never seen *Sesame Street!* That's hard to believe."

"Not when you consider the nomadic life they lived. Packed from one fleabag rooming house to another, following that ragtag band, singing on the streets of San Francisco for small change," Edra said indignantly.

Lane was too stunned by her words to do more than murmur, "I . . . I didn't know."

"I'm sorry. Of course you didn't. How could you?" the other woman said. "I'm not sure, but I may be the only person to know the whole of Annie's story."

"I wish I had talked to you long ago, Mrs. Hardy, but I only found out about you today," Lane said regretfully. "Annie got upset when I asked her questions, so I kept putting them aside. I'd be more than grateful for anything you can tell me about her."

Leaving a glass of lemonade on the counter for Cheyenne, who darted through the door to grab it as the first strains of the *Sesame Street* theme song sounded from the next room, Mrs. Hardy brought a small tray with iced tea, sugar and lemon to the table.

"Just knowing Annie is at your market, where she's not going to get in a lot of trouble, takes a big load off my mind when I'm at work all day, Miss Fielding," she said, offering a glass from the tray to Lane. "I'll be glad to tell you all I know about Annie. But please call me Edra."

"I will if you'll call me Lane."

"I can't hardly tell you about Annie without first telling you about her mother," Edra Hardy said over a background of cheerful irrelevancies from the TV in the next room. "You wouldn't know about *her,* either, of course."

"Only that she's dead and her name was Marigold."

Edra smiled wryly. "That was my name for her. Her real name was Frances Fairchild, but she hated it. She said it made her sound like she sucked on a lemon, so I called her Marigold. When she got older she dropped the Fairchild and started calling herself Marigold Luna after a moon goddess she read about in a book."

"Then you knew her for a long time," Lane re-marked.

"I was the Fairchild cook."

"Not the Fairchilds who own that zillion-dollar mon-strosity overlooking Gull Cove?"

"The very ones," Edra said. "I worked there from before Marigold was born until after her mother died and her father remarried. Fourteen years in all."

As the sad story of Marigold/Frances and her child, Cheyenne, unfolded, the two women became so absorbed in Edra's recollections that the glasses were forgotten and the ice slowly turned the robust tea into a pale, watery brew.

It was the old story of an aging father who, in a futile grasp for lost youth after his first wife's death, married a very young woman who proceeded to make life miser-able for his child.

Marigold fled to the kitchen, where Edra took the un-loved little girl to her bosom and tried to provide a buf-fer against the neglect upstairs. Left by her father for weeks at a time while he indulged her stepmother's pas-sion for travel, high living and international play, Mari-gold grew into a bitter, rebellious adolescent. As one after another governess clashed with the stepmother and de-parted, it was Edra who gave Marigold most of the care she received. A year into the marriage, Edra was re-placed by a chef imported from France by the step-mother, and went to work at Brennan Memorial Hospital in Seahampton, where she had worked as head cook ever since.

But Edra had remained Marigold's confidante. Often the older woman would find the troubled teenager wait-ing on her front porch when she arrived home from work.

Listening, Lane felt a growing respect for this woman, who, while raising her own three children and sending them to college—one of them through medical school—had responded to the deepest needs of a young person set adrift.

The summer Marigold was sixteen she ran away from home.

"I didn't think anything special when she quit coming by, though I missed her," Edra said. "I just figured Mrs. Fairchild had found a way to keep her from seeing me."

It developed that the Fairchilds were, in fact, away on one of their extended foreign junkets. It had been weeks before anyone knew Marigold was missing. Heartbroken and steeped in guilt, the father had in the end offered a big reward for information leading to her return.

"I should have seen it coming," Edra told Lane regretfully.

"Don't be hard on yourself, Edra. She didn't tell you what she was going to do, did she?"

"What she *told* me was that she was in love," Edra said. "Poor kid. She was so happy. She used to take her guitar and hang out down at the marina in the summer, which is where she met him. When she told me they were talking about getting married, I thought she meant *someday*. I never dreamed she had it in her mind to run off with him then and there."

After Marigold's departure, Edra's only contact with her had been through letters. The first, from Chicago, said that she was with someone who called himself Wolf, the leader of a small-time rock band, and that he'd promised if she came away with him, he'd make her their lead singer.

*The Wolf Annie remembers in her nightmares,* Lane thought grimly.

The second letter reached Edra a few months later from somewhere in Wyoming and told of the birth of Cheyenne. After that, sporadic notes and postcards, no two mailed from the same place, told only of disillusionment and shattered dreams. As she spoke of them, Edra's eyes filled with tears, and she paused to fumble for a handkerchief and wipe her eyes.

"Then I didn't hear from her all last year, and the last letter I wrote came back stamped No Forwarding Address," Edra said. For a moment Lane feared the woman's grief would not let her go on.

When she spoke again Edra's voice was flat from held-back emotion. "In March this year Marigold finally wrote, and when I got the letter, I'll be honest with you, I cried. She wrote that she was dying of leukemia. She wanted me to know she'd arranged for Cheyenne to be put aboard a plane and sent here to me after she passed away. Two days after I got the letter, I got Annie."

Lane drew a soft breath of sympathy, sadness wrenching her heart as she pictured the dying young mother agonizing over the welfare of her little girl in the last hours of her life. *Poor Marigold,* she thought. *Poor Edra. Most of all, poor Annie.*

"The past four months have brought you some traumatic changes," Lane said quietly. "It couldn't have been easy on such short notice to rearrange your life to include a child."

To Lane's distress, Edra's composure suddenly collapsed.

"I'm ... too ... old," the woman said brokenly, "too tired. I've been cooking in somebody else's kitchen nearly every day for the past fifty years." She paused in a visible effort to get herself in hand. Bringing out the handkerchief again, she blew her nose. "I'm sorry," she said. "I didn't aim to let myself go like that."

"It's all right," Lane assured her gently. "I understand."

"I was going to retire this fall," Edra said when she had regained control of her emotions. "With my social security and the hospital's retirement plan I could quit working and still be able to get by, but there's no way I can support a child. All I can do now is go on working."

"But surely her mother didn't expect you to take care of Annie until she's old enough to take care of herself!" said Lane in disbelief. "What did the letter say?"

"That the man she married wasn't Cheyenne's father and not ever to let her fall into his hands...."

"That would be Wolf?"

"Yes, more's the pity," Edra said disapprovingly. "It went on to say if I couldn't keep Cheyenne myself, she'd trust me to find a good home for her." She stopped, gazing at Lane despairingly. After a long pause she lifted a shoulder in a gesture of defeat.

"What can I do? People looking to adopt want babies, not half-grown kids. Even if I knew how to go about finding a home for her, how could I be sure it would be a good one?"

"Have you thought of going to Mr. Fairchild?"

"I'll be honest with you. I might have—even though she asked me not to in the letter—if Mr. Fairchild hadn't died in February," Edra confessed. "Marigold was afraid if Cheyenne was left in their care, she would grow up as neglected and unloved as she had."

"What about the stepmother?"

"Never. That's one place I won't turn. With her father, I can tell he cared—keeping that big reward offer going all these years. I like to think he realized his mistakes and had a change of heart," Edra said. "But that stepmother! The child could be a lot worse than just neglected if she ever got in *that* woman's way."

Numbed by Edra's painful recital, Lane stared blindly into her half-empty glass, caught up in problems that, having been heard, had suddenly become hers.

Edra sighed. "She should have been in school, but there were only a few weeks left when I got her, and after the last move before Marigold died, she took to teaching the child at home, so she doesn't have any records," she said. "I didn't think it would hurt to wait until fall to start her. That gives me the summer to run down her school records."

"Annie's smart. You needn't worry about her catching up," Lane said reassuringly.

"I pray every night for a good home for the child," Edra Hardy said, and Lane raised a hand against a mist that clouded her eyes. Taking a last sip of tea, she prepared to leave.

Then, as she rose to her feet, she caught a fleeting glimpse of Annie's stricken face at the doorway before the child turned and slipped silently back to the living room across the hall.

How long had the child been listening? How much had she heard?

## CHAPTER FIVE

"DEAD? Whatdya mean he's dead?"

"I don't know a better way to put it," the gatekeeper said.

From out of his broad lexicon of obscenities, Wolf spat a single trenchant syllable of frustration.

He'd been screwed! He'd listened to Hugo the drummer and done everything Hugo told him to do. He'd spent the better part of two months running down the stuff Hugo said he had to have. Now here he was at the gate of the million-dollar pile of stone they called the Fairchild Cottage, ready to start negotiations with Goldie's old man for the reward, and this twelve-hundred-a-month gate guard was telling him Fairchild was dead.

It was all Wolf could do to keep from opening his mouth and howling like his namesake. If the son of a bitch was dead, the reward went with him. Wolf could kiss the money goodbye.

Out of the corner of his eye Wolf watched sullenly as the guard left the gatehouse and walked over to the car to take a closer look. Wolf hated the feeling that things were closing in on him. He squirmed inside the unfamiliar confines of the brown double-breasted polyester suit he'd bought at the Goodwill to show Goldie's old man he was a dude to be listened to.

Leaning closer, the gatekeeper stared fishy eyed through the window at Wolf and said, "He died in February. If you're his son-in-law, it looks like his widow wasn't in a hurry to let you know he was dead."

The widow? That'd be Goldie's mother! Wolf felt a mild flurry of returning hope. Maybe he was wrong that she'd already passed away. Suppose she was still around—offering the reward money would have been as much her idea as his. The offer could still be good.

The promising thought was cut short by the gate man. "If you think I'm going to let you in to see Mrs. Fairchild, you better think again. I've got orders that she doesn't want to see *any*body."

He was at the car window, looking pleased with himself, his face so close Wolf caught the stale smell of onions on his breath. Wolf flexed his hands and considered the satisfying prospect of shooting one arm out and jabbing two fingers in the bulging eyes. Containing himself, he reached for the briefcase Hugo'd given him to carry.

"She might change her mind if she knew what's in here," he said. "It's about her daughter...."

But the guard wouldn't listen. "So that's what you're up to," he interrupted with a snort of laughter. "Get outa here! If it's the reward, even if I let you in, which I'm not about to do, it won't do you any good to talk to her."

"If you knew what's in this briefcase—"

"I know this—the missing daughter was Mr. Fairchild's child from his first marriage. The second Mrs. Fairchild couldn't care less. The first thing she did after the funeral was cancel the reward.... You still think you got something to say to her?" When Wolf didn't answer, the guard backed away to let the car move on. "Now git!"

Seeing his last hope dwindle to nothing, Wolf felt for a moment as if he'd been poleaxed. He sat motionless behind the wheel, uncertain what to do.

"Hey! You heard me," yelled the gatekeeper, turning surly. "I told you to get the hell outa here. If you're not gone in the next thirty seconds, I'll call the police."

IT WAS EARLY EVENING when Wolf got back to Greenwich Village and went looking for Hugo, knowing there'd be no settling down for him until he'd told him about the day's debacle. Climbing the four flights of stairs to Hugo's walk-up, Wolf braced himself for the abuse he'd have to swallow when he told the drummer the scam had failed.

Hugo was a bastard, but he was smart and he was a lawyer, even if he wasn't *licensed*. He'd never taken his bar exams, but he'd been through law school. He made as much on the side as if he *was* a lawyer, giving advice to people who, for their own reasons, didn't want to deal with a real one.

If the widow had canceled the reward, it meant she sure as hell didn't want to hear about a grandchild that wasn't even hers. He'd be damned if he could see any more in it, but maybe Hugo would. It wouldn't be the first time.

Breathing hard, Wolf pulled himself up the last two steps and rang Hugo's doorbell, then waited and rang again. Though he hadn't especially expected to find Hugo in, he swore and pounded on the door. When that brought no response, he swore again, then gave a departing kick to the door and plodded back down the stairs to the street. There he started making the rounds of Hugo's favorite watering holes and found him drinking cheap wine at a back booth in a place called Guido's.

Wolf slammed the briefcase down on the table in front of Hugo, slumped into the bench across from him and wasted no time breaking the bad news.

"I got there too late," he announced sourly, with a sudden perverse feeling that the whole mess was somehow Hugo's fault. "If I hadn't wasted the best part of two months scuddin' all over the goddamn country looking for the 'proof' you said I'd need..." Something in the back of Wolf's mind reminded him that it wouldn't have made any difference—Fairchild was already dead before he'd started looking, but it felt better, blaming it on the drummer.

"You mean somebody got there ahead of you?" Hugo demanded. "What the hell are you trying to pull, Wolf? I don't believe it."

"I mean you can kiss your share of the reward money goodbye. Old Fairchild died last February."

"Well, you don't say."

Wolf was prepared for anything but the gradual change he saw in the other man's face. Angry suspicion turned to satisfaction, and there was a growing glint of speculation in Hugo's eyes.

Hugo was on to something. Wolf felt a stir of excitement and leaned across the table in sudden impatience to hear what the drummer had to say.

"You want to bet he left a bundle for Goldie in his will?"

"For all I know, he never even left a will," Wolf said glumly.

"Don't be stupid. People that rich always leave wills. Furthermore, any man who'd pay a hundred grand to locate his missing daughter is a sure thing to name her in his will. Might even hope an inheritance would bring her home after he was dead."

Wolf eyed Hugo malevolently across the table and took back everything he'd thought about his intelligence a while before. Couldn't the bastard see? Fairchild could have left his whole goddamn estate to Goldie, but what good would it do them? Goldie was as dead as her old man, and *she* sure as hell didn't leave any will.

"Yeah, and George Bush is going to invite the Wolf Pack to play at the Kennedy Center," Wolf said derisively.

"Shut up, Wolf. We're on to something. Take the kid—"

"*You* shut up. Fairchild didn't even know there was a kid."

"That doesn't matter. Let's say he left half of his estate to Goldie, who died a couple months later," Hugo said. "Now listen carefully, because it's what we're going to build on." He stopped long enough to take a cigarette from the package on the table and light it on the butt of one he then stubbed out.

"It doesn't matter if old Fairchild didn't know about the kid," he continued. "The kid would be Goldie's heir and could inherit by what the courts call 'right of representation.'"

Wolf stared at Hugo sullenly, trying to get a clear picture in his mind of what the drummer was telling him. Gradually he felt better. He wasn't sure he understood, but if Hugo saw something in it...

"Yeah...well...how do we get into the picture?"

"You go into court as the kid's father and claim her share of the estate on her behalf," Hugo told him. "Damn it, you *are* her father, aren't you? Don't lie to me, because you may have to prove it with a blood test, or worse yet, a DNA test."

"You were with the band. You know damn well I'm the kid's father. It's my name on her birth certificate," Wolf said, bridling. "The kid came a little early because of how sickly Goldie was when she was pregnant. That don't mean the kid's not mine."

"I'll say this much. Nobody ever accused Goldie of sleeping around," Hugo said. He took a drag on his cigarette and picked up where he left off. "Okay. So you get the court to appoint you trustee of what she's going to inherit. I'll tell you later what you do from there.

"Right now, you're going to need proof Goldie was Fairchild's daughter as well as the kid's mother, and evidence of your connection with them both. Let's see what you've got in here."

Opening the briefcase, Hugo spilled its contents onto the table and shuffled through pictures of Goldie and pieces of her handwriting, a copy of Cheyenne's birth certificate naming Goldie as the mother and Wolf as the father, a license for their marriage, a death certificate for Frances Fairchild, a.k.a. Goldie Luna, and a locket containing a picture of Frances/Goldie as a child, with her mother.

Hugo finished looking over the stash and gazed at it thoughtfully.

"It'll do," he said at last, scooping up the papers and pushing them back in the briefcase. "You know where the kid is?"

"At Seahampton. I've got my eye on her."

"Good. Find a place to rent out there and start making noises like a father. Make her come live with you."

"I don't know if I can."

"Do as I say. Bribe her if you have to. Say you're her father and she has to, and if she won't, the police will see that she does. If worse comes to worst, you're bigger than she is. Scare the hell out of her until she'll say anything you tell her to," Hugo said grimly. "But first we go through the public records at Seahampton for Fairchild's will and make sure he left something to Goldie."

"And after that?"

The pseudolawyer gave him an appraising look, and Wolf could taste the bile rising in his throat. *Like I'm yesterday's garbage,* Wolf thought bitterly.

"After that we'll get you into some decent clothes and go to work making you respectable."

# CHAPTER SIX

STILL TRYING to sort out the elements of his recent encounter with Lane Fielding, Matt was deep in thought on his return from the market. He entered the house and walked through the kitchen. The sight of Cora through the open doorway of the sun room, sitting straight-backed in her favorite rocker, cleared his mind and brought him to a stop. Her stockinged feet were resting on a footstool, beside which lay her orthopedic shoes. Her glasses sat squarely on her nose.

As solid as Plymouth Rock, he thought affectionately, and was about to speak up to let her know he was there when he saw that her book lay facedown in her lap and realized she was fast asleep.

*Way to go, Cora,* he muttered softly. He had long suspected these never-acknowledged catnaps were the source of Cora's seemingly endless energy.

Not wanting to disturb her well-deserved rest, he was moving away when he saw her chin drop and watched her draw a shuddering breath and wake with a start. She made a grab for the book as it started to slide off her lap and caught sight of Matt in the doorway.

"I was reading," she said defensively.

Matt resisted a temptation to tease her and said instead, "Remember our little sea-drenched Annie? I found her at the beach again this morning."

"Good heavens, you didn't have to fish her out of the water again, I hope."

"No, but I had to pull her out of a hole, and something had scared her pretty bad. When I brought her with me to get the car, she wanted to see you, but you weren't here. I loaded her and her bike in the Chevy and took her to the produce market, which seems to be her haven."

"I was out shopping," Cora said, and went on worriedly, "What can her folks be thinking of, letting her run loose this way?"

"There doesn't seem to be much evidence of 'folks,'" Matt said, explaining as best he could the misconceptions Annie had managed to establish about her parentage.

"We just found out about it today," he said.

"But doesn't anybody know where she comes from?"

"It doesn't look like it. She showed up unannounced at the market one morning about two months ago and has been going there every day since."

"Two months? All that time and no one's taken the trouble to find out where she comes from or who her parents are?" Cora said critically.

"Well, you see there's been this misunderstanding," Matt explained. "Lane has thought all along she belonged to me, and I thought she belonged to Lane. Neither one of us had the guts to accuse the other of child neglect until this morning, when it all finally came out in the open."

"Lane? Who's Lane?" Cora asked, a glimmer of new interest in her eyes.

"Elaine Fielding. The woman who runs the market," Matt said quickly, not caring to encourage Cora's romantic penchant for putting one and one together and coming up with wedding bells. "She was on her way to start looking into Annie's home life when I left the market a while ago."

Cora bent down to reach for her shoes and slipped them on. When they were laced and tied, she pushed herself stiffly to her feet.

"I wish I'd been here to see the child," she said as she started for the door. "I've got something I found the other day. I'm sure it belongs to her."

Curious, Matt followed her into the kitchen, where she opened a drawer and brought out what looked like nothing more than a shapeless blob of melted red plastic. Upon closer examination he saw it had once been a child's miniature coin purse, not much bigger than a tea bag, with a metal clasp at the top.

"It was in the bottom of the dryer the day after I dried her clothes. It must have fallen out of one of her pockets," Cora said, handing him the purse. "It won't open. Looks as if the heat ruined it."

Matt worked at the clasp with his thumb and forefinger before handing it back with a shrug.

"You keep it," Cora said. "If the child's at the market every day, you can take it to her the next time you're there."

"I don't know that I'll be going anytime soon." A shadow of his own inquietude crept into Matt's voice at the memory of the sudden cooling in Lane's manner a short time before. He fingered the bit of plastic absently.

"I guess we might just as well drop it in the trash can," he said. "She probably hasn't missed it, and she's not apt to want it anyhow after it's been through the dryer."

"I wouldn't be so sure about that," Cora demurred.

As Matt bent to open the lid of the trash can, his fingers felt some small object inside the plastic.

"Wait a minute," he said and let the trash lid fall back into place. "There's something in here. Feels like a penny... or a dime... or a candy." *And a legitimate excuse to see the elusive Lane.* As quickly as the truant thought skated across Matt's mind, he rejected it.

Aloud he said, "Even if she doesn't want the purse, she might feel differently about whatever's inside." He dropped the bit of red plastic into a pocket of his windbreaker and turned to go up to his office.

"Is the rug dry yet?" he turned back to ask Cora.

"It should be, but you might take off your shoes before you go in."

By the time Matt reached the third stair, Cora was right behind him, carrying a large roll of brown wrapping paper, which she thrust under one of his arms for him "to walk on, just in case."

He was hardly surprised upon reaching the door to his office to find the carpet still unmistakably damp. With a grunt of annoyance, he left his shoes in the hallway and started laying brown paper ahead of himself as he walked into the room that had once been a sleeping porch and had solid walls of windows on three sides.

Halfway in, Matt saw the windows were all wide open. To let in the breeze for the purpose of speeding the drying, he presumed. The effect was not unlike that of a wind tunnel. Documents and letters he'd spread out on his desk and table that morning in more or less orderly sequence lay strewn like autumn leaves all around the room.

By the time he'd closed the windows and harvested the last of his scattered papers, his feet were cold and his humor testy. When finally he settled down at his desk, it was all he could do to sound reasonably pleasant as he returned the several calls awaiting him on his answering machine.

The last call, from Cliff Harris, whom Matt had left in charge during his absence, had to do with a program of procedural changes Harris had talked Matt into letting him initiate. The conversation left Matt vaguely uneasy, and he went to the fax machine to read the progress report on the program Cliff said he'd sent Matt that morning.

It was Matt's own plan. He knew its provisions by heart. He had worked up the proposal from observations and ideas that had been germinating in his head in the years he'd been goofing off. There'd been a time when he had believed in the plan so completely he'd counted on it as his passport to the position left by Birch's resignation. But when his father saw the program he called it "sophomoric," and Matt had quit believing in it himself.

He'd regretted discussing his idea with Cliff Harris, assuming that Cliff, too, had found it lacking but was too kind to say so. But he'd come to find out, after his father was gone, that Harris had believed in the program almost more than Matt had.

They were talking about major changes that in theory would greatly benefit the company but in practice could play hell. What if his father had been right?

Resolving to call Cliff after the market closed and talk the program over with him again, Matt sat down at his desk, reached for a notepad and pencil and turned on the computer to catch the last hour of the market before the Exchange closed for the day.

As the hour moved on, he found his attention faltering. Figures faded into fruits and vegetables, and a long-limbed, green-eyed woman with reddish-brown hair came stealing across the computer screen to block out the all-important, ever-changing numbers.

When trading was over and the Big Board shut down, Matt turned off the computer and stared down at the still-blank notepad at his elbow with a sense of frustration. He pushed back his chair and stood. One sock foot came down outside the paper, and he felt the dampness seep through the wool to the sole.

Swearing, he lifted his foot off the rug and at the same time became acutely aware of the wet smell of rug cleaner that permeated the room. He swore again. A Seahampton beach house with Cora Meigs in residence was no place to run a business.

Unexpectedly, the situation struck him as funny.

"To hell with it," he muttered, laughing. He'd better go into the city and talk things out with Harris. That way he could hang out at the office for a few days and see how everyone was adjusting to the initial change. If nothing more, it would give Cora time to get her rugs clean and her curtains washed without getting in his hair.

Stepping gingerly across the floor and out, he put on dry socks in his bedroom and went downstairs to tell Cora he was leaving for a few days. Twenty minutes later, he was on the road.

THE DAY AFTER her visit with Edra Hardy, Lane kept one ear cocked for the muffled roar of the old Chevy's motor that would announce Matt Cheney's arrival.

Under other circumstances, she told herself, she wouldn't even have noticed if he stayed away, though it never dawned on her he would. He'd rescued Annie twice and shown concern for her. Wasn't it natural he'd want to hear the little girl's story; natural that she should share what she'd found out with him?

In any case, she had a market to run—farmers arriving with fresh produce to deal with, bins to be filled, an occasional early customer to be waited on. She set Annie to work polishing the first of the new summer crop of apples and showed her how to build a pyramid for an apple display.

But she worked absently, a troubled eye on Annie, who seemed unusually subdued. Lane's thoughts returned time and again to Edra Hardy's unsettling disclosures the day before. And beneath it all, she waited.

Every old car that rattled into hearing range sent her pulse leaping into high gear only to slow back to normal when the car came into view—another color and a different make. The day ended, and Matt Cheney never came.

Three days passed, and still no Matt. She couldn't believe he'd washed his hands of the child after they'd cleared up their crazy misunderstanding. She began to wish she hadn't dismissed him quite so summarily.

She hadn't meant to freeze him out. All she'd intended was to put him on notice that she wasn't one of the women standing in line for a place on his list of female companions. Maybe she should have made it clear she had no objection if he'd like to check back and find out what she'd learned about Annie. It shouldn't have been that hard to get the message across without compromising herself or making him see her words as a come-on.

"You've been as restless as a bead of water on a hot skillet all week," Angus said that evening as she lowered the awning and prepared to close up shop. "Best you get a good night's sleep tonight, lass."

But Lane hadn't had a good night's sleep since her disturbing conversation with Edra. This night was to be no exception.

A home for Annie. There was the problem, she thought, staring blindly into the darkness from where she lay. Only two people in the whole village of Seahampton gave a damn about finding a home for Annie—Edra and herself—and poor Edra had already given up. Which meant it was up to Lane.

One way would be to go to the juvenile authorities and let them give Annie to anyone who wanted to take her, but this was not an orphaned kitten to be handed over to the first comer. This was Annie.

No doubt there were churches and social-service societies that might be able to put Lane in touch with couples looking for a child, but it was all so impersonal, and if and when such a couple appeared, how could she know they were right for Annie?

In the darkness she shivered. It was too much like playing God. She couldn't do it alone. If only there were someone to talk with who cared about Annie but could see the problem objectively. She needed a sounding board, she thought, and out of the night's stillness a name came to her, a name she had refused to acknowledge until now.

Next morning Lane screwed up her courage, swallowed her pride and picked up the phone book to look for a number for the third person in Seahampton who knew—and might conceivably be interested in—Cheyenne: Matt Cheney. She punched the numbers, her heart thundering in her breast. After four rings, just as she was thinking of giving up, a woman's voice answered in a polite, impersonal tone.

"This is the Cheney residence."

Braced for Matt's voice, Lane blinked in surprise.

Collecting herself, she said, "Could I speak to Mr. Cheney, please? My name's Lane Fielding."

There was a moment's pause at the other end of the line before the woman, her voice now warm and friendly, spoke again.

"This is Mr. Cheney's housekeeper, Cora Meigs, Ms. Fielding. I'm terribly sorry, but he's not here."

"Oh." More of a sound than a word, the single syllable betrayed her disappointment.

"He had to go into the city on business. I don't know when he'll be back."

"His vacation's over?" asked Lane with an unaccountable feeling of disappointment.

There was a wry laugh at the end of the line. "It's not so much over as never started," the woman said. "I wouldn't call what he's been doing since he got here 'vacationing.' He spends most of his time shut up there in his room with the telephone and the computer and the fax machine. The little girl, Annie, has provided the only diversion he's had."

Lane murmured in puzzlement. The housekeeper's words didn't fit her image of Cheney.

"I worry about him," Mrs. Meigs confided, as if to an old friend. "He's so wrapped up in his work I'm afraid he's forgotten how to play. Even when he's out for a walk on the beach, it doesn't mean he's relaxing. It only means he's working out some business problem in his mind."

Lane gave a sympathetic cluck, wondering at the new note in the housekeeper's voice.

"But I'm probably telling you something you already know," the housekeeper said. "Let me give you his home and office numbers in the city. I'm sure you can reach him at one of those."

"Oh, no, that won't be necessary," Lane said quickly. "It's nothing important. I'd really rather you didn't tell him I called." With a polite word of thanks, she hung up and leaned her head on her hand for a moment in a state of confusion.

Mrs. Meigs's words threw a quite different light on Matt Cheney. She made him sound altogether unlike Roz's womanizing playboy "hunk." If what she was looking for was a sounding board, she wasn't sure one persona was a lot better than the other.

Through the office window she caught sight of Annie bobbing up and down in an aimless game of hopscotch outside the market area, and knew the little girl was killing time until Lane came out. She'd promised to show her how to braid the garlic into strings for hanging when Annie had finished her regular chores. As Lane rose from her desk to go, the phone rang and she paused to answer.

On the other end was her friend Roz.

"I just called to tell you I'm going to be your neighbor," Roz said, a note of barely contained excitement in her voice.

"Here in Seahampton? Wonderful! Where? When?"

"On Swan Road. A friend and I are renting a cottage from one of my customers for the next four weeks, starting Wednesday."

*Friend?* No need to ask the gender. Roz's voice was a giveaway.

"Anyone I know?"

"No. His name's Neal Roberts. He's an attorney."

"How about having supper at the farm with me next Friday? That'll give you a couple of days to settle in," Lane said.

"Love to," Roz replied. "I've got a lot to tell you. I can hardly wait."

They talked for another minute and were about to hang up when Roz said suddenly, "Oh, by the way, guess who I saw going into the Beaumont Theater at Lincoln Center the other night? That old heart-stopper Matt Cheney."

Lane couldn't think of a thing to say. Not seeming to notice, Roz rattled on.

"The woman with him looked as if she'd just stepped out of a Saks window. Must be your Annie's mom."

Before Lane had a chance to set the record straight about Annie's parentage, Roz put an end to their talk.

"Here comes Neal. I gotta go. 'Bye, darling, I'll see you soon." Lane stared at the dead phone in her hand a moment and placed it carefully back in its cradle.

So much for a sounding board, she thought with a touch of regret. Not that the idea wasn't a good one. She just hadn't taken into account what a busy man Matt was.

STANDING in the huge window of the main room in his midtown loft apartment, Matt gazed across the lighted darkness toward the Empire State Building in the near distance and wrestled with the notion of calling Lane. He had a perfectly honest excuse for doing so. He'd tell her he'd been wondering all week what she'd found out about Cheyenne and hoped she wouldn't mind that he was calling.

But suppose she *did* mind? Suppose she told him in a few short sentences what she'd found out and then hung up? It would leave him without so much as a crack in the door. He'd be damned if he'd let her shunt him off again. Next time she blew cold on him, he was going to know why. It was time he got back to Seahampton and decided what to do about Lane.

Heading toward Seahampton early the next afternoon, Matt gradually became aware of a growing feeling of well-being. For one thing, he realized he was whistling as he turned the car off the Long Island Expressway on the last lap to the beach. As nearly as he could recall, he hadn't whistled since he was a schoolboy.

Letting down all the windows, he breathed deeply, filling his lungs with the tangy breeze off the ocean. Why did he feel so good? he wondered. He'd been at his Wall Street office four full days and hadn't accomplished what he'd gone into Manhattan to do—except escape the rigors of Cora's housecleaning fervor. And that had been an excuse for taking off to the city—not a reason.

It was a crock—telling himself he had to discuss the new company procedures with Cliff Harris in person. The truth was, he'd gone into the city for only one purpose. To prove to himself that Elaine Fielding was just one more attractive woman in a world full of attractive women.

Dinner and a show with Tan Piper the first night had shown him what a stupid idea that was. The evening had been...what could he say? Forgettable. It wasn't that Tan had lost any of the charm that had captivated him back in the days when she was a deb. It was that he found his attention straying, and before the ordeal was over, it was all he could do to keep from yawning in Tan's face. By then, the supreme foolishness of trying to equate Lane with other women was clear.

It would take more than a bizarre experiment to make him see Lane Fielding as just another pretty face. Not a woman who had the guts to throw over a Manhattan career to rescue a failing farm for a widowed aunt and the wit to parlay it into a flourishing produce market. Not a woman who had the heart to take on the troubles of a lonely waif and a cranky, old arthritic Scot.

Adjusting the Taurus's cruise speed as he approached the cloverleaf for Seahampton, it occurred to Matt that he wasn't being quite fair. He'd known other women as beautiful and accomplished, as overall remarkable as Lane. It was just that there was something special about the sweet, husky voice that made him want to take her in his arms and never let her go. There was something about her long-legged, curvy body, her bright, humorous face and intelligent eyes that made her special, too. Special, anyway, to him.

Arriving on the outskirts of town, he turned off the highway on Shell Road and five minutes later coasted into the graveled driveway at the back of the beach house. As he stepped out of the car, Cora's head appeared at the back door.

"Well, it's about time," she called out. "I'd decided you'd given up on vacationing."

Matt laughed and came bounding up the back stairs to give her a peck on the cheek.

"The Pope will be relieved to hear you've just spoiled your record for infallibility," Matt teased.

Cora sniffed. "Don't be smart," she said reprovingly. "I've a notion not to tell you who called you yesterday."

His arm across the woman's shoulders, Matt reached around her, opened the screen door and escorted her into the kitchen. "I'm all ears."

Clearly hoping to be coaxed, Cora didn't answer at once. When no more was forthcoming from him, she said smugly, "Lane Fielding."

Matt's face reflected his astonishment. Quickly hiding his feelings, he said with a show of composure, "Did she want me to call back?"

"If she did, she didn't say so," Cora said.

"She didn't happen to mention what she was calling about?" Matt couldn't help asking.

"No. She just said it wasn't important. Oh, dear," Cora broke off unexpectedly, her face suddenly flushed in embarrassment. "I forgot. She did say she'd rather I didn't tell you she called."

Matt gazed at her, delighted. "It's all right, Cora. As long as you've got your loyalties straight. Thanks for the information," he said. "I just wish I knew what it meant."

He reached to take a plum out of a basket of fruit on the counter and bite into it.

"Would you like something to eat?" Cora asked.

"I stopped for a hamburger along the road, but thanks anyway," he said. "I'm going out again. There's an errand I've got to run."

Leaving the kitchen, he climbed the stairs to his room. A few minutes later he left the house. In the pocket of his tan sailcloth jacket, he carried the remains of what had once been a little red plastic purse.

Under a sudden compulsion to get going, he didn't bother to try his Seahampton car of preference. Instead he stepped back into the Taurus and set out in the opposite direction from which he'd come.

Stepping into the market, he savored the outdoor smells of the freshly picked farm goods mingled with the spicy fragrances of cinnamon rolls and flowers. He scanned the area in search of Lane.

He didn't see her at first. When he did, he was unprepared for the staggering jolt of pleasure that struck him.

She was wearing a yellow men's shirt that hung loose like a smock over white cotton pants, and her hair was tied back from her face with a length of red-and-green tartan ribbon. She was knee-deep in a rainbow of flowers she was in the process of moving onto a tier of shelves directly in front of where she stood.

She bent to pick up a bucket of huge fluffy-headed pink and purple blossoms. In a purely reflexive movement, Matt stepped forward to offer his help. By the time he got to her, she had hoisted the huge bouquet onto the bottom shelf.

"If the bottom ever drops out of the produce market, you could make a career for yourself as a freight handler," he said. He let a hint of the admiration he felt for her self-reliant style surface in his teasing.

At the sound of his voice she turned, and he was relieved and reassured to see a smile of welcome light her eyes. He saw no trace of the cool send-off she'd given him the last time he was here. Nevertheless, they took a moment to size each other up before either spoke.

Smiling, she asked without preliminaries, "You came to hear about Cheyenne?"

Matt said, "If you can spare the time," and wondered what she would say if he told her what he'd really come for: to learn about himself, and her, and what he sensed was happening between them.

Lane glanced around. The market was busy. It was not a good time. Even so, she started, "She's an orphan, Matt, at least functionally. Her mother's dead and the father took off before she was five. Look—" she broke off suddenly. "It's a long story and here comes Cheyenne. This'll have to wait for another time. Call me and we'll arrange to talk when she's not around."

Matt looked up to see the little girl hopscotching randomly along the sand-strewn aisle that led up to the flower stand, her pale yellow pigtail bobbing up and down with each jump. Nearing them, she raised her eyes. At the sight of Matt, she came to a stop and walked on slowly.

"Hi, Annie," Matt said. She eyed him with no particular show of friendliness. For a moment he wasn't sure she was going to speak.

"Hullo," she said finally. Then to Lane, on a faintly accusing note, she said, "I didn't know *he* was here."

"I brought you something," Matt offered, and in a shameless effort to curry favor, reached into his pocket for the damaged purse. "Cora found this in the dryer after she'd dried your clothes. She figured it must be yours." He held out the blob of red plastic to Annie, who let out a squeal of joy and snatched it from his hand.

"I'm sorry the dryer was ruinous, but if you'll tell me where it came from I'll try to get you another."

But Annie wasn't listening. All her attention was focused on opening the purse. Frantically she worked at the clasp with her fingers. When it wouldn't yield, she brought the plastic up to her mouth and tried to force the frame open with her teeth.

"Stop that, Annie. You'll break your teeth," Lane said sharply.

Matt's hand went out and firmly reclaimed the purse. He reached into his pocket and pulled out the miniature Swiss army knife given him by Birch. Watching him, Annie jigged up and down with new impatience.

"You're sure you want me to cut it open?" Matt asked. Annie answered with an emphatic nod.

Forcing the point of the main blade deep into the plastic, he slit open the purse and handed it to Cheyenne to explore. Relaxed, he watched amused as she poked her finger into the hole in search of something and with a cry of delight, fished out the small object she found inside. With a soft, crooning sound she pressed the treasure against her cheek and then to her lips in a shower of noisy kisses.

Tears glistening in her eyes, she looked up at last and said to the watching grown-ups, "It's Marigold's ring." She held it up for them to see, an unusual bit of craftsmanship fashioned of gold mixed with four different alloys to create intertwined strands of green, white, yellow and red.

At the sight of the ring, Matt suddenly remembered another place and time. He was in a metal-crafts shop in Sag Harbor, looking into the round dark eyes of a woman with the sweet face of a child. He was slipping the ring onto her finger, saying, "Now you belong to me."

As if waking from a dream, he became aware again of Annie, hugging him fiercely around the legs with both arms.

"I love you. I love you. I love you," she was caroling blissfully. "You found Marigold's ring!"

And, as if from afar, he heard Lane say, "Matt, are you all right? You look as if you've seen a ghost."

Like a diver coming up for air, he fought his way back to the surface. Quickly he regained his composure.

"Sorry. I just thought of something. Please excuse me. I've got to go," he said, fighting for control. He turned and left without a backward glance, knowing only that he had to get away.

## CHAPTER SEVEN

WITH AN UNREASONABLE feeling of rejection, Lane watched him drive away. For a moment she stared after the car, then went to look for a piece of bright-colored string, hoping to avert further tragedy by securing the precious ring safely around the child's neck.

She returned to the work of the market but couldn't get Matt's strange exit out of her mind. Something had taken place that she did not understand. He'd been all charisma up to the moment of departure. Then, like a light, he'd turned it off and all but fallen over his feet to get away.

Had he been paying her back for walking out on him the last time he was here? she wondered uneasily, and at once thought not. It had been more as if something unexpected had come over him, not as if he had suddenly decided to be rude.

That night she dreamed about Matt Cheney, an incredibly erotic dream she clung to and lost as she awakened to the pounding of her heart, and over it the peal of the telephone. Still under the spell of the dream, she stretched voluptuously and reached blindly for the phone. The sound of Annie's voice hit her like a dash of cold water.

"Lane..." She heard desperation in the word, a cry for help. It brought Lane upright and wide-awake, the word *Wolf* in the forefront of her mind.

"Annie! What's wrong?"

"Edra's on the floor, like she's asleep, but I don't think she is. I can't get her to wake up."

"Oh, my God," Lane muttered under her breath. Annie sounded on the verge of hysteria.

"I'll be there, honey, just as quickly as I can," Lane said, already out of bed and extending the long phone cord to its limit as she flung open her closet door and grabbed for clothes.

Cheyenne's frightened voice continued from the other end of the line. "Lane, I'm scared. D'you think she might be . . . ?"

*She can't say the word,* Lane thought, and realized there was nothing of reassurance she could truthfully say. A swell of pity for the little girl filled her heart and a growing anxiety speeded her hands as she dressed. If Edra was dead, Annie shouldn't be there alone with her.

"She's probably just fainted," she said encouragingly, hoping what she said was true. "It'll take me about fifteen minutes to get there. You'd better go to a neighbor's until you see my car."

"I don't know anybody," said the forlorn little voice at the end of the line, reminding Lane that Edra had said they had only recently moved to this house from a smaller apartment so Annie would have her own bedroom. She saw it was daylight and automatically noted it was 6:15 by the bedside clock.

"Then wait out on the front steps for me."

After a moment's hesitation, Annie said, "If she wakes up, she might be afraid. I'd better stay here inside."

"Do as you like," Lane said, knowing she had no time to waste challenging Annie's indomitable will. "I'll call Emergency to send an ambulance when I hang up. As soon as I'm dressed I'll be on my way."

As a precautionary measure—for who could predict what the ever-resourceful Annie might think to do before she arrived?—Lane added, "Oh, and Annie, don't try to move Edra or wake her up. If she should waken, tell her I'm coming and that, for her own good, she must stay right where she is until the ambulance arrives."

When Lane pulled up in front of the Hardy house a short time later, the ambulance had not yet come. The front door was open and Cheyenne was watching for her through the screen.

"Edra's awake," the child called out. "She's on the floor in the kitchen. You said not to let her move, but I don't think she wants to much."

Lane found Edra sprawled on the confetti-patterned linoleum in the kitchen, clearly in great pain. A ladder-back kitchen chair lay tipped over on the floor beside her. A cupboard door above the nearby counter swung wide open to expose shelves filled with home-canned fruit.

With a stifled moan, the injured woman said weakly, "I sure do appreciate your coming."

Lane dropped to her knees beside her. "Don't talk," she said. "Stay quiet till the ambulance gets here and we find out how badly you're hurt."

"I reckon it's my hip," Edra said in a labored voice. "The chair. I climbed on it to...get a jar of peaches out of the...cupboard for breakfast. I've done it a hundred times. I must have been a little off balance."

"Shh. Please," Lane said. "Save your talking for the medics...." She broke off at the sound of Annie's voice from outside, where she had gone to watch for the ambulance.

"They're here," the child called, and Lane rose and stepped aside to make room for the two white-uniformed men to get to Edra. Annie hovered nearby, watching with troubled eyes. Lane put a comforting arm around her shoulders. One of the medics knelt on the floor and began a cursory examination of the injured woman, who was clearly in pain as she answered his questions.

"We'd better have a doctor look at this, ma'am," the medic said presently, rising to his feet. "We'll take you to Emergency at the hospital."

Edra let out a cry. "But I *can't* go to the hospital," she wailed. "They're expecting me at work."

"You're not going to work today, lady," the medic said bluntly. "Let's have a doctor look at you. He may want some X rays before he decides what you can do." Turning to Lane, he asked, "Does she live here alone?"

Before Lane could answer, Edra's thin voice spoke out. "There's Cheyenne..." she started, and stopped as if she realized the full magnitude of her problems.

"Oh, Lordy, Lordy. *Cheyenne!*" she cried out in anguish. "I forgot all about her. What am I to do with Cheyenne?" She broke down and began to sob.

Without consciously willing herself to make the move, Lane was on the floor beside the distraught woman again, taking her hand and smoothing it gently with her own.

"Don't worry about Cheyenne, Edra."

She spoke impulsively, thinking only to comfort Edra, and realized as the words left her mouth that she had nothing to back them up. *My God, the poor woman has every reason to worry,* she thought. Then unexpectedly she was struck by an idea so simple, so obvious, she wondered why it hadn't occurred to her before.

"I'm going to take her home with me," she said to Edra. "Just forget about everything else and go to the hospital. I'll keep Annie as long as you need me to. I live by myself in an old farmhouse that has three extra bedrooms, and I'll enjoy having her with me.''

As Lane talked she became aware that the little girl was on the floor beside her, leaning around Lane to get Edra's attention.

''She really means it, Edra. She really does. We're kinda like . . . sisters,'' she cried out excitedly, her tongue tripping on the words in her haste to get them out. ''I won't be any bother. I promise. I'm a lot of help. Lane says so, herself.''

Edra's tears had stopped, and she lay quietly watching the medics jockey a gurney through the door into the kitchen. With nothing to ease the pain but her own determination not to give in to it, the woman lay still. Annie watched her with anxious eyes, as if waiting for some kind of release, but Edra said no more. She sighed, closed her eyes and appeared to yield to the inevitable.

''I'm sorry you got hurt, Edra,'' Annie said in a small, apologetic voice, as if somehow it were all her fault.

THE MORNING AFTER he returned the little red purse to Annie, Matt had no mind for the work that had stacked up during his absence in the city. The questions that had woven in and out of a restless night's sleep had nothing to do with his business affairs and everything to do with Annie's ring.

Shortly before six he pulled on an old pair of white duck pants and a faded blue polo shirt and slipped out the back door and around the house quietly, so as not to awaken Cora. Then he headed down the path to the beach, where he'd wandered late the night before, searching for half-lost memories of the first time he'd seen the ring and of the woman he had bought it for.

Deaf to the screeching gulls that wheeled down to prey on surf fish swept along by the incoming tide, he settled down on the breakwater. Under the hypnotic spell of the ebb and flow of the sea, a picture of the fragile, sweet-faced woman with her long brown hair and dark, wistful, sometimes pain-filled eyes gradually began to take shape in his mind. For a moment he saw the small, slender body, the pale, fair skin. The image blurred and fragmented. Try as he would, he couldn't hold the pieces together in a complete image of the Marigold he had known.

*Marigold.* He wondered suddenly if he'd said her name aloud yesterday when he saw the ring. He'd heard the sound of it in his ears, of that he was sure; but it could just as well have been the voice of Cheyenne. The ring was hers. Who but Marigold could have given it to her?

Could Annie be her child?

He found it hard to envision Marigold as a mother, yet he couldn't think of any other reasonable explanation for the ring being in Annie's possession. And if Marigold was Annie's mother, then Marigold must be . . .

He left it there, but it wouldn't stay. The thought he had avoided until now pushed its way to the surface. *Hadn't Annie told Lane her mother was dead?*

The truth hit him at last with the force of a physical blow. He came to a stop, his head reeling from the shock. She'd had such a hunger for life. He'd intended to give her a feast, but he'd failed her. Before he knew what had happened, his chance was lost.

With a deep feeling of regret for the lost relationship he'd never fully understood and now never would, Matt accepted what had to be the truth: Marigold was Annie's mother, and now she was dead.

Driven by a sudden urge to get out of himself, he left the breakwater and walked down to meet the tide, stopping to shy a piece of driftwood at the gulls, then jumping back to escape an incoming breaker. The action broke his tension.

He moved slowly along the hard-packed sand at the water's edge, the sadness still with him; but as he walked he gradually began to realize that his sadness lacked all feeling of personal loss. His sorrow was for the child, Annie, left alone, and for the woman, Marigold, who'd been cheated out of her fair share of life.

Twenty-one she'd been when he knew her eight years before. Dead at twenty-nine. Too young by far.

Twenty-one, and yet there'd been a shadow of disillusionment in the dark eyes that asked for nothing, expected nothing, that had made her look older, even soul weary. By the same token, there'd been something childlike about her, too, a vulnerable quality that had set her apart from the teenage girls who flocked like seabirds around the marina where he kept his boat. She had seemed a refreshing naïf next to the blasé career sophisticates who'd been regular fixtures in his life at the time.

It had been one of those summers when he was at loose ends and feeling sorry for himself, he remembered as he paused to poke a foot absently at the empty shell of a horseshoe crab. One of those summers of getting even with his father. The irony was that the chic, sleek young women he partied and sailed with—the whole playboy scene he'd adopted to get his father's goat—bored him out of his skull. Remembering, Matt grinned in spite of himself.

Into this monstrous boredom had come Marigold with her guitar and her sweet, smoky little voice, singing ballads on the dock at the marina. A kind of kinship of discontent had grown between them, and before he knew it her troubles had made him forget his own. He'd wanted to take care of her. God, how he'd wanted to take care of her. She'd made him feel needed. No one had ever needed him before. For a while that summer his only goal in life had been to make Marigold happy.

She'd seen the ring in the window of a craft shop at Sag Harbor where he tied up one day when he'd taken her out for a sail. He remembered how he bought the ring and put it on her engagement finger and how later, back on the boat, they'd made love for the first time. All he'd wanted after that was to find a job with another investment firm and marry Marigold.

At least he'd had sense enough to know he couldn't support a wife without a job, he thought wryly, stopping to tie a shoe. Sense enough to realize that Marigold would provide a good excuse for his dad to give the prodigal the old heave-ho.

He would never forget how his father had summoned him back to the city and sent him to the West Coast for a four-week investment seminar without notice. There'd been no time to find Marigold to tell her, and he'd never known where she lived. When he got back weeks later, Marigold had gone off with a rock musician. He never saw her again.

He still remembered how broken up he'd been, blaming his father for taking him away from Marigold, blaming Marigold for abandoning him for another man, despising himself for loving Marigold with such fervor when she apparently hadn't loved him at all.

He wondered now if his father had shipped him off that summer because he'd gotten wind of what was up between them. A flicker of resentment stirred in him and snuffed itself out. It was too late to matter.

But it had mattered then. Mattered enough that he'd loaded his sloop with provisions and sailed alone up the Atlantic coast to Cape Cod. He'd licked his wounds and searched his soul and damn near got caught in a hurricane. His father had never really forgiven him for taking French leave, but at the end of the summer he'd come back a healed man.

A pall of melancholy settled over him now, and he turned away from the sea and trudged through the heavy sand toward the path that would take him back to the house.

It was as if Marigold and their relationship were something he'd read in a book. A book with the ending missing. Unexpectedly he wondered if Elaine Fielding had uncovered anything in her inquiry about Annie that would fill in some of the lost pages. "A long story," she'd said. And not a happy one, he thought, since it surely had to do with Marigold's death.

What possible good would it do him to revisit old sorrows? he asked himself, half-inclined to leave the matter alone. But his step quickened. Was it too early to find Lane at the market? He rubbed a hand over the early-morning stubble on his face. Not if he took time first to shower and shave.

Of a mind now to hear what Lane had found out about Cheyenne's background, he took off at a jog. His interest had been peripheral before. Now a nagging need to know propelled him on his way.

BACK IN THE PICKUP after learning that Edra had suffered a broken hip and seeing her settled in a hospital room to await surgery, Lane at once started making lists in her mind of all the things she had to do.

She'd talked to Edra's son, a doctor in a small town in New Jersey, who'd promised to be at the hospital with his mother well before she went into surgery that afternoon. She'd called the hospital kitchen where Edra worked and told them why Edra had not shown up this morning. Next on her agenda was moving Annie's belongings from Edra's house to her own.

First she must stop by the market and make sure everything there was under control. Had she told Angus about the shipment of honeydew melons due in from California today? And shouldn't they be picking the green beans a little earlier, before they got so big? And what about...?

Not until Annie, buckled into the seat beside her, broke the silence did Lane realize she'd been so preoccupied with problems, she'd hardly spoken to the child all morning.

"I guess when Edra quits hurting so much she's gonna be glad she broke her hip," Cheyenne said abruptly. A worried note in her voice caused Lane to turn her eyes away from the road in a quick glance at the little girl's face.

"Why would she be glad, Annie?" she asked cautiously.

"She won't have to have me around anymore," Annie said in a voice so still Lane had to tilt her head closer to make sure she heard the words. For a moment she was at a loss for something to say that would restore the little girl's damaged sense of self-worth. How was she to explain that Edra was too old and too tired, that she had raised too many children and worked too hard for a well-earned rest to give it up for the sake of another child?

"You heard her say she wanted to find a home for you, and you thought that meant she just wanted you off her hands. Isn't that right?" she asked the child.

"Well, that was what she said," Annie replied quietly.

"You're dead wrong, sweetie," Lane said, and saw Annie shoot her a look of sullen disbelief. "That may be what you think you heard, but don't forget I was the one she was talking to. I may not remember Edra's exact words, but I remember exactly what she meant."

She waited a moment for her words to sink in, and when she spoke again her tone was gentle.

"We don't lie to each other, Annie. You know that. What I'm going to tell you is the truth. What Edra was saying to me was that you are a special little girl who deserves a real home and young parents who have enough time and energy to give you the love you need and deserve. Things that will never be in her power to give you."

Encouraged by a look of willingness in the child's eyes, Lane continued, doing her best to explain the situation from Edra's point of view. When she had run out of words, she was relieved to see that some of the uneasiness in the round blue eyes had vanished.

"So you can see why it's not a very good idea to listen to what other people say when they don't know you're listening," Lane felt obliged to say in conclusion. But she sounded disgustingly priggish to her own ears.

Annie slumped pensively within the strictures of her seat belt. "Well, all right. If you say so," she said finally. "But I don't see how I'm ever suppose' to find out what's going on if I don't."

They were nearing the market, and Lane decided she'd better leave well enough alone.

"I called Angus to open up, but I want to run in and see if anything needs my attention. Then I'm going over to Edra's and move your stuff to my house. You can come with me if you like, or stay and help Angus with the usual chores. Edra said you have the key and that everything I find in your room is yours."

Annie wriggled to straighten herself in the seat. "I sure feel sorry for Edra after what you said," she told Lane in an uncommonly sober voice. She hesitated and went on thoughtfully, "Living with her was all right, I guess, only she was awful tired, and she was always mending or sewing or doing something with her hands. It would have been nice if she'd ever made a lap that I could sit in."

A minute later Lane turned into the marketplace, parked the pickup in front of the office and got out. She was totally unprepared for the small, pigtailed dervish who came tearing around from the other side of the vehicle and caught her in a flying tackle around her waist.

"I'm really sorry about Edra, but oh, Lane, I'm so glad I get to come live with you," Annie cried joyously, hugging the wind out of Lane. "I want to live with you for always."

A feeling of panic rose inside Lane, and she fought it down. This was no time to be fainthearted, she told herself. If there was one thing Annie didn't need right now, it was more rejection.

"Let's take it one day at a time, Annie baby," she said softly, laying a kiss on the crown of the pale golden head as the little girl detached herself and went cheerfully off toward "her" corner of the market.

As Lane scanned the marketplace in search of Angus, she noticed a dark blue Taurus that looked vaguely familiar. She watched the car turn into a parking space, then caught her breath as the door opened and the long, easy-moving body of Matt Cheney stepped out from behind the wheel.

Her pulse gave a sudden rush. *Nothing doing,* she told herself, resisting an impulse to run out and welcome him. This was the guy who had walked off and left her standing with her mouth open the day before.

He was looking for her, she realized. She stayed where she was. He finally caught sight of her and started forward. She noticed that his unruly hair was damp, as if from a recent shower. She certainly couldn't call him handsome, but there was a vitality about the strong, irregular face she found tremendously appealing, catching her attention in a way handsomeness alone seldom did.

"Could we talk?" he asked without preliminaries when he was near enough to be heard without shouting. The lines of his face were taut, his eyes shadowed by some inner conflict, but the vitality was still there.

"I suppose that could be negotiated," Lane replied.

He responded with a blank look, as if he'd forgotten about yesterday, but in the next moment he managed an uncomfortable grin.

"Oh, that," he said. "You'll have to forgive me for running off that way."

"The hell I will," Lane muttered inwardly.

He offered no explanation for yesterday's hasty withdrawal but stated the purpose of today's visit bluntly. "I came to hear about Annie."

Why the sudden rush? thought Lane testily. He'd been in no such hurry to hear Annie's story the day before.

"Not a chance this morning," she said crisply.

A shadow of disappointment flickered across his face.

"When do you think you could find time?" he asked, an almost beseeching note in his voice.

Unexpectedly, Lane's defenses collapsed.

"This has not been the usual morning," she said more graciously. "You catch me at a very bad time, and this is not a good place to talk. Even in my office, there are interruptions, and it's not that easy to avoid Annie."

"Let me take you to lunch," Matt said. "You *do* eat lunch, don't you?"

"Usually a sandwich between customers, but thanks for the offer. I really don't have time today." Then, to her surprise, she found herself relenting. "I do have to take some things to my house in a couple of hours. It's a good place to talk if you'd care to meet me there."

Matt gave her no time to change her mind. "Say around twelve-thirty? I'll be there if you'll tell me where you live," he said.

When she'd drawn a map of the country lanes that would take him to the farm, Matt went on his way, leaving Lane to take care of sundry chores that awaited her before going back to Edra's house to collect Annie's belongings. The chores done, she called the hospital and was told that Edra would be sleeping under sedation until her son arrived.

Relieved of further responsibility for Edra, and assured by Angus that the market could carry on without her for a while, Lane saw she had just time enough to move Annie's things to her house before Matt arrived at the farm. Annie was expecting to go with her but she couldn't tell him Annie's story with the child listening in. As she puzzled over what to do, Mrs. Brandon in the bakery booth unwittingly solved the problem by asking Annie if she'd like to cut out cookies for her. Annie, who loved nothing better, begged to be left behind.

"Be sure and get Marigold's picture," Annie called after her anxiously as Lane got in the pickup. "Be sure you get *everything*. Don't leave anything behind."

"I'll take you back to get it if I do," Lane promised.

Assembling the child's meager belongings a short time later, Lane was disappointed to find almost nothing in the way of playthings other than a dilapidated Pooh bear, held together by a network of patches, and a tattered copy of *A Child's Garden of Verses* with the back cover missing. There was also a badly scarred guitar and a picture in a heart-shaped plastic frame of an ethereal-looking woman with large, haunting eyes and a wreath of daisies around her head—a kind of latter-day "flower child," Lane thought, and guessed her to be the late Marigold. Other than that, there was a motley collection of clothing—T-shirts, sweaters, jackets, sweatshirts, coveralls, jeans and underwear—most showing some signs of wear but all of them clean and in reasonably good shape. She found no shoes, so assumed the child owned only the pair she was wearing.

Everything fit into a large canvas carryall, which Lane was in the act of packing when the telephone rang.

"Mrs. Hardy?" a woman at the other end asked when Lane answered.

"No. I'm sorry, Mrs. Hardy's not here," she said. "May I ask who's calling?"

"My name is Susan Craddock, and I'm calling from California," the woman said. "I don't actually know Mrs. Hardy, but this is in regard to the little girl who lives with her. It's important. When will Mrs. Hardy be back? Or better yet, is there someplace I can reach her now?"

"Mrs. Hardy had an accident this morning and is in the hospital," Lane said.

"Oh, God, how awful. What do I do now?" the woman muttered, her voice distraught.

"Excuse me, but if you are calling about something that concerns Cheyenne, perhaps you'd better tell me,"

Lane said. "My name is Elaine Fielding. I own and operate a farm produce market just outside of Seahampton. Cheyenne will be staying with me until . . . actually, I don't know just how long, but it may be several weeks."

"Then you know all about Annie? Is she all right?" Susan Craddock asked anxiously.

"Mrs. Hardy has told me a lot. As much as she knows, I think. And Annie's in good hands and doing fine."

"You know about Wolf?"

"Enough to understand he's a most unsavory character who may or may not be Cheyenne's father."

"Marigold said he's *not,* and I believe her. I'm Marigold's friend and was with her when she died." There was a sound of something close to hysteria in the woman's voice. "She left a few things with me for safekeeping and asked me to see that Cheyenne gets them when she grows up."

"Keep them, by all means. Certainly for the time being they are much better off in your hands," Lane assured her.

"But they're not in my hands. Wolf has them."

"Wolf?"

"That's what I'm calling about. Marigold's husband—the rock player who calls himself Wolf Wilding—came to my apartment to get Annie." The woman began hesitantly at first, then the words came crowding out in a rush as if she couldn't stop them. "I told him she was gone, and he forced his way in and tried to get me to tell where I sent her. I wouldn't, and he pulled out a switchblade knife and said he'd slit my throat if I didn't tell him where she was. . . ."

She was crying now. Lane was too horrified to speak. There was a long moment of silence on the line.

"And I...told him," the woman said at last in a broken voice that was hardly more than a whisper.

"He didn't give you much choice," Lane said, a sick feeling in her stomach, an uneasy shiver along her spine.

"He made me give him everything Marigold left me to give to Cheyenne, which was mostly pictures and papers."

"When did all this happen?" Lane asked. Again there was a long silence on the line, and Lane was beginning to wonder if Susan Craddock had left the phone when she spoke again.

"He started hitting me and made me promise I wouldn't tell anybody he'd been here. He said if I ever did, he'd have me killed, and, honest to God, I was so scared at first I really thought he *would*," she said. "But lately I've been thinking he'd never know if I told Mrs. Hardy he's out to get Annie, and I knew if I didn't do it pretty soon I'd go out of my mind."

Gooseflesh prickled the back of Lane's neck as the full import of what Susan Craddock had just told her swept over her.

"How long ago was he there?" Lane asked, gripped by a sudden ugly suspicion that Wolf might already have been stalking Annie, biding his time, for whatever reason.

"Three weeks ago. I should have called right away, but since you say she's all right, I guess no harm's been done. Just the same, I'm really sorry."

"Please don't worry about it," Lane said, striving to keep the sound of her apprehension out of her voice. "If it's any comfort, I'm in the process of moving Annie and her belongings away from the address you gave Wolf, so he'll have to locate her again. And if and when he does, he'll discover she couldn't be safer if she had her own security guard.''

"That really takes a load off my mind,'' the woman said, her voice almost cheerful for the first time. "Maybe I can finally get a decent night's sleep. I just wish I'd screwed up my courage to call sooner.''

*So do I,* Lane said to herself as she hung up, deeply disturbed but seeing no purpose in admitting to Susan Craddock how shaky she felt. It took more arrogance than she possessed to feel certain she could protect the chick she was taking into her nest from the marauding Wolf.

A restraining order, she thought. She could at least have Colby Strawn—the Fielding family attorney since before Lane was born—get a court order to keep Wolf at bay. He would have to hire a detective, of course, to find where Wolf hung out and serve the papers.

Driven by a sudden sense of urgency, she looked up Colby Strawn's number and dialed. To her surprise, the lawyer himself answered. The office was closed for lunch, he said, and he'd be tied up all afternoon. Could she come now?

Though she realized that would make her late for her meeting with Matt Cheney, her anxiety would not let her wait another day. Hesitating only a moment, she told him she would leave at once.

Ten minutes later Lane pulled into a parking space at the rear of the small Victorian cottage that housed Strawn's office, glad she'd chosen not to wait. It wasn't the first time she'd been given a sense of solid comfort simply from knowing she had Colby standing by. Nor was she alone in that, she thought. The doughty attorney was a venerated institution around the small east Long Island town of Seahampton.

She smiled now as she looked up to see his balding head and stout, medium-tall frame, impeccable in one of the gray worsted suits that were his uniform, standing in the open door waiting to greet her.

The business that brought Lane to his office took only a few minutes. The lawyer heard Lane's story and assured her there would be no problem getting a judge to sign an order to keep Wolf away from Annie and her. It might take time for a detective to locate Wolf and serve the restraining order, he warned, and strongly advised her in any case to be constantly on guard.

What he said came as no surprise. The knowledge that he would take care of obtaining the order and see it through gave her a new feeling of security. Nonetheless, she left Colby's office a short time later feeling disheartened and a little lost, thanks to a bit of information casually dropped by the attorney on her way out.

After nearly sixty years of practicing law alone, Colby was looking for a young lawyer to work with him and gradually take over his whole practice so Colby could retire.

It was the first time she'd ever thought of age and retirement in relation to Colby Strawn. She'd known him forever. During the sometimes stormy settling of her Uncle Charlie's affairs, she'd come to count on his wisdom. Her adviser and her friend. He seemed ageless. Somewhere in the back of her mind she knew he was pushing eighty. That he was old had never entered her mind. The thought disturbed her immeasurably.

The fact was, she was going to miss Colby Strawn.

She'd never been one to worry a lot about her ability to make the right decisions when it came to business, but the problems of finding a home for Annie and keeping her safe from Wolf were different. These were decisions that affected the welfare and future of another human being.

More than ever now she needed Colby. With Colby retired, whom could she turn to to tell her what she was doing right and what she was doing wrong?

"Matt Cheney," she said aloud. He had shown a real concern over Annie's welfare, and who else was there?

She wasn't looking for a husband or a yes-man, or a committee to tell her what to do. All she was looking for was what Colby Strawn had given her—sound advice and a listening ear.

# *CHAPTER EIGHT*

HOMEWARD BOUND a few minutes after she left Colby Strawn's office, Lane pressed hard on the gas pedal and hoped some zealous cop wouldn't come charging out of nowhere and nail her for breaking the speed limit. She'd tried to call Matt before she left Edra's house to let him know she'd be delayed, but no one had answered. Now she had an anxious feeling Matt Cheney might not have been inclined to wait for her if she wasn't there when he arrived.

Slowing down, she left the main highway for Mill Road and turned shortly into Fielding Lane, a graveled private road flanked by farmland on either side that led to the old family farmhouse where she lived.

Lane hated being late. Even more, she hated finding herself, because she was late, on the defensive with Matt Cheney. She was doing him a favor, after all, agreeing to talk to him on an already hectic day. Between the Craddock woman's call and her new concern about Colby Strawn's retirement, she felt none too sociable. Still she knew she needed Matt as a sounding board when it came to Annie.

Once she was past the apple orchard, the faded yellow farmhouse that had been her haven from the time she was a child came into view. As always, the sight of the old house gave her a comforting feeling of homecoming. Except for the specter of the man named Wolf that had hung over her since her conversation with Susan Craddock, she could almost forget the scramble of problems the morning had brought.

The building had grown up around a simple four-room core that dated back nearly a hundred years. Later generations had added wings and gables, turning the structure into an architectural anomaly that Lane couldn't have viewed with more pride had it been designed by the great Frank Lloyd Wright.

The rambling farmhouse, built on a slight rise, nestled among ancient trees and overgrown shrubs that hid the driveway from the road. Not until Lane nosed the pickup around the last huge clump of lilac bushes could she see the now-familiar Taurus Matt Cheney sometimes drove, parked in the shade at the front of the house. Pulling up beside the car, she was a little surprised to see there was no one inside.

As she stepped from the pickup, she noticed that the day had grown hot and muggy and realized the climate must be stifling in the parked car. Matt had no doubt taken refuge on the porch. She started toward the house, but when she reached the low wrought-iron fence that separated the big yard from the graveled driveway, she saw the porch was empty.

Opening the gate, she moved on, peered into the shadows cast by ancient trees in and around the yard and came to a full stop. A strange syncopation in her heart made her head feel suddenly light.

At the sight of Matt Cheney asleep under the old mulberry tree she used to climb as a child, she had an eerie sense she was back in her early-morning dream.

She drew a quick breath and hesitated. Spurred by a sudden awakening within, she stepped quietly forward through the grass. A few feet away from where Matt lay she came to a stop and gazed down at the sleeping man.

Not Adonis exactly. Adonis sculpted by a rough, primitive hand, she decided. Yet there was something almost beautiful about the lean, muscular body and rugged features that held her spellbound.

She stood for a long moment watching the steady rise and fall of Matt's breathing until she began to feel like a voyeur. With a conscious effort, she tore her gaze away. The golden yellow of an oriole's feather that lay like a sunbeam on the grass near her feet caught her eye.

She retrieved the bit of brightness and moved toward the sleeping man. His slightly parted lips, sensuous, relaxed, seemed infinitely inviting. She reached out, and in an impulsive faux kiss, brushed the oriole feather lightly across his lips. He stirred in his sleep and slapped irritably at the feather. In sudden panic, Lane backed off a few steps and stopped, unable to look away from Matt as he pulled himself to a sitting position and stared at her owlishly with sleep-dulled eyes.

After a moment his mouth stretched in a prodigious yawn. He hoisted himself lightly to his feet and rubbed a hand across his face. Raising an arm, he mopped beads of perspiration from his forehead on the sleeve of his knit shirt and combed his fingers through the wheaten thatch of hair, damp and disheveled from the heat.

When their eyes at last met, and Lane saw he was now fully awake, she felt unaccountably self-conscious. What in the world had she been thinking of? she wondered, shocked and a trifle undone as she groped for something to say to break the uncomfortable silence that grew between them.

"Have you been here long?" she asked.

"Long enough to catch up on some of the sleep I lost last night," he said with a grin.

Reminded of her own restless sleep the night before, Lane felt a new heat rise to her cheeks. A perverse impulse tempted her to say, *That's what you get for messing around in my dreams.*

Instead she said properly, "This humid heat makes everyone drowsy." Then, eager to escape the uneasy feeling that somehow he knew she'd been watching him, she turned abruptly and made for the house, saying over her shoulder, "Let's go inside. It's ten degrees cooler in there."

"What did we do before air-conditioning?" Matt said, contributing his share of small talk.

*She said. He said.* It was up to her now to say something or risk drowning in her own silence. Why must she suddenly come down with a tied tongue in the presence of Matt Cheney?

"I don't know what you did, but we did what I still do," she said, her voice sounding artificial to her ears as they climbed the three broad steps leading up to the porch. "Most of the rooms have cross ventilation, and the house is situated so it catches the breeze off the ocean every night. I open the windows when the sun goes down and close them in the early morning. It works so well we've never felt any need to go to the trouble and expense of installing air-conditioning."

"Aren't you afraid of being robbed?"

"Not here. We're very low-crime around here. I keep the doors locked, and the screens are wired to an alarm that would scare off the devil himself."

She opened the front door and motioned him to come as she stepped inside.

*"Voilà,"* she said and came to a stop. "That's funny." The house was almost as warm as the air outside.

"Darn! I forgot," she said in sudden disgust. "I went off in such a hurry this morning, I forgot to close the windows. I'm sorry. I was dying to prove my point."

"Why the special hurry this morning?"

The question reminded her of why Matt was here. Since that first glimpse of him asleep in the grass she'd been behaving as if their meeting was some sort of tryst. Now everything came back into focus, and she was suddenly once more at ease.

"It all has to do with Annie," she said. "I'll tell you, but first let's find a cooler spot. The best I can offer is the kitchen, which has a big ceiling fan. Under the circumstances, it's probably the coolest room in the house."

"Sounds fine to me."

Leading the way past the staircase landing and down the hallway to the kitchen at the end, Lane remembered she hadn't had anything to eat since the night before. The grandfather clock struck one, and a rumble in her stomach reminded her she needed food.

She took the two steps that led down to the big tile-floored country kitchen and paused to look up at Matt. He was directly behind her on the bottom step, and she was startled to find him so near.

"Before I try to tell you the strange, convoluted story of Annie, I've got to have something to eat," she said. "Will you join me? It's only fair to warn you that when my stomach's empty, I turn into a terrible grouch."

Before she could turn to go into the kitchen, Matt tipped her face up with his hands to meet his. He kissed first one corner of her mouth, almost roughly, and then the other.

Lane was caught completely unawares, and a warm wave of excitement washed through her. She closed her eyes, suddenly light-headed and lacking the will to move. Dazed, she was conscious only of the rush of heat through her body as she waited for the kiss to deepen. When nothing happened, she opened her eyes, and found them mirrored in Matt's questing look—a look that set a wild pulse throbbing in the deep, sensual core of her body.

Slowly he withdrew his hands, but she was powerless to break away from his compelling gaze until she saw his eyes cloud with uncertainty and look away. Irrationally, she felt cheated. Searching for words to strike out against the small betrayal, she heard Matt utter a strange muffled sound and heard in it a note of yearning that matched her own unwelcome longing.

Then she was in his arms, her breasts pressed hard against his muscular chest as his mouth came down to cover hers with a fierce, sweet hunger that brought their tongues together in frantic, caressing strokes. Then, with one final, lingering thrust of his tongue, he pulled away from her with a groan. He stood looking down at her, and she gazed back, bewildered at first, too shaken to speak.

Out of nowhere she heard the voice of her friend Roz Kramer saying *"That old heart-stopper Matt Cheney."*

She drew a sharp breath and walked across the kitchen to open the refrigerator.

Matt watched her go before moving to stand at the big bay window that jutted beyond the east wall of the kitchen. He stared out moodily, wondering at his own response to their kiss.

He'd been following her down the hallway, still groggy from his interrupted sleep, when suddenly she was smiling up at him, and he was lost. He hadn't been ready for the jolt that hit him when his mouth touched the magnetic softness of her skin, nor for the intoxicating taste of her lips and the delicious satiny hollow of her mouth.

Something extraordinary was happening inside of him where this woman was concerned. Something that had never happened before. Not just the familiar, insistent, raw sexual arousal he knew well, though there was plenty of that, too. Something was happening in his head, in his heart. Something that implied involvement he was in no position to undertake. It scared the hell out of him.

He had only to remember his mother to know that until he could fulfill his obligation to the family firm without selling the woman short, he had no right to get involved in an affair of the heart. In a company shaped by his father, he wasn't even sure a time would ever come, but that wasn't something he could explain to Lane even if he thought she'd believe him.

Venting his dissatisfaction in a deep sigh, he turned away from the window and took stock of the big, cheerful kitchen for the first time. There was a simple homeyness about the rustic tile floor and counters, the natural-wood cupboards, the many-windowed walls, that spoke of a contentment quite at odds with the prickle of tension he felt in the air.

His eyes came to rest uneasily on Lane, now occupied at the sink, her back to him so all he could see of her head was the sorrel hair. Something in the set of her shoulders and the prideful lift of her head told him he wasn't the only one shaken by the sudden unleashing of hidden passions.

She was rinsing garden greens under a running faucet and dropping the leaves into a salad spinner on the drainboard beside her. He felt an almost irrepressible urge to cross the room and seize her in his arms and . . .

Swearing inwardly, he stifled the images that crowded seductively into his head. As if he weren't already in enough trouble, he thought.

Her silence was beginning to get to him. Why the devil didn't she turn around and say something? Anything. Give him hell, if that was the way she felt. Granted, he had no business coming on to her like some adolescent who'd learned all he knew from X-rated movies, but he'd be damned if he'd let her think he'd meant to demean her.

He started across the room. At the sound of his steps on the hard tile floor, Lane turned her head. Her eyes met his in a level look that brought him to a stop and held him there.

"All right. I shouldn't have come on like I did," he said crustily. "I could say I'm sorry, but it would be a lie. I can't be sorry for doing something I've wanted to do since the first day I saw you." He was stopped by a new thought and surprised to discover that it mattered. "I got the impression somehow that you didn't exactly hate it yourself, but if I was wrong . . . if I offended you . . . well, I *am* sorry about that," he finished.

Her gaze left his, then returned. He was unsettled to see that her eyes held an expression that was both cool and a little cynical.

"The last thing in the world I wanted was to make you mad," he said, feeling more clumsy with every syllable.

"Mad? Should I be?"

Her voice had that delicious bluesy break in it that played hell with his psyche. It was all he could do to stifle his sudden resurgent desire, let alone find a response to the wickedly innocent question.

She waited a moment for him to answer, and when he didn't she said with a hint of sarcasm, "It's really my fault. I should have made it clear when I asked you here that this was to be a meeting, not a date."

"Now wait a minute, Lane," Matt broke in, coming to his senses with unexpected heat. "I resent your innuendo. Think what you like, I didn't plan that pass. It just happened. Those damned dimples at the corners of your mouth... all I can say is they drive me nuts."

Lane eyed him skeptically. After a moment her face yielded a weak grin.

"I *told* you I get mean when I'm hungry. Let's take our plates in to the table and I'll tell you what I know about Annie while we eat."

AT ONE END of the trestle table that spanned the width of the big bay window, Lane toyed idly with the fork on her plate and lapsed into silence, unable to detach herself at once from the story she had just finished recounting to Matt.

Sitting at a right angle next to her, Matt gazed out the window to the strip of silver along the far edge of the landscape where the sea began, his mind too full of the strange account he had just heard to speak.

*So it was true. Marigold had been Annie's mother, and Marigold was dead.*

Rising, Lane took Matt's empty plate, stacked it with hers and reached for the casserole with the microwaved remains of last night's pasta.

Automatically, Matt got to his feet. His mind only vaguely on what he was doing, he cleared what remained on the table and followed absently, unloading the bowl and glasses on the counter near her. Pulling a tall stool out from under the counter, he sat and watched in silence as Lane made order out of confusion around the kitchen. His thoughts were on the poor, lost Marigold, who, that one short summer, had been the focal point of his existence. Would things have worked out better for her if his absence hadn't given Wolf the opportunity to play Svengali?

"About Annie," he said aloud. "You say you're bringing her here to stay with you? For how long?"

Lane looked up as she loaded the dishwasher beside her.

"I'll keep her for as long as she needs to stay, of course," she said, and he was disconcerted to hear a note of reserve in her voice, as if to remind him she hadn't forgiven him and warn him to keep his distance.

"Then Annie doesn't have an immediate problem?"

Lane paused in the act of scraping the last shreds of pasta into the garbage disposal and gave him a look of disbelief.

"The poor kid's life is nothing *but* problems, Matt," she said indignantly. "She needs a permanent home and parents she can count on. She needs the security of a real mother and father, committed to her as truly as if she'd been born to them."

"You're talking about adoption?"

"What else is there? I won't put her in the hands of some public service to be passed endlessly from one foster home to another for the rest of her juvenile life."

"Adoption is pretty damn permanent," Matt protested with unexpected heat, at a loss to understand his gut reaction against putting Annie up for adoption. "It sounds to me as if you're in one hell of a hurry to turn her over to strangers."

"You're darned right I'm in a hurry," Lane flared. "Annie's been shuttled from place to place like excess baggage from the day she was born. It's about time somebody found her a permanent home. If you have a better idea, let's hear it."

"Couldn't you...?" Matt began, and lapsed into silence, uncomfortably aware that he could hardly suggest Lane hold off for a while on the chance that... Oh, hell, he didn't know what. The kid was in good hands with Lane. Like the old saying, Why try to fix it if it ain't broke?

When he didn't finish his sentence, Lane said caustically, "You're a big help." After a moment's silence she sighed and said, "It's not your problem. Ever since I first talked to Edra I've known it was up to me to find Annie a home."

"Why you?"

"Who else is there?" she asked flatly. "Her mother and her grandfather are dead. She's scared to death of the man who claims to be her father. Edra's got her own problems. I'm the only one around in any position to do something about Annie."

She turned back to the sink and gave a last swipe at the casserole, tucking it away in the dishwasher before she started on the silverware. Matt watched her in silence, his mind on the woman as much as on what she was saying. Like Marigold, she was unique; yet she was as different from Marigold as a deep, sparkling river from a shallow brook.

Lane's words caught his attention again.

"...make sure the couple who get Annie are warm, loving people who want a child for the right reasons and can keep one step ahead of a very bright little girl," she was saying.

"Are there *wrong* reasons?"

"To save a marriage, or because adopting is the 'in' thing, or because someone on an ego trip wants a child to turn into an extension of themselves."

"I suppose the adoption agency looks into all that."

Lane looked at him in dismay. "You don't think I'm going to let an *agency* find parents for Annie, do you?"

"You mean you expect to go out and find a couple to adopt her yourself?" Matt said. The stubborn look on her face told him that was exactly what she expected to do. "How do you think you'll find this paragon couple, Lane? Put an ad in the paper?" he asked.

She glared at him resentfully. "I'll talk to the kinds of people a childless couple might confide in if they were looking for a child—doctors, lawyers, judges, ministers, counselors," she said, her voice chilly.

As surely as Lane felt it was up to her to find a home for Annie, Matt suddenly felt it was up to him to save Lane from the pitfalls he could see in the course she was setting for herself.

"There are official channels to be gone through, you know," he reminded her, frustration creeping into his voice.

"Of course I know, but until the papers are ready to file, I intend to be in control," she snapped. "They can deal me out later, but unless I'm absolutely sure a couple is right for Annie, no papers will be filed."

"Things just don't work that way, Lane," Matt said in exasperation, not relishing the role of devil's advocate.

"I don't see why not."

"Because they won't let just anyone handpick a couple to be Annie's parents. You're not her mother. You're not even a relative."

"But she's in my care, and there's no one else," Lane said stubbornly.

"I'm not sure even the most devoted bystander has any right to offer a child for adoption. Officialdom is going to slap you down if you try to go through with any such plan."

Lane turned angrily, about to speak, then reconsidered. She bent and took a box of dishwasher detergent from beneath the sink and filled the dispenser. Slamming the door with a bang, she turned to face him.

"You've been dead set against everything I've said since I first brought up the subject of adoption," she accused, her eyes flashing with anger.

"Not dead set," he said, knowing it was only half-true. "I'm simply questioning the way you plan to go about it."

"At the risk of sounding rude, may I ask why you suddenly think you should have a say in what I do about Cheyenne?"

Matt hesitated, not quite sure himself. Was it because Annie was all that was left of Marigold?

He said at last, "You're not the only one interested in what becomes of Annie, you know." As he spoke the words, he realized that his tie to Annie through Marigold was only part of what was motivating him. The other part, God help him, was Lane herself.

HEADING BACK to the market a short time later, Lane traveled once more at a speed beyond the legal limit. She drove automatically, impelled by anger and guilt to hurry. Anger at "that old heart-stopper Matt Cheney" and at herself, because what had happened between them was as much her fault as his. Guilt because she should have been back at the market an hour ago. It wasn't fair to Angus, who was first of all a farmer, to keep him from his fields for so long. This was his busiest season, too.

Reaching the market, Lane berthed the pickup in its usual parking spot and noted with satisfaction and renewed compunction that the place was abuzz with customers. She hopped down from behind the wheel to meet Angus, making his labored way around shoppers toward her. His flushed face showed agitation and told Lane that whatever had been going on during her absence was more than the old fellow could handle. It had been thoughtless of her to leave him so long, she told herself.

She hurried forward, an apology on her tongue, but Angus raised his voice to speak first.

"Come, lass. You be needed. I was aboot to call the police." The Scottish burr thickened his words as always when he was overwrought. "There's a mon talking to our Annie over there. I ken trouble when I see it, but I dinna have the power alone to throw the mon oot."

Before his voice left off, Lane was already on her way toward where Angus was pointing, her heart suddenly hammering with alarm. She'd caught a glimpse of Annie, half-hidden by the man who stood in front of her, his back to Lane. She'd seen enough to realize that the child was cowering on the bench before him.

From behind, the man looked formidable—rawboned and somehow shaggy in spite of custom-styled hair. Though he was little more than average height, to Lane he appeared to loom over Annie like a behemoth. A circle of howling wolves silhouetted against a full moon beneath the words Wolf Pack was silk-screened across the back of the T-shirt he wore.

Approaching unnoticed with Angus at her side, Lane was shocked at the sight of an Annie she had never seen before; an Annie paralyzed by fear, an Annie who appeared to have lost all will to defend herself. What she saw told Lane more about the child's past experiences with this man than anything she'd heard from Susan Craddock and Edra, and sent adrenaline spurting through her system.

"You there," she ordered. "Get away from the child." Realizing she'd had the luck to catch the intruder off guard, she pushed herself between him and Annie, at the same time avoiding all contact with the creature she assumed to be Wolf.

He turned at the sound of her voice. She was surprised to see that he'd looked bigger and more formidable from the back. There was a telltale weakness in his face that spoke of hard living—a self-indulgent puffiness that fortified Lane's courage. He was a bully, she decided, appraising him, but soft—a type who could be stared down.

"Just trying to get this kid to come home with her old dad like a good girl, the way her mother would want her to," he said in an ingratiating tone, his eyes shifting as they met Lane's. "Like I was telling her, I went out and found us a nice new home just so her and her old dad can live together now that our mommy's gone. It's lonely...."

"Spare me your histrionics, Wolf. I would as soon turn her over to Jack the Ripper," Lane broke in contemptuously. To Annie, whose round, frightened blue eyes gazed on the scene in an almost catatonic state, she said, "Cheyenne, run to the office, darling. Go! I'll be with you in a minute or two."

Wolf let forth an obscenity and shot out an arm to seize Annie and yank her to her feet. It was a measure of the child's terror that even then she made no sound.

"Let go of her," Lane ordered coldly, putting a reassuring hand on the child's shoulder. To Angus, who had closed in with her, she said, "Go call the police."

At the word *police,* a change came over Wolf. Swearing again, he looked around frantically as if officers might surround him at any moment.

Because Annie's bench was at the back of the market and away from the flow of shoppers, the confrontation had gone unnoticed. Now the sounds of brewing violence attracted attention. People were turning to see what was going on, moving closer.

Wolf let go of Annie's arm. As if some inner source of power had suddenly been released in her, Annie lit out like a scared rabbit, racing past the bins and the tables to the office. There she shot inside and slammed the door behind her.

"You're not going to get away with this," Wolf snarled. "I got rights. I'm her father. I got the papers to prove I am. I'll get the kid yet."

"Not without a court order and a police escort," Lane said, stalling for time. She was relieved to see Angus walking back toward them, pausing to coax curious customers back to their shopping. "And speaking of the police, here's Angus," she went on triumphantly. "They'll be here any minute."

With a final obscenity, Wolf stalked off to a maroon-colored van in the parking lot and skidded away in a shower of gravel.

Simultaneously Lane's control gave way, and she began to shake. Suddenly her legs were two pieces of garden hose that threatened to buckle under her weight. Only the intervention of Angus, arriving back on the scene in time to put a firm hold on her arm and help her to Annie's bench, saved her from sinking in her tracks to the ground.

"You're a bonnie lass," the old Scotsman said gruffly.

From Angus it was the equivalent of a citation of valor. Lane managed a shaky smile.

"I doubt that Wolf would agree," she said dryly. "I'm fine," she added in answer to the anxious look in the old man's eyes. "A little shook up but okay. Go on back to your farming."

Her trembling had quickly subsided, and to reassure Angus, she rose from the bench and started for the office to call off the police, to do what she could to put Annie back together and to satisfy her customers' curiosity.

Thank God Susan Craddock had finally mustered the courage to call her and put her on notice about the kind of man she was dealing with. This time Wolf had been easy enough to rout, but she had no illusions that she'd seen the last of the man. It seemed improbable that he would choose the busy market again for his next appearance. A prickle of fear raced up her spine. In all likelihood, next time it would be just Annie and her and Wolf.

And a switchblade knife.

# CHAPTER NINE

A RESTLESS SADNESS hung over Matt in the days that followed his meeting with Lane. A sadness made up of a strange mixture of sorrow for Marigold and frustration for that unattainable fulfillment he'd begun to envision with Lane.

Like a mourner after the funeral of someone who has profoundly affected his life, he found himself living in a kind of vacuum. Now that Lane had given him the missing pages, he could not close the book on Marigold until he understood what his relationship with her had been about. More important, he needed to understand to what extent it might be possible for him to care for Lane, and what his options were if it turned out he could care too much.

Dazed by the magnitude of what he faced, he retreated to his upstairs office at the beach house, put personal problems on hold and escaped to the world of trade. A hundred miles or so from the head office of Cheney, McCrae in Manhattan, he launched an ongoing dialogue with Cliff Harris and other key people in the family firm via telephone, computer and fax machine. As long as he was plugged into that great gambling arena of business and finance, he could tune out personal complications that waited to grab him when he let his mind roam free.

He could tune them out, but he couldn't tune out Cora Meigs, who harangued him with a sporadic diatribe about the ruinous effects of overwork.

A day finally came when Cora delivered the coup de grace. She issued an ultimatum—something Cora was not wont to do.

"I'm giving you fair warning, Matt Cheney," she said. "If you're not out of this office before noon tomorrow, I'm going to have your carpet cleaned again. It looks like the only way I can pry you away from those machines of yours. You're as bad as your father."

To have Cora, whose opinion he genuinely respected, tell him he was like his father made him feel as if he'd sold out.

"I can think of worse things," he said, and meant it, in a way. His father, in matters of business and finance, had been a genius. When it came to heading the family firm, the old man had always been Matt's role model. But there his admiration ended. He wanted never to be like his father in any other way.

It seemed suddenly a matter of great urgency to prove Cora wrong.

NEXT MORNING at the breakfast table there was a certain static in the air that told him Cora was biding her time to launch a new attack. He finished a leisurely browse through the *Times* and the *Wall Street Journal* and got to his feet to go up to his office when he was stopped by the baleful look in Cora's eyes.

"Uncle," he said promptly.

Cora continued to glower. "Are you trying to tell me something?"

"I just cried 'uncle,'" he said. "Don't bother to call the rug cleaners. I promise I'll spend the day in wanton idleness."

Cora gazed at him in disbelief.

"Word of honor," he swore. "Give me a few minutes to take care of a couple of things upstairs, and then I'm off."

Cora sniffed. "I'll believe it when you walk out that door. Once those electronic gadgets get hold of you, you may as well kiss the day goodbye."

Upstairs, Matt stopped outside the door to his office and looked in, tempted, in spite of his good intentions, to check a couple of stocks in Value Line before he carried out his promise to Cora. He sighed in resignation and moved on down the hallway to the bedroom that had been his since childhood. Inside, he came to a stop again and looked around.

Freed finally from the constraints of business he'd imposed on his mind the past few days, his thoughts turned inevitably back to the very concerns that had sent him into self-exile earlier in the week.

He'd done a fine job of screwing things up with Lane, he thought with disgust. She'd been as turned on as he was when he got carried away by his lusty impulses the other day. He was sure of it. Until he made the fatal mistake of telling her they wouldn't let her handpick a set of parents for Annie. Before he knew it, he was in Siberia. He could see her face now—the curve of her chin set in a stubborn, unaccepting line, the stormy sea-gray eyes turned on him resentfully.

The urge to see her was almost too strong to resist. The morning was early. The market would be quiet. Maybe he should drive over and try to set things right with her. But a wiser instinct told him he'd better give her time to learn from someone else how the adoption process really worked.

The decision left him with a day to be filled with vacationlike activity or risk losing face with Cora.

His gaze traveled around the room, seeking inspiration in walls so familiar he hadn't actually seen them in years. His eyes came to rest on a framed watercolor of a sailboat. He moved closer as if to greet an old friend.

It was the *Wanderjahr,* the sailboat he'd bought with bonds his mother had put away for him when he was a boy, kept secret from his father, that had matured while Matt was in grad school. That he'd spent all that money on a sailboat instead of reinvesting it seemed bizarre to him now. He'd never considered doing otherwise at the time.

He found himself grinning nostalgically at the thought of the penniless young hedonist he once had been. He felt a twinge of regret that he'd sold the boat after his father died.

With a last lingering look at the painting, he suddenly knew what he was going to do with the day. Impatient to be off, he changed into a pair of boat moccasins, grabbed a light canvas windbreaker out of the closet and headed for the stairs.

On his way through the kitchen he stopped to have a word with Cora, who still sat at the table working the *Times* crossword puzzle.

"Don't bother with lunch for me, Cora," he said. "I don't know when I'll be back. I'm going to the marina."

She turned her eyes from the puzzle and said curiously, "I thought you sold your boat."

"I did. To Luke Shields, but I think he still keeps it at the Seahampton Marina. I wouldn't mind seeing it again."

"That's good," Cora said with a satisfied smile and went back to her puzzle. "Have a nice day."

MATT HADN'T BEEN BACK to the marina since he sold the *Wanderjahr*. Driving the Nomad into the marina parking lot a few minutes later, he saw that the familiar horseshoe-shaped boat basin had been enlarged in the years of his absence to accommodate several dozen boats of all sizes and descriptions. A boat shop and a small restaurant and bar had been added. The snack bar looked much the same as when he'd been one of its daily clientele. It was busy with customers, most of whom were in their late teens and early twenties as in the old days.

As he reached the bottom of the plank steps down to the landing where the *Wanderjahr* had once been berthed, he had an eerie feeling that he had only to look back over his shoulder to see Marigold sitting on one of the steps where he'd first noticed her, strumming away at her guitar.

A light blue ketch now occupied the space where he had kept the *Wanderjahr*. Disappointed, he turned away from the sturdy, two-masted boat and climbed the steps back up the quay.

The morning calm still lay on the water as he scanned the moorings in search of the graceful one-masted sloop that had once been his. When he glimpsed a flash of yellow among the boats tied up on the far side, his steps quickened. A minute later he was down on the dock, reaching out to lay an affectionate hand on the smooth bow of the *Wanderjahr*.

What a beauty she was, he thought with a surge of pride in the grace and pizzazz of the sleekly designed boat. He felt a renewed sense of satisfaction in the bright, straightforward yellow of the hull and was pleased to see that Luke had been giving the boat the same loving care Matt had lavished on her when the sloop belonged to him.

Immersed in nostalgia, and struggling to recapture some half-remembered moment from the time the boat was his, he was roused out of his daydream by a familiar voice calling down to him from the quay above.

"Well, if it isn't Matt Cheney."

Looking up, Matt broke into a surprised smile at the sight of Luke Shields standing at the top of the steps. Luke was a psychiatrist in Manhattan with a thriving practice that normally kept him away from the water on weekdays.

"I never thought I'd find the old workhorse so far from the plow," Luke said.

"I might say the same of you."

"I'm playing hooky, and Dorrie's up in the Catskills. How about having some clam fritters with me at the restaurant while I wait for the wind to come up?" Shields said. "It's too early yet for a good breeze."

"I'm with you," Matt replied. He gave a last glance at the sloop and climbed the steps to join Shields on the quay. "I was just admiring the *Wanderjahr.* I haven't seen the boat since I signed her over to you. She couldn't look better if I'd kept her myself."

"Thanks. She's a great boat," Shields agreed. "If you have the time, maybe you'd like to go out with me when the wind comes up."

"You're on," Matt said, hoping he didn't look as much like an eager kid as he felt.

Falling into step, the two men walked on to the restaurant. There, over clam fritters and beer, they filled each other in on events that had taken place in their lives since they'd last seen each other at Shields's wedding two years before—a successful marriage, by Luke's account, but for one small flaw.

"Dorrie, God bless her, has given up going out with me on the boat," Luke told Matt dolefully. "I no more than get the *Wanderjahr* into the bay than the poor gal turns pea green. She's tried every seasick remedy known, but nothing works."

An hour and a half passed while they consumed two orders of clams apiece and exhausted topics of mutual interest. When at last the two walked out of the restaurant, the air currents had whipped up a perfect afternoon for sailing.

"I appreciate your company," Luke said as they started for the boat. "Now that Dorrie doesn't come with me, I get tired of sailing alone."

Boarding the *Wanderjahr* was like coming home after a long absence, Matt thought, as Luke started the auxiliary motor and maneuvered the thirty-foot cruiser through the traffic of the boat basin to the open water.

Soon they were on the bay, the motor silenced, running before the wind. Like the wind-filled red-and-blue spinnaker that billowed out ahead of them, Matt's spirit soared with a kind of joy he'd almost forgotten. He felt suddenly young and vibrant, his body surging with a vitality he'd thought he'd never know again.

What he'd give to be out here on the *Wanderjahr* like this with Lane, he thought unexpectedly, never doubting she would share the same joyful sense of rebirth that sailing brought to him. He had a feeling that somehow he wasn't getting through to her now. He imagined that if the two of them shared the wind like this together, she might come to understand the nature of the man he was. But what difference did it make? His days here would soon be over. His time with Lane Fielding was surely a passing thing.

It was late afternoon, and the breeze had begun to die down when the two men reluctantly headed back to the marina. As if they'd said everything over lunch, they'd spent most of the afternoon in silence, each deep in his own thoughts.

"Dorrie's inherited this summer place she's crazy about in the Catskills on a fine little natural lake," Luke volunteered musingly as they doused the sails and prepared to come into the boat basin. "Maybe if I got something like a catboat, she'd be able to go out with me there. The lake's a lot quieter than the bay. And even if she couldn't, she loves just being there. It wouldn't make me feel so damned guilty when I leave her behind to go sailing."

"You wouldn't care to sell me the *Wanderjahr*, would you?" Matt said impulsively.

Shields turned his head to look at Matt curiously. "It's only a matter of time before I sell to someone, I suppose," he said morosely. "I'd sure as hell like for it to be you. D'ya really want to buy her back?"

Matt was silent for a moment. "I . . . don't know. I honest to God don't know. The words just came off the top of my head." But even as he talked, the thought of buying the boat took hold, and he wondered how he'd managed to live so long away from the water.

"My God, what am I waiting for?" he burst out suddenly. "Of course I want to buy the boat. I never should have sold her in the first place."

"You've got a deal," said Shields.

GIVEN THAT she could expect no support from Matt in her quest for adoptive parents for Annie, Lane set forth on her own agenda the morning after their stormy parting. The memory of his kiss still burned her lips. Resentment churned within.

She'd been so sure he'd give her his wholehearted cooperation. All she had wanted from him was a little friendly encouragement. She hadn't been prepared for the static she got instead.

Borrowing time from the market, she juggled the next week's calendar to squeeze out time for canvassing respected acquaintances and friends in the fields she'd mentioned to Matt, explaining her mission, asking them to refer any likely parental prospects they might know to her. To her chagrin, she was met by a blank wall as one after another advised her to put the adoption in the hands of professionals who were trained in the task she had chosen to undertake.

Before the week was out, the last of her rancor toward Matt had disappeared. By then it was all too evident that the only candidate interested in adopting an older child was solely concerned with acquiring a built-in nanny for her brood of under-fives.

Settling down at her desk to catch up on the market's bookwork one morning, Lane finally accepted the fact she was getting nowhere. She saw no other course but to follow Matt's and everyone else's advice to put Cheyenne's adoption in the hands of the authorities.

Wolf would be back. An involuntary shiver ran down her spine, and she craned her neck for a reassuring glance out the screen door to where Annie sat on the step, playing jacks and humming contentedly to herself.

Once adoption proceedings were under way, Wolf would have to prove he was Annie's father or take himself out of the picture.

But suppose Edra and Susan Craddock were wrong? Suppose the wretched fellow actually had a legitimate claim to Annie? Suppose he arrived one day with the police and confronted her with an order to turn Cheyenne over to him?

If it came to that, she vowed, she would take Wolf to court and, with the help of Edra and Susan, prove he was an unfit father. At the same time, deep inside, she refused to give credence to the dreadful possibility. There was a chance, of course, that Annie's mother had lied to Edra and Susan, but some deep, instinctive wisdom told Lane that the Neanderthal Wolf was not Annie's father.

Furthermore, Lane was sure Wolf didn't have a shred of proof to back any such claim. If he could prove Annie was his child, he would go after her through legal channels instead of trying to sneak her away. He would look to the police to help him instead of taking off the minute he knew they'd been called.

As she pondered her problems, Annie came bounding through the screen door, breathless with excitement. Grabbing Lane's hand, she pulled her from her chair and over to the door.

Pointing a finger, she said, "See that lady over there by the potatoes? That's Cora."

Lane saw a pleasant-faced gray-haired woman in her midseventies, whom she'd seen in the market before. Her figure was round and solid and there was a look of cheerful, no-nonsense competence about her that one didn't forget.

"Cora who?" Lane prompted, turning back to Annie.

"The lady I told you about that warmed me up that day and dried my clothes and gave me the best cookies," Annie said, obviously pleased to see the woman.

"Oh, yes," Lane murmured, remembering. "So that's Cora Meigs. She comes here often for strawberries and vegetables. Aren't you going to run out and say hello to her?"

Annie hung back, suddenly shy.

"She's nice," Annie said, but she made no move to follow Lane's suggestion.

"Go on, honey. I'm sure she would like to see you," Lane urged.

The big blue eyes looked up at Lane beseechingly. A small hand reached out to grasp hers.

"You come, too," Annie said softly.

For a moment Lane hesitated, suddenly shy herself for no reason she understood. Then she laughed and gave the child's hand a gentle squeeze. "Of course."

The woman had moved on to the section of the market that had become Annie's domain and was about to put a bunch of radishes in her basket. As they approached, she looked up and saw the child. "Well, if it isn't Annie," she said warmly.

"Hi," said Annie in her smallest voice. "It was me that tied up those radishes and washed them. Some of them were real dirty."

"Well, they're not now. You did a very good job. I don't think I've ever seen cleaner radishes."

Annie beamed.

"I've wondered what became of you," Cora told her. "I look for you every time I come to the market, but you're never around."

"I'll be here now," Annie assured her with an unexpected show of confidence. "I live with Lane." Taking hold of Lane's hand, she fixed her blue eyes on the older woman and said stoutly, "This is Lane. She's my sister. . . ." The eyes moved uncertainly and caught Lane's. "Sorta," she finished.

Caught off balance, Lane looked helplessly at the other woman and swallowed the lump that rose in her throat. Holding out her hand in greeting, she said, "I'm Lane Fielding. We've talked on the phone." She hesitated, for a moment embarrassed, then added quite seriously, "As she says, Annie and I are 'sorta' sisters."

"That sounds like the relationship I have with Matt. He's 'sorta' my son," Cora said with a chuckle. "I guess you know my name's Cora Meigs."

"I've noticed you in the market. It's good to meet you . . . to know who you are," Lane said. "Now I can thank you for taking care of Annie in her hour of need. It was very kind of you."

"Those were the *best* cookies," Annie said. "Better even than the ones Mrs. Brandon and I make."

"Come again. I'll make some for you while you play on the beach," Cora said.

"Thanks. That's very nice of you, but don't look for her," Lane said before Annie could answer. Trying to disregard the disappointment that sprang to the child's eyes, she added, "She's promised she won't go back there again alone."

"And wisely so," Cora agreed. "How would it be if I came and got her one day? Matt can take her to the beach while I make cookies."

With her back turned to Cora, Annie was hopping on one foot as she looked hopefully up at Lane and mouthed the words "Say yes. Say yes." Though Lane had mixed feelings about the proposal, she hadn't the heart to refuse her outright. She settled for a time-honored cop-out.

"We'll see."

THE APPLES WERE FIRM, round and a delicious pale green in color, touched on one cheek with a splash of pink, the first of the summer to ripen. Annie had climbed the tree early that morning to pick a small basket of the fruit and pass it down to Lane.

They were at the foot of the tree, munching apples and gazing up at a bumper crop, when Matt paid an early visit to the nearly empty market. Spotting the Chevy wheeling into the parking lot, Annie let out a small squeal of delight.

"It's Matt," she cried, and raced across the lot to meet him.

After their strained parting the week before, Lane had seen no more of him. What had brought him here today? she wondered, and was suddenly glad he'd come.

Bemused, Lane held back, letting Annie do the greeting. Before Matt had found and returned her ring, Annie had treated him with undisguised suspicion. Now she flew to his side as if he was a long-missing friend.

Watching the man and child walk toward her, Lane sensed in the man a new vitality, a new joie de vivre that hadn't been there when she saw him last. She felt herself starting to smile in spite of herself.

On impulse she picked an apple out of the basket she held and, without warning, tossed it his way.

"Have an apple," she said.

Deftly, Matt caught the flying missile and turned the fruit in his hands, admiring it from all sides before he bit into the pale crispness with a crunch that sent a spurt of juice flying into the air.

"Now that's what I call a perfect apple," he said.

"I'll climb up and get some for you," Annie volunteered, and went scampering off to look for another basket.

# NO RISK, NO OBLIGATION TO BUY...NOW OR EVER!

# CASINO JUBILEE
## "Scratch'n Match" Game

## Here's how to play:

1. Peel off label from front cover. Place it in space provided at right. With a coin, carefully scratch off the silver box. This makes you eligible to receive two or more free books, and possibly other gifts, depending upon what is revealed beneath the scratch-off area.

2. You'll receive brand-new Harlequin Superromance® novels. When you return this card, we'll rush you the books and gifts you qualify for, ABSOLUTELY FREE!

3. If we don't hear from you, every month we'll send you 4 additional novels to read and enjoy before they are available in bookstores. You can return them and owe nothing, but if you decide to keep them, you'll pay only $2.96* per book, a saving of 43¢ each off the cover price. There is **no** extra charge for postage and handling. There are **no** hidden extras.

4. When you join the Harlequin Reader Service®, you'll get our subscribers-only newsletter, as well as additional free gifts from time to time, just for being a subscriber!

5. You must be completely satisfied. You may cancel at any time simply by sending us a note or a shipping statement marked "cancel" or by returning any shipment to us at our cost.

**YOURS FREE!**

*This lovely heart-shaped box is richly detailed with cut-glass decorations, perfect for holding a precious memento or keepsake—and it's yours absolutely free when you accept our no-risk offer.*

# CASINO JUBILEE
## "Scratch'n Match" Game

SCRATCH HERE

### CHECK CLAIM CHART BELOW FOR YOUR FREE GIFTS!

**YES!** I have placed my label from the front cover in the space provided above and scratched off the silver box. Please send me all the gifts for which I qualify. I understand I am under no obligation to purchase any books, as explained on the opposite page.

(U-H-SR-08/92) 134 CIH AFPC

Name _____

Address _____ Apt. _____

City _____ State _____ Zip _____

▼ DETACH AND MAIL CARD TODAY!

# HARLEQUIN ''NO RISK'' GUARANTEE

- You're not required to buy a single book—ever!
- You must be completely satisfied or you may cancel at any time simply by sending us a note or a shipping statement marked ''cancel'' or by returning any shipment to us at our cost. Either way, you will receive no more books; you'll have no obligation to buy.
- The free books and gift(s) you claimed on the ''Casino Jubilee'' offer remain yours to keep no matter what you decide.

If offer card is missing, please write to: Harlequin Reader Service® P.O. Box 1867, Buffalo, N.Y. 14269-1867

When Annie was out of earshot, Lane said, "I'm glad you're here before people start pouring in. I've been wanting to talk to you. I owe you an apology. A little research proved you right on the subject of adoptions. I'm afraid I wasn't very nice."

"Well, I wasn't very diplomatic, so it was a standoff. Let's forget about it," Matt said. "Anyhow, that's not what I came to see you about. I came to see if you'd go for a boat ride with me."

"A boat that's got sails?" asked Annie breathlessly, coming up with her basket.

"Right. A boat with sails."

"Wow! We sure would," squealed Annie, dropping the basket in her excitement.

When Matt broadened his attention to include Annie as if she'd been part of his invitation all along, Lane had to admit to a grudging respect for his grace in accepting the unexpected.

"I thought I might prevail on you two hardworking ladies to take a day off and try out my sailboat."

"You have a new sailboat?" Lane asked.

"Not really new," Matt said. "I just bought it back from a friend. I thought you and Cheyenne might enjoy a sail if you can cast off your moorings here."

"Thanks, but I simply can't take any more time off," Lane said politely. "I've been away from the market too much in the past few days." She was disconcerted by the look of sharp disappointment on Annie's face.

"I see I'm going to have to bring Cora over here to deliver her number-one lecture on how all work and no play makes Jack a dull boy," Matt said.

"That may be very well for Jack, but if Jill doesn't settle down to business pretty soon, this market's going to be in big trouble."

"Please, Lane, don't say no," Annie begged from beside her. "I want to go on a sailboat. I've never been on a sailboat. Marigold used to sail. I want to *so much.*"

How could she say no to those huge, pleading eyes?

"Please, Lane. Please, please. Puh-lease," Annie begged. "I'll fold the laundry and put it away when you do the washing, and I'll tidy up my room and put my stuff away and hang up my clothes *forever,* and you won't even have to ask."

"Let's don't get carried away, Cheyenne," Lane said dryly, knowing these to be Annie's most hated chores. "Don't make bargains you're not going to want to keep. I might hold you to them."

Annie seized the moment. "Does that mean we can go?"

Lane gave Matt a weak smile that admitted she'd been outmaneuvered.

"It'll take some doing. I couldn't possibly make it this week, if that's what you had in mind," she said, and heard a sigh of resignation from Annie. "Give me time to arrange for a day away from the market. Next week, maybe?"

"Monday?"

"Tuesday would be better. Mondays are for cleaning up the market after the weekend rush."

"Tuesday it is, then," Matt said with a smile that left Lane feeling as eager for the excursion as Annie was.

TUESDAY SEEMED an aeon away to the man who had been thinking in terms of tomorrow. Leaving the market, Matt shook off a let-down feeling. Tuesday was still better than the flat-out "no" he'd half-expected, and he could use the time, he reminded himself. He still had miles to go on the journey of self-discovery he'd launched in the days after he bought back the *Wanderjahr*.

It took only the old sailcloth dungarees he wore, still almost white after many washings, the skid-proof deck shoes and the faded red-and-blue striped rugby shirt that had become his uniform to remind him how the pattern of his life had changed. The wardrobe, left from early sailing days and unearthed from the bedroom closet, fit him as comfortably as his own skin.

No more did he spend all his waking time closeted in his upstairs office. As a sop for his conscience, he gave the becalmed hours of morning to the world of business and finance, but when the first midday breezes began to stir on the bay, he headed out to the marina.

As he approached the crossroads to the marina now, he gave his office a dismissive thought and turned toward the bay. The morning was half-over, he rationalized to assuage his guilt. Too late to get anything worthwhile done today.

At the boat basin snack shop he bought a fat Reuben sandwich and a six-pack of beer from the deli and headed for the *Wanderjahr*. Aboard, he stowed his lunch in a cooler near the tiller, made sure the sails and lines were handy to the helm and checked to see that everything from a spare sail stop to sunburn cream could be reached from the tiller. When the first whisper of breeze became strong enough to swell a sail, he cast off and made for the open bay.

His sailing followed the pattern that had become almost a ritual in the days since he'd reclaimed his boat. Far out in the bay by early afternoon, when the wind currents were at their best, his mind cut loose from all thought except for the joy and technique of sailing. He raced the wind while the currents held strong. In the midafternoon slackening, he picked an untrafficked spot and dropped anchor to eat his sandwich, washed down with beer.

Creature comforts satisfied, he stretched out, closed his eyes and let his mind wander on a voyage into himself in search of that other man—the Matt Cheney he'd almost forgotten and wondered sometimes if he'd ever been.

Along the way he'd begun to recover and revise the lost vision of Marigold and to wonder more and more if his interlude with her had really been the one great romantic love of his life after all. Today again, his thoughts returned to that golden summer, seeking a name for what he had felt for Marigold, calling into question the depth and quality of his own emotions as memories came reeling back across the years.

He'd seen something in the waiflike, sad-eyed face that had challenged him to...do what? he wondered today. To make her feel good, he guessed, at a time when he'd had an overriding need to feel good about himself.

He'd taken her sailing and taught her how to handle the boat. If he brought a smile to her face it was as if he'd earned a medal. Making her laugh had been as good as being knighted. He remembered nights when he'd lain awake testing his wits to beat his own record for pleasing Marigold.

In the beginning there hadn't been anything sexual about the attraction. Other women had catered to his libido at the time, and in spite of her world-weary attitude, he hadn't really looked at her as a woman. She'd seemed more like the kid sister he didn't have, to be enjoyed, adored, cosseted, sheltered.

That was the way it had been until the day she'd spotted the ring in the window. He'd seen the look of hope and yearning in her eyes as he slipped the ring on her finger. Though she'd never said anything about her home life, something had told him at that moment that she needed him, that he was the only person in her world who cared about her.

The idea that this woman actually *needed* him had been overwhelming. He'd slipped the ring off whatever meaningless finger he'd put it on and changed it to the ring finger of her left hand. It meant they'd be married, he'd told her, his voice so charged with emotion he could hardly speak.

And with those words everything had changed. Back on the boat she wanted him to make love to her, and he'd taken her below and undressed her as they explored mutual delights.

He remembered a little sadly that she'd wept joyously. He had promised himself he'd give her everything in his power she asked for. He was in love for the first time in his life. Looking back, he couldn't think of a more apt way to describe his state at the time than "head over heels."

Then out of the blue it was over. He'd been ordered off to the West Coast, and when he got back from doing his father's bidding, she had already run away with a rock-band musician. Wolf. At the time, he'd fully expected to carry the pain the rest of his life.

Now at last, after many hours of solitary contemplation on the sailboat, Matt understood and felt no shame for the honest emotions that had motivated him through his summer affair with Marigold.

It was as if a great weight had been cast off his spirit.

In the dying breeze of late afternoon, he pointed the *Wanderjahr* for home, knowing that the love he'd felt for Marigold had never been the great love he'd let himself believe. Seeing the affair for the first time without romantic blinders, he knew it at last for what it had been—protective, affectionate and, *face it, Matt,* intensely physical. Never having experienced the kind of love that binds a man and a woman together for a lifetime, he had misunderstood his feelings for Marigold.

The wind had died down to no more than a whisper by the time he neared the boat basin. He brought down the sails and started the motor, coming into the basin under power.

He felt good. He'd found the Matt Cheney he'd put aside. He'd found he wasn't as bad a guy as his father had made him believe he was. And he'd found the Marigold he'd been looking for.

# CHAPTER TEN

IN THE SHADOWY INTERIOR of Guido's in Greenwich Village, Wolf crossed his arms on the red Formica table-top and swore.

"Damn you, Hugo! You're not the one who has to mix it up with that Fielding broad. She never lets the kid out of her sight. Let her catch me around the market and she'll call the police, then I'll be back in the slammer. If you'd just listen . . ."

Hugo held up a hand in weary acceptance.

"All right already. So you've got a new scam," he said. "You can tell me all about it, but it better be good. In case you've forgotten what we read in Fairchild's will, the old geezer left half of that ten-million-dollar estate to Goldie *by right of representation.* That means now that Goldie's dead, all that bread goes to the kid, remember?"

"I remember, and I remember something else. The widow Fairchild," Wolf said sullenly. "If we don't go after it, the whole ten million goes to her, so I come up with this idea how to get the money without mixing it up with the police or the courts."

Hugo gave a consenting grunt. "Go ahead," he said with a noticeable lack of enthusiasm. "Let's hear it."

"Well, you know all about the widow Fairchild," Wolf said. "She gets ten million dollars if Goldie never shows up to claim her half. Right? Only what she don't know is

Goldie's not going to show. You wanta bet that widow is awake nights scared silly that one of these days Goldie's gonna come popping in.''

"Get to the point."

Wolf curled his lip in a malevolent smile. "So the widow's ripe for a good-news, bad-news scam. I tell her she don't have to worry about Goldie claiming her half. I got proof for her Goldie's dead . . . for a price. I collect, but she still don't know about the kid. Then I tell her there's this kid, and I tell her all that stuff you said about right of . . ." He groped for the word and gave up. "Whatever . . . I tell her no one knows about the kid but me, not even the kid herself, and for a price I can guarantee my lips are sealed.''

"Is that it?"

Wolf appeared reluctant to answer.

"Well, there's one catch, so I thought I'd better talk to my 'lawyer' before I go ahead," Wolf said with a feeble laugh.

"Which is?"

"I can't get anywhere near the widow. She lives in a fort. The bastards that answer the phone won't connect me with her. The only way I can get through to the broad is to write her a letter."

"You do, and you'll buy yourself a one-way ticket up the river. That's blackmail, you know. A dumb bastard like you would never get away with it."

"She wouldn't have to see me, and I'd use a post office box and another name." Wolf's voice was surly. "You're so smart, *you* can write the letter."

Hugo stared at Wolf, a look of disbelief on his face. He seemed to be struggling to find his voice. Then he swore violently.

"Know what's wrong with you, Wolf?" he said at last, his voice bitterly controlled. "You're a stupid bastard, and you're a coward. Furthermore, you're mean. That's why you can never hold a band together. We had a pretty good outfit, back when we called ourselves the AWOLS and Marigold was lead singer. Before you fried your brains on crack and started beating up on Goldie. Before you pissed off the best musicians and changed the name to the Wolf Pack.... And there went the band."

"Damn you, Hugo. I don't have to sit here and listen to that crap," Wolf said shrilly, starting to rise, but the drummer lunged across the table, put both hands on Wolf's shoulders and pushed him back in his seat.

"Oh, yes, you do. Stay where you are," Hugo ordered in a quiet, deadly tone. "I've got too much invested in you to let you go now, you son of a bitch. I've paid good money to set you up in a respectable middle-class house out there at Seahampton just to convince a judge you're the kid's father."

"Now, Hugo—" Wolf began, but Hugo cut in.

"Shut up, Wolf. I've got you all set up, and it's up to you to get your kid and hang on to her. Keep her at the house with you and don't let her out of your sight. Show yourself around the neighborhood as a doting father with a sick kid who has to be kept inside. Got that?"

"Yeah," Wolf said sullenly.

"Don't try to weasel out of this, Wolf. There's a lot of money at stake, and I promise you unless you go after it the way I'm telling you to, I'll see you back in the slammer, and this time they'll throw away the key."

"You can't threaten me, Hugo," Wolf protested weakly. "I'm clean. I haven't done drugs since I got out. You can ask my probation officer if you don't believe me."

"Does your probation officer know about the crack you've been dealing on the side? Because I do. Does he know about the times you've left the state?"

For a second Wolf stared at Hugo, too stunned to speak.

"You wouldn't... That's *blackmail*."

Hugo stared back icily. "So it is."

## CHAPTER ELEVEN

"WHAT DO YOU MEAN by an undocumented person, Neal?" Lane asked uneasily.

It was the night of Lane's promised dinner for Roz and her friend Neal Roberts, now established in the house on Swan Road for the month. Dinner over, the three sat on the front porch watching Cheyenne and her new friend, Geraldine, from a neighboring farm, at a game of croquet on the south lawn.

"An undocumented person is what Annie appears to be," the attorney replied. "If you don't have any papers for her, such as a birth certificate or some other kind of official acknowledgment that she exists, she is an undocumented person."

"Well, I don't have documents, but I do have Annie. It's plain to see she exists," Lane protested, only half in jest.

"Not enough. You could run into problems if you suddenly had to admit her to a hospital, for instance. And some kind of documentation will be necessary when you enroll her in school."

Lane's heart lurched. It had not been a good week.

"What do you suggest I do?" she asked weakly, unable at the moment to consider one more problem she would have to solve.

"Have mercy on her, Neal," Roz protested. "Everything's coming down on her at once. School doesn't start for another six weeks, and Annie looks as healthy as a young colt. Can't this wait a few days?"

"Of course. But it might be a good idea to have your-self appointed guardian, since Annie's in your care. If you'd like, I can take care of filing a petition for you right away," Roberts said amiably.

"I *would* feel more secure if I were her legal guardian until the adoption gets under way," Lane admitted. "Surely there's more to it than simply filing a petition, though."

"It'll take a little time. The matter will be put in the hands of a social worker, who'll check out you and An-nie. Then it goes to a judge for approval," Roberts ex-plained. "I'll be glad to do the legwork."

"I'm tempted to impose on you, since I'm in between lawyers, in a way," Lane said. "Our family attorney is getting ready to retire. Under the circumstances, I hesi-tate to bring him something new that calls for immediate action."

"No problem, and certainly no imposition," the at-torney assured her. "On the contrary. I'll be glad to take care of the matter. I've never taken such a long vaca-tion. This will keep me from feeling like a drone."

Sitting beside Roberts on the porch swing, Roz took his hand and smiled at him fondly. "Okay. That's settled," she said. "I challenge you to a game of croquet."

Looking out, Lane saw that the two little girls had abandoned the croquet set and were taking turns push-ing each other in the swing Angus had hung from the lo-cust tree for Annie.

"You two play. I don't have the energy to swing a mallet," Lane said, and was met with little protest.

Her low-energy plea was no lie, she thought. She couldn't remember a worse week, quite apart from the fact that it had been the busiest she'd known in produce sales. The physical work at the market had given her a welcome release from the frustrations of the search for parents for Annie.

In that respect, the week had been a write-off. She should have accepted what Matt Cheney had told her in the first place, she thought, disgusted in hindsight at her own perversity.

As twilight turned into darkness, Lane rose and went to turn on the floods that lighted the croquet court.

"Sorry," she called out, laughing as she saw that the sudden illumination had caught her guests in a stolen embrace. A moment later a car turned off the country road and into the driveway, and Lane walked down the steps to greet the parents of Annie's friend.

"Your mom and dad have come to get you, Geraldine," Lane called. In a minute the two little girls left the swing and came giggling across the lawn.

Lane and Annie watched Geraldine drive off with her parents. Then Lane put her arm around the little girl and together they walked back to the porch.

In the darkness Lane settled back on the porch swing with Cheyenne snuggled in close beside her and watched the fireflies. Unexpectedly a flood of emotion welled up in her, and she wrapped her arms around the little girl, pulling the small, warm body closer.

"You are something special, Annie," she said.

"Mmm," Annie murmured, half-asleep. She rolled her head down into Lane's lap and closed her eyes.

"Something very special," Lane repeated softly.

IT WAS EARLY MONDAY evening by the time Lane left the market after a strenuous day spent getting the place in order for the week ahead and her coming absence. Beside her in the pickup, Annie chattered away like a little squirrel as they started off. A mile or so on their way, Lane became suddenly aware that Annie had grown unusually quiet.

Out of the corner of her eye she saw that the child kept looking back, and she realized Annie was watching another vehicle not far behind them. When she turned the pickup into Fielding Lane, the van turned, too.

She pulled off the road onto the shoulder bordering the cornfield and was startled by a shrill cry from Annie.

"It's Wolf!" the child wailed. "He's following us!"

Curbing her growing panic, Lane steered the pickup along the bumpy shoulder, wondering frantically what to do. Her answer came in the field of corn that rose like a dense forest beside them on the passenger side.

"Hang on tight, Annie," she said quickly. "I'm going to speed up and raise a cloud of dust that'll keep us out of sight from the van. When the pickup stops, you jump out and hide in the corn. Do you understand?"

Wide-eyed, Annie nodded.

"I'm as close as I can get to the field. In a minute I'll stop. Jump out and run as far into the corn as you can. I'll call you when he's gone."

The truck plowed through the loose, rutted dirt for a few more yards until Lane was satisfied that the screen of dust the pickup was stirring up would hide Annie's takeoff.

"Brace yourself, honey. We're going to stop," she said. "Now scoot."

Annie tumbled out and landed running, lost at once in the thick cloud of dust that billowed up around them. A few seconds later the van pulled to a stop some yards ahead of the pickup, gradually becoming completely visible as the dust settled.

Fighting the explosion of panic that burst in her breast at the sight of the large, threatening figure emerging from the van, Lane stepped out of the pickup. She realized too late that she might be safer if she locked herself in the truck. About to turn back, she knew she dared not. If she did, he would surely go looking for Annie.

Backing up a step, she gripped the bed of the truck for support and called out, her voice breaking in an unsettling quaver. "This is a private road. Unless you have business with the Fieldings, I must ask you to leave."

Wolf stopped in his tracks and glared at her. "Cut the bull. I came to get my kid. Call her back out of that corn."

"I'd bite out my tongue first," Lane said grimly, her voice gaining strength with the words.

Wolf started forward, thrusting a hand into a pocket and drawing out a knife. At the touch of a button, a vicious-looking blade shot out, and Lane's heart missed a beat.

Knife in hand, Wolf stalked on toward the terror-stricken Lane. Casting desperately around for something to defend herself with, she noticed a short-handled hoe in the pickup. In a flash, she leaned into the bed of the truck to grab the implement and rocked back on her feet, planting them firmly on the ground as she faced the advancing hulk, hoe swinging. Wolf came to an uncertain stop.

"Stay where you are," she called, her voice more menacing now that it had lost its croak. "The hoe's as sharp as a razor. I've killed snakes with it. I promise you it can put a Wolf out of commission."

Wolf looked around him as if suddenly confused.

"Don't think I'm afraid to use it," Lane said, gripping the hoe firmly and taking a threatening step toward
the man. He hesitated, then backed away.

"Drop the knife," she ordered. He backed up another step and Lane advanced two. Swearing bitterly, he
dropped the knife.

"Get out of here and don't come back," she said
grimly. "If I catch you on Fielding property again, I'll
turn you over to the police."

Wolf bent as if to pick up his knife, but before he could
get his hands on the weapon, Lane started after him
brandishing the hoe. Cursing, he edged toward his van.
She quickened her steps aggressively. Wolf began to run.
She stopped. He turned back. This time Lane took after
him at a run and sent him fleeing all the way back to the
van.

He gunned his engine and skidded in a shower of dirt
into a U-turn that pointed the van toward her. At the last
second the van veered and passed her, heading back out
Fielding Lane to the country road from which it
branched.

Lane grabbed hold of the pickup, leaning against the
door for support while she caught her breath and waited
for her body to quit trembling and the strength to come
back to her legs.

She remembered Wolf's knife lying in the road and
hesitated. If she left it there, it could be picked up by a
child, or by Wolf, for that matter. Obviously she had to
retrieve it.

Not caring to touch the wicked-looking tool, she used
a length of paper towel she kept in the pickup as a glove
to pluck it out of the dirt and retract the blade before
wrapping the knife in toweling and slipping it into her

pocket. She would drop it in the bay while she was out in Matt's sailboat tomorrow.

She trudged back to the truck and yelled for Annie. She called twice and waited. Soon she heard the cornstalks rustling not far away.

"Annie?"

"Here I am."

Annie's small body emerged from the forest of corn. She came running across the rough ground to throw herself, trembling, into Lane's arms.

"I was so scared," she said in a squeaky voice. "I heard him holler that I'm his kid. I'm *not* his kid." The child was sobbing now. "Don't let him get me, Lane."

"Don't worry, love. I won't," Lane said.

Holding the wiry little person close in her arms, Lane stroked her until her trembling subsided.

"Come on, sweetie," she said. "Let's pick some corn and go home and fix dinner."

THE WHITE DENIM JEANS and shell-pink T-shirt, a near match to the pants and shirt Annie wore, had seemed a small enough indulgence when Annie had talked Lane into wearing them "so we can be twins." Seeing their attire through Matt's eyes as he drove into the marketplace now, Lane wished she'd worn anything else. We look like a Mutt-and-Jeff version of the Bobbsey Twins, she thought, feeling a bit foolish.

"By the time we get to the marina the wind should be about right for sailing," Matt said as he reached to take the tote bag from Lane's hand. He gave an astonished grunt as he felt the full weight of the bag.

"Good Lord, what have you got in here?" he asked. "A kedge?"

"What's a kedge?"

"A small anchor," Matt told her.

Lane laughed. "Sorry. No kedge," she said. "Bath ing suits and towels and straw hats and sunscreen, b cause Annie and I both have that kind of skin.... Oh, ye and Maiden Blush apples. But no kedge."

Under the soothing spell of the water and Matt's eas good humor as he set out to initiate the land-rooted La and Annie into the esoterica of sailing, Lane quick forgot everything else.

Where was the self-centered swinger Roz had d scribed? Not this warm-spirited, considerate host wh managed to jolly a protesting Annie into a brand-nev looking safety vest Lane suspected he'd bought esp cially for the occasion.

As he acquainted Lane with the whims of wind an sail, she began to sense a kind of team spirit betwee them and to feel a new harmony with the boat.

"Would you like to try your hand at the helm?" asked after a while.

"You think I can?"

"Of course. Later I'll show Annie how we work t tiller."

"You're going to let me drive the boat?" Annie sa eagerly.

"You can help. I'll teach you how it works."

It was early afternoon before Matt took the helm aga from Lane and brought the boat about. She was su prised to find her hands and legs shaky from the ten concentration required to keep up with the helmsman quick, incisive, often urgent commands.

"You learn fast, but I don't want to wear you out, Matt told her with a look of such warm approval brought a rush of heat to her face. "What do you say take a break?"

Annie let out a wail. "No-o-o. What about me? You said..."

"I haven't forgotten, but we've got all day," Matt said. "Let's tie up now and go for a swim, and then we can eat the lunch Cora packed for us. Later you can help me sail the boat."

"I want to sail the boat now," Annie said, her face clouding over. "I'm not hungry."

"Too bad. Cora baked some special cookies for you," Matt said.

"I'd rather sail the boat," Annie said stubbornly. "The cookies'll still be there."

"So will the boat," Matt said. "All in favor of pulling into that little cove across the water and having lunch say 'aye.'"

Her lip a little pouty, Annie followed Lane's resounding "aye" with a reluctant one of her own. A few minutes later the *Wanderjahr* lay at anchor off the sandy beach of the cove, and Matt was inflating a small rubber boat to take them ashore.

"What about the water?" Lane asked. "Is it all right for me to swim to the beach?"

"It's deep here, but there's no undertow. It's sandy bottomed and shallow near the beach," Matt told her. "If you want to swim, Annie and I'll take the stuff over in the dinghy. You can change into your bathing suits here."

"Me, too?" asked Annie eagerly, already peeling off her life vest.

"Come along," said Lane, heading down to the cabin.

In a matter of minutes Annie strutted back up proudly in a new red, white and blue bikini Lane had bought for her the week before when she'd taken the child to purchase missing items in her wardrobe.

Blinking as she came up into the sunlight in last year's blue one-piece tank suit, Lane swallowed a small gasp of pleasure at the sight of Matt pushing the dinghy through the shallow water. She paused a moment to watch him vault into the rubber boat and head back toward the sloop on a return trip from the sandy beach, where he had dumped a hamper and a cooler and blankets.

The long, sinewy body, clad now in sleek black swimming trunks that fit like a second skin, seemed to Lane for a breathless moment as beautiful as any sight she had ever enjoyed. She could see the ripple of muscles under golden skin. Double golden where the hair on his legs, chest and arms turned red-gold in the brightness of the afternoon sun.

Nearing the boat, Matt came to a sudden stop and looked up at Lane for a deep, appreciative moment as if committing her to memory. Lane felt all at once brazenly underdressed.

"Well, if it isn't Miss Liberty," Matt called up to Annie in her patriotic colors. She giggled, and before Lane realized what she was about to do, scrambled to crawl over the side of the boat.

"Stay where you are, Cheyenne," Matt ordered sharply. Annie clung to the railing, suddenly afraid. Matt came on through the water and stopped below her, looking up at the child with grave and reproving eyes.

"You don't pitch yourself blindly off a boat without knowing what's below, Annie," he said sternly. "Do you know how to swim?"

"Kinda," Annie said, hanging on for dear life. "Aren't you going to catch me?"

"You should have made your arrangements before you went over the side," Matt admonished. "I'll catch you. You can let go." Hesitating, Annie looked down uncertainly at the water. Reluctantly she relaxed her grip and dropped into Matt's arms. He lowered her into the dinghy.

From where she stood on the boat, Lane observed the scene angrily at first, her sympathy all with Annie. Still, she made no effort to interfere. She felt like a traitor, letting Matt take Annie to task, even when she knew it was for the child's own good.

With Annie sitting before him in the dinghy, Matt continued seriously, "Don't ever do anything like that again when you're on a boat, Annie. Not until you've checked with the skipper. You're too smart a kid not to look before you leap. That's the way people get hurt."

Annie's countenance had been a study in injured feelings. Watching, Lane had been afraid she was going to cry. Now as Matt came to the end of his lecture, she saw a streetwise look gradually spread over the small, stormy face.

"Yeah," Annie said, thoughtful at last. "It's like Marigold said when we used to have to stay at the shelters. We wouldn't have to live like that if she hadn't jumped before she knew where she was going to land."

At the mention of Marigold's name, Lane saw a new look in Matt's eyes.

"Come on, kid," he said more gently. "It's about time someone taught you to swim."

CHATTERING TEETH finally brought the swim lesson to a halt. While Lane and Matt swam out to a buoy that marked the cove entrance and back, Annie lay wrapped in a towel and watched from the beach.

Ravenous by then from their workouts, the three of them devoured Cora's chicken sandwiches and potato salad and deviled eggs and pickles and fudge cake.

Now, wrapped in an enormous, brightly patterned towel, Annie lay fast asleep on a blanket spread out in the shade. Lane sat on a second blanket, hugging her knees, watching Matt, who was stretched out beside her, one arm over his eyes. Was he asleep? she wondered drowsily.

Unexpectedly Matt took his arm from his eyes and pulled himself to a sitting position beside her, his face on a level with hers. "So, what do you think of the *Wanderjahr?*" he asked. His voice sounded anxious, as if her answer might matter a great deal to him.

"The boat's beautiful," she said. "Where did you get the name?"

"I didn't," Matt said. "I bought her secondhand from a fellow who had German roots. *Wanderjahr* was the name she came with. I almost didn't buy her because of the name."

"Can't boat names be changed?"

Matt laughed. "It's bad luck to change the name of a boat, they say. Not that I'm superstitious, but somehow I didn't want to be the one to do the changing. Then I found out that, roughly translated, *Wanderjahr* means a kind of retreat from whatever life a person's been leading. I knew then the boat was for me."

Lane gave him a curious glance and was surprised to catch a fleeting look of embarrassment in his eyes.

"I was pretty sour on life at the time. My father didn't seem to appreciate what a treasure he had in me," he said with a laugh that poked fun at the person he had been then.

"I may have been the only gofer on Wall Street with a master's degree in business administration from Harvard," he continued. "Looking back, I suspect the boat was a place I could go to feel sorry for myself and lick my wounds and tell everyone to go to hell. When I didn't need that anymore, I sold the boat.''

"When was that?"

"When I got what I'd been wanting all my life."

Lane waited for an explanation, consumed by curiosity.

At last he said, "The board made me head of the company when my dad died."

"But now you've bought back the boat."

With a puzzled shake of his head, Matt said, "Right." He paused and added with a wry grin, "By rights, I shouldn't be taking time for a vacation. Dad never did. I don't know what I was thinking of when I bought back the boat." He sighed, his ebullient mood of the morning suddenly gone.

"You probably did it for the same reason you bought it in the first place. You need an escape," Lane guessed aloud.

"Escape?" Matt repeated the word as if he'd misheard. "Escape from the only real goal I've ever had from the time I used to sneak into the stock exchange with my brother, Birch, as a kid? What's to escape from?"

"The work you're so crazy about, maybe," Lane ventured, feeling like the voice of experience, though she'd only stumbled on the answer as it applied to her a moment before. "You can't be a complete person without a balance between work and play."

Unexpectedly, Matt reached over and took her face between his hands and drew her head down until his lips met hers in a soft, fleeting kiss.

"You are very pretty when you expostulate, you know," he said, touching the corner of her mouth with a forefinger. "It's too bad what you say sounds so much like Cora Meigs."

"Cut that out, Matt," Lane said, slapping his hand away as if it were an offending mosquito.

"Mmm," Matt said, and before Lane knew what was happening, his arms were around her, pulling her smoothly back onto the blanket, her body on top of his. Where her ear pressed against his chest, she heard the strong, steady pounding of his heart over the hard-beating sound of her own. A sudden rapturous tumult within held her still for a moment.

Then his hand touched her bare leg and moved over the skin toward her thigh, and she came to her senses and rolled away. In instant reflex, his fingers closed on her leg, but when she pulled free, he didn't try to restrain her. Their bodies no longer touching, she lay still.

Matt was still that old heart-stopper, she thought. Being with him was better than being with anyone else she had ever known.

From the moment he'd driven up to the market in that wonderful relic of a car that morning in May, she'd been conscious of an almost palpable sexual tension between them. Today she'd been glad of the demands of sailing that had kept the sensual dynamics in check. Umpteen times that morning she'd reminded herself she was quite comfortable without a man—without *this* particular man in her life.

Now, suddenly, she wasn't so sure. Acutely aware of his male presence beside her, she relived the moments immediately before.

Until Matt, it had been a long time since she'd felt herself carried away by that earthshaking upheaval of senses that lay dormant deep within her. Too long, she thought, and held her breath, aware suddenly that Matt had raised himself on one elbow and was looking down upon her.

"'Elaine the fair, Elaine the lovable, Elaine the lily maid of Astolat,'" he said softly, his deep voice sweetly seductive.

*Elaine the fair...* She knew the passage—assigned to be committed to memory in junior high. To her ears it didn't ring quite true. She suspected he'd misquoted and swallowed a strong impulse to giggle.

"English lit, tenth grade, Alfred Lord Tennyson, *Idylls of the King,*" she said smugly.

Matt blinked in surprise. After a moment she heard a chuckling sound in his throat, heard it roll up and out in a burst of solid laughter, and then she was laughing, too.

Struggling to sit up, they leaned together and their laughter gradually tapered into companionable silence. Lane raised her eyes to find Cheyenne looking down at them, sleepy eyed and accusing.

"You woke me up. Now can I sail the boat?"

THE SUPPLY OF SUNSCREEN was running low, and the three fair-skinned sailors took the precaution of covering up when they returned to the boat. Matt pulled on his shabby almost-white sea pants over his bathing trunks and brought Lane's and Annie's pants up from the cabin below.

When they were under sail again, Matt made good his promise to Cheyenne, letting her place her small hand with his on the tiller while he explained the tiller's part in steering the boat. It was not long before Annie saw that she was still too small to duplicate the crewman paces she'd watched Matt put Lane through, and she lost interest. She went below to forage through the lunch basket in the galley for Cora's cookies and in the tote bag for books and diversions Lane had brought for her entertainment when sailing palled.

When Annie was safely occupied below, Matt reached in his pocket.

"Ever see this before?" he asked. In his hand lay Wolf's switchblade knife, in the plastic bag she'd transferred it to this morning because the paper towel was bulky in her pocket.

Lane gulped. "Where . . . ?"

"It dropped out of your pants when I brought them up."

"You weren't supposed to see that," Lane said unhappily, reaching to take the knife. Matt pulled his hand back.

"Do you realize that in the eyes of the law this thing you've been carrying in your pocket is a concealed weapon?"

"It's not as if it's an automatic pistol, but I suppose you're right," Lane said. "I was going to drop the thing overboard this morning, but I forgot."

"You shouldn't be walking around with this, Lane. Where did you get it?"

Lane was quiet for a moment. Finally she said tightly, "I'd really rather not talk about it, Matt, if you don't mind."

"Damn it, I *do* mind. You don't find one of these in the pocket of the average, decent, law-abiding American citizen, Lane. I want to know where you got it."

"And if I don't tell you? I suppose you'll think I'm planning to bump someone off," she said acidly.

"Don't be ridiculous."

With a sigh of resignation, Lane gave in. "Well, if you must know, the knife belongs to that horrible creature who claims to be Annie's father."

"Wolf?"

"He dropped it in the dirt last night after I chased him away from the corn patch with a hoe. He was trying to get Annie."

"Oh, my God!" Matt exclaimed, and Lane knew she was not going to get off now with anything less than the full story.

When her account was ended, she said firmly, "Now, please give me the knife and let me drop the blasted thing in the bay. Maybe then I can forget the whole god-awful business."

To her consternation, Matt still did not relinquish the tool.

"Did you put your hands on the knife, Lane?" he asked.

"Certainly not," she said with a shudder. "The thought of touching anything of Wolf's makes me sick, let alone something so horrible. What difference does it make?"

A freakish gust of wind brought Matt's attention back to the sails. Instead of answering, he glanced at the clouding sky.

"It's about time we headed in," he said.

Encouraged by his sudden preoccupation, Lane reached again for the knife he'd laid down. This time he made no effort to stop her.

"That knife's undoubtedly got Wolf's fingerprints all over it, Lane," he said, speaking quickly as he concentrated on sailing the boat. "Please don't throw it in the bay. It should be in the hands of the police."

"Unless I can show there's a crime involved, which I can't, the police aren't going to be interested," she protested.

"Not now, maybe, but someday that knife might be Wolf's undoing."

Lane lapsed into deep silence, absently watching Matt work with the rigging. When at last she spoke, she raised her voice slightly to be heard above the rising sound of the wind on canvas.

"You might be right," she said. "Tomorrow it goes to the police."

She saw Matt lift his hand, thumb and forefinger forming a circle in a signal of approval.

A moment later, he called out, "If you can give me a hand now, we'll take this baby in ahead of the storm. I'll be telling you what to do, so listen up. We're getting ready to come about. Don't forget to watch out for the boom."

## CHAPTER TWELVE

THE AUXILIARY MOTOR brought them into harbor under power and ahead of the storm. They were on the Montauk highway heading home before it broke. Rain and hail pelted the old Chevy wagon in a continuous bombardment until Matt pulled off Fielding Lane into the driveway that led to the farmhouse. There the deluge ceased. A minute later, as Lane nudged the lethargic Annie up the steps of the house, she raised her eyes to see a full spectrum of colors arching over the barn to the field beyond.

Before she could call Annie's attention to the rainbow, the little girl began to whimper.

"I don't feel so good," she said, and tore away from Lane to throw up in the bed of impatiens at the foot of the porch.

When the siege was over, Lane wrapped her in one of the huge towels from the tote bag and let Matt carry the child to the rose-sprigged room upstairs.

"Too many of Cora's cookies," he said quietly to Lane over the bedraggled head of the little girl as he lowered her to the bed. Annie lay still, her eyes closed, her knees curled halfway to her chin, not so much asleep as in a state of cautious quietude.

"Don't blame it all on the cookies," Lane said softly, smoothing her hand over the moist little head. "Too much everything. Too much sun. Too much fun. Too much excitement. Poor kid's not used to such a surfeit of pleasures.''

"You sure she's going to be all right?"

"I doubt if it's anything a good night's sleep won't cure. She may be over the worst already," Lane said. "I'll give her a quick sponge-off and put her to bed. Wanta bet she'll be her sparky self in the morning?"

"Are you telling me it's time to go?" Matt asked bluntly.

Under his gaze, she felt a sudden warmth flush her cheeks. She turned her eyes back to the child on the bed before she answered.

"If you're not in any hurry, I'll find something for us to eat when I've got Annie tucked in." In her effort to make the invitation seem casual, she was suddenly afraid it sounded as if she'd just as soon he didn't stay. She was relieved when he accepted without demur.

"Fine," he said. "I'll be downstairs when you're through here."

Her eyes still on Cheyenne, Lane heard him cross the landing on his way down. When the sound of his footsteps faded away, she roused the little girl enough to get her up on her feet.

"Come on, Annie, love," she said, gently pulling the windbreaker off over the pale blond head. "Let's peel you out of these clothes. You'll sleep better if we wash off some of the sand."

She took her time getting Annie ready for bed, in part to make sure the ailment was no more serious than an upset stomach, in part because of a certain uneasiness she felt as to what Matt might have read into her willingness to let him stick around.

By the time the child was bathed and in bed, it was evident her illness had passed. Lane leaned down to lay a good-night kiss on the cool forehead. In a wink, Annie had nodded off.

Aware of her own grubby condition, Lane took a few minutes to step under the shower and wash away what was left of the day's sunscreen and sand. She towel-dried and combed her hair, leaving it to curl in damp tendrils around the base of her neck. Dressed in a short, cotton knit dress the color of sunflowers, she slipped her bare feet into sandals and went to peek in on Cheyenne.

Assured by the child's regular breathing that all was well, Lane stepped out on the stair landing and quietly closed the door behind her.

A wonderful earthy smell of garlic and herbs and onions and a potpourri of other garden comestibles wafted up the stairs from the kitchen below. Puzzled, she stopped to sniff the aromas, identifying herbs and vegetables as her nose picked up their scent.

Curiosity overcame her. She started slowly down the stairs and crossed the hallway, breathing in the mixed bouquet as she went.

Matt stood at the stove looking as much at home in her kitchen as in the cockpit of his own boat, his attention focused on a large heavy skillet.

What in the world was he up to? Lane wondered. She realized for the first time that each new perspective from which she saw Matt Cheney added a further dimension to the person she thought she already knew. She felt an unexpected lilt of excitement knowing she was discovering yet another facet of this remarkable man.

With one hand he wielded a broad wooden-handled tool to turn the contents of the skillet. With the other he salted, peppered, tasted; salted, tasted, peppered; whistling softly, contentedly, tunelessly as he worked. After a minute he adjusted the burner heat and covered the skillet with a large aluminum lid.

"Tomatoes, parsley, green peppers, basil," Lane sang out blithely as she started toward him.

At the sound of Lane's voice, Matt glanced at her quickly and added, "And potatoes and zucchini and whatever else you had squirreled away in the vegetable bin in your refrigerator."

"That could be dangerous. Nothing with little green whiskers, I hope," Lane said with a laugh.

He turned fully to look at her, then without hesitating, reached back to fiddle with the burner control and crossed the kitchen. He caught her in his arms so tightly her body became at once startlingly aware of his contours under the thin layers of clothing that separated them.

Lane instinctively did what her body told her to do. As his head came down, her arms flew to clasp him around the neck. Their mouths came together in a hard, clinging kiss that softened and melted when her lips parted under the questing thrust of his tongue. She tasted the fresh flavor of basil that lingered from the savory mixture he'd just sampled from the stove.

As if from off in the distance somewhere, her instinct for self-preservation cautioned, *Easy does it.* Trying not to hear, she stayed a moment longer before she dazedly pulled away, only to see that he had not come this far to be easily diverted. Her fragile resolve stiffened. Turning her head from his, she gave a gentle push against his chest with both hands. He blinked and let her go, looking surprised.

"No, Matt," she said.

"What's that supposed to mean?"

"As far as I know, the word has only one meaning."

"Do you mean 'No, you're off bounds to me forever' or 'No, try again another time'?" he asked trenchantly. "Because if what you intended to convey is 'No, cut that out, it leaves me cold,' your eyes tell me you're lying."

In spite of herself, Lane laughed. "Actually, I mean 'No, I'm starving.' Isn't that good-smelling stuff on the stove about ready to eat?"

"It wasn't that kind of no, either," he said stubbornly, and reached to bring her back into his arms, but she stepped away quickly.

"I—I'm just not ready, Matt," she said.

She started toward the stove. Matt followed, his eyes puzzled.

For something to say, she asked, "Aren't you afraid this is going to burn?"

"Not especially," he said a bit stiffly, then giving in with good grace, he grinned. "Ever since I set my counter on fire, I never walk away from a stove without turning off all burners."

Still somewhat shaken by the unexpected contretemps, Lane watched him turn the burner back on under the skillet and reach for the spatula.

"I didn't expect to find you slaving over a hot stove when I came downstairs," she said after a moment, beginning to feel intimidated by the silence she felt growing between them.

Matt made a dismissive move with his shoulders. "I thought I might as well be doing something while you put Annie to bed. I hope you don't mind."

"Mind? Of course not. What is it?"

He looked at her blankly. "As I told you, stuff you had in the fridge, cut up and browned in some of the olive oil out of the cupboard. Some tomatoes and the green...you know, the *herbs*. You just let them cook up together with the lid on till it's done."

"How do you know when it's done?"

"When it tastes right."

Matt turned back to the stove and took off the lid of the skillet, sampling the vegetables gingerly and trying to cool the overheated dab he was tossing around on his tongue.

"Wow!" he exclaimed. "That's hot!"

Lane opened a drawer and pulled out a spoon. "Let me taste it," she said.

"Watch out," Matt warned. "You'll burn your tongue."

Forewarned, she approached the spoon more circumspectly, blowing the sample cool before she put it into her mouth. When it finally seemed safe, she let the food stay on her tongue long enough to give her taste buds time to enjoy the subtleties.

"Pretty good stuff for something you whipped up while I was putting Annie to bed." Dipping her spoon into the pan for more, she held it to cool while she said teasingly, "I bet Cora made it. It was in the hamper and you heated it in the microwave, then whisked it into the skillet when you heard me coming."

"You have just lost your bet, my sweet," he said smugly. "And don't think I won't collect."

He leaned over and ran his tongue softly over one corner of her lower lip. A shiver rippled through her. Caught unawares, she couldn't think of a thing to say.

"Tomato," he said. She gazed at him blankly. "In the corner. It's been driving me crazy." He leaned closer. "Wait. I think I missed a smidgen."

In spite of herself, Lane's tongue darted to the corner of her mouth and explored her lower lip. She ducked her head away and eyed him suspiciously.

"You're a fraud, Matt Cheney."

He gave her a look of hurt innocence. "Why do you say that?"

"If a kiss was what you wanted, why didn't you just say so?"

"Because you would have just said . . ."

The temptation was too great. Lane cut off the final word by bending forward and touching her lips to his in a kiss as light and swift as the touch of a butterfly. Then she danced away from his reaching hands and across the room.

Opening a cupboard, she said, "I'll set the table. How about eating outside? It looks like a gorgeous sunset in the making, thanks to the storm."

Pleasantly aware of Matt's frustrated gaze upon her, Lane gathered place mats and napkins and headed out the back door. The air was warm and balmy after the brief summer storm; the heavy, unmowed grass wet.

Stepping out of her sandals on the porch stair, she walked across the ankle-high grass, as soft as plush carpeting to her bare feet. The sandy loam had quickly soaked up the rain, but the tall grass held the moisture and felt wonderfully cool to her feet.

Back in the kitchen, she found Matt juggling garlic bread hot out of the oven in a napkin with one hand and opening cupboards in search of a bread basket with the other. She rushed to the rescue.

Spooning up a bite from the skillet, he held it out for Lane to taste.

"Think this stuff's done?" he asked. "Watch out. It's still hot."

Without taking the spoon from his hand, she blew on the steaming food.

Matt made a sound between a sigh and a moan. "God, if you only knew how tempting you look...."

Quickly Lane slipped the still-hot bite into her mouth and rolled it around on her tongue to avoid getting burned. "Tastes done to me," she said.

They filled plates with Matt's nameless gustatory offering, uncorked a bottle of cold chardonnay, loaded bread, glasses, plates and wine on a tray. With teamwork and good timing, they were outside at the table in time to see the sun touch down on the horizon in a spectacular crimson-and-orange streaked sky.

WHAT'S TO SAY about a sunset after you've exhausted the "magnificents" and "spectaculars" and "fantastics"? Lane wondered. But after the first brilliant glow began to fade, she was relieved to find that instead of becoming mired in a bog of awed silence, she and Matt were volleying conversational trivia back and forth as easily as if they had known each other for years.

The brilliant colors faded to a faint blush on the western horizon while they finished the last of the food and sipped from their wineglasses. The first fireflies began to flicker in the beginning dusk, and they lapsed into a lazy, companionable silence as they watched the tiny lights.

After a while Lane said lazily, "As Annie would say, 'This is neat!'"

In the light from the citron candle put out to discourage mosquitoes, she saw Matt turn his head to look at her with a quizzical smile.

"Is that a general statement, or have you something specific in mind?"

Lane drew a deep breath of satisfaction. "General," she said and stopped, not sure that she wanted to say more. But then, why not?

"Specific, too," she added hesitantly. "Earlier I was thinking how... good... it was to be around someone I can talk with so easily, but I just realized that it's even better to be comfortable whether we talk or not."

From the look on his face, she thought he was about to move closer and touch her. She felt a shadow of disappointment when he reached instead for the chardonnay bottle and filled their half-empty glasses with wine.

"According to this morning's tide chart, there should be a full moon coming up pretty soon," Matt said. "I suppose the grass is too damp to lie down in?"

"Definitely. What's that got to do with the moon?"

"According to a wise old sage, the only position for watching a full moon rise is supine."

Lane drew in a soft breath and thought about it a moment.

"I have never heard *that* one before," she scoffed.

"Well, if he didn't say it, he should have."

Rising to her feet, Lane said, "Excuse me a minute, please, Matt. I really should go in and check on Annie. I think I could hear her, since the window's open, but I'll feel better if I take a look."

ANNIE WAS SOUND ASLEEP and showed no sign of her earlier upset when Lane went to her room. Looking down on the sleeping child, she suddenly remembered Marigold's letter telling Edra of Cheyenne's birth. She'd found it the day she moved Annie to the farm, the day Matt had come to hear Annie's story. Matt had shown an interest in seeing the letter, but in her pique she'd forgotten to show it to him.

On her way out she stopped to take the letter from Annie's small box of treasures, her mind again on Matt. Though her early resolve had weakened, a small voice kept saying, *Watch it, kid. Don't let yourself become vulnerable.*

She came downstairs intending to act as if she hadn't understood his subliminal message, and found him clearing up the remains of their meal. Together they made short work of the cleanup, and though Matt didn't renew his advances, by the time they'd finished Lane had had a change of heart.

As they headed outside again, she opened one of the big storage closets that lined one wall of the porch. She pulled out a large sausage-shaped bundle and tossed it to him as he reached for the door.

SUPINE on the big unzipped sleeping bag spread out on the grass, they awaited the moon. Darkness settled in around them like black velvet, soft and warm and twinkling with brilliants as the fireflies sparked the night.

"I remember the first time I saw fireflies," Lane said dreamily. "It was the first time I came to the farm. I thought I was in fairyland."

"Didn't you grow up on the farm?" Matt asked in surprise.

"That was later. My father was a geologist. Until I was five, and my mother came to live in Manhattan, we lived all over—South America, Africa, Texas. I don't remember much about any of it, except that wherever my parents were was a battlefield. When my mother brought me here to see her sister, Aunt Mercy, for the first time, I was five and the place looked like heaven to me."

"You lived with your aunt from the time you were five?"

"Oh, no. I lived with my mother in a tiny apartment in the city. Except when I ran away."

"How old were you?" Matt asked intently.

"When I ran away? Eight, maybe. I'd take the subway down to Penn Station and get on the Long Island Railway for Seahampton. When I got here, I'd call Uncle Charlie to come get me. And then Aunt Mercy would call my mother. Most of the time my mother hadn't noticed I was gone." Lane was surprised to discover that for the first time she could voice the humiliation without feeling bitter. "I'd stay here until Mom came to get me. Sometimes I'd be here a month."

"On a regular basis?"

"Until I was ten and I talked my mother into letting me go live with my aunt and uncle. This has been my home ever since, except for the few years I was away at college and working in the city," Lane said. Sometime, while she was talking, he had taken her hand in his. He raised it now to his lips.

After a while he said, "Come to think of it, I used to run away, too. Only I was a lot older. I used to run away from my job as flunky at the family firm, or maybe from my father's contempt. Sometimes I just ran away from myself."

"Where did you run to, Matt?" Lane asked softly.

"Like you, to Seahampton. The *Wanderjahr.* The beach. I had the beach house to myself. My mother was killed in a car crash years before. After Birch and I left home, Cora didn't come to the beach again until after my father died."

So, in the shadowy intimacy of the darkness they talked about themselves and each other. They talked about things known only to them: about fathers who had failed them and mothers who weren't there; about uncertainties, frustrations, and fears—things close to the quick neither had ever voiced before. They talked about good times, too—hopes and dreams, satisfactions and rewards.

When the first edge of the full moon appeared on the horizon they lay in thoughtful silence and watched the luminous sphere climb into the cloudless sky.

In the emotional sense, Lane thought sadly, they had both been neglected children. That alone had left them equally wary of marriage; left each with the fear they would be no less hurtful to spouses and children than their parents had been. Left them afraid, perhaps forever, to take the one step toward commitment.

There must be a name for it, she thought with a touch of bitterness. It was as much a phobia as acrophobia or claustrophobia. Matt called his "the family business," and she called hers "I don't trust men," but they were actually both the same. Thank God they were in it together. With all her heart, she hoped that together they could work out a cure.

Was Matt thinking about the same thing? Lane wondered, her heart filled with a strange new warmth for this man whose secrets she'd shared. It was as if she had known him all her life.

In the mystical brightness of the moon she could see his face across the small space that lay between them almost as clearly as if it were daylight. So near. So dear.

She lifted herself and moved closer to him, pressing his hand to her face, knowing as she did that she was making herself vulnerable again.

She didn't care. All she cared about now was the look of yearning on his face as he put out his arms and gathered her to him. For a moment he did nothing but hold her close. Then, with an exultant intake of breath, he buried his face in the hollow of her throat.

In the mysterious center of Lane's body, a quiver of rapture kindled and flared and radiated through her. Suddenly it didn't matter that she might get hurt. She had been hurt before, and without ever feeling such a perfection of joy. Surely the trade-off was worth the risk.

Lifting his head, Matt began clumsily to undo the top buttons of her dress. Trembling with haste, Lane's hands came to help. Halfway down, impatience overtook her, and she slipped the half-buttoned garment over her shoulders to fall in folds around her waist, unashamedly baring her breasts.

She heard his intake of breath, felt a stillness beside her, and then he cradled her with one arm and cupped one of her breasts in his hand. As if under a spell, she watched the erotic play of his thumb and forefinger on the breast's softness as the nipple rose out of its areola. He lowered his head and guided the readied nipple into his mouth. Deep within, Lane felt the sweet, poignant sting of passion and caught her breath.

At the sound Matt lifted his head, rolling her almost roughly out of his arms in a sudden need to see her. Resting on his knees, he looked down on the long, slender body that lay before him, silvery white in the moonlight. He'd never seen anyone so beautiful, he thought with a feeling of awe. Her legs emerging from the bunched-up clothing around her hips seemed incredibly long. They tapered from knees to ankles to slender bare feet, with an almost ethereal grace.

The legendary name bandied with hilarity this afternoon returned unexpectedly to his mind. All at once the name seemed infinitely appropriate for the moon-burnished woman who lay before him.

"Lily maid . . . lily maid," he murmured, with no fear now that she would laugh.

He leaned over and slipped the rest of her clothes down over her hips and pressed his lips to her navel. Moving to bury his face in the fragrant, silky mound of hair between her thighs, he heard a soft wail from above.

"Oh, Matt, I . . . can't."

Afraid, not wanting to hear, for a moment it was as if he hadn't. With an effort he raised his head to look at her, wondering what he would do if she'd had a change of heart.

"I . . . forgot. Oh, God, Matt," she whispered. "I forgot. I'm . . . not . . . prepared."

Understanding then, he was overcome with a rush of relief.

"When there's a chance I might be with you, I will always be prepared," he said quietly.

Lingering no more, he undressed quickly. She reached out eagerly to bring him down to her, and a great gladness sprang up inside him. Their bodies fused, and he carried her with him on a mighty, pulsing wave that swept them to its crest.

AFTERWARD, they lay together in a kind of haze. When rapture gradually subsided and passion quieted, Lane's thoughts turned in wonder to the time of talk they'd shared before they made love. Without the talk, she could never have soared with him to sublime heights beyond the reach of dreams.

A night breeze stirred the leaves above them, cooling them as it whispered across their moist bodies. She shivered and fumbled to rearrange the sleeping bag in an effort to give them some cover.

"Don't go," he said drowsily, reaching to bring her back to him. His arms around her, he rolled her with him to one side of the sleeping bag and covered them with the other half. Her head buried in the hollow of his throat, they drifted together into a sweet, tender sleep.

## CHAPTER THIRTEEN

WHEN MATT WALKED into the kitchen that morning, still in a state of euphoria from his interlude with Lane, he was met by a smiling Cora, holding out a color snapshot for him to see.

"Where have you seen this face before?" she asked. From the pleased note in her voice he knew she was on to something she wanted him to discover for himself. It was not unlike Cora to snap the trash man with her camera because she saw a resemblance to Tom Selleck. Then she'd want Matt to guess who it was.

But he hadn't had enough sleep last night to be up to one of Cora's games. It had been long after midnight when he got home. Then he'd read the letter from Marigold Lane had given him as he was on his way out. The rest of the night he'd spent trying to figure out if what he'd read could have something to do with him.

"Good morning, Cora," he said, pausing to give the picture a passing glance. "Why, it's..." he started, and came to a dumbfounded stop. He reached out and took the picture from Cora, staring at it transfixed. "Oh, my God," he exclaimed softly.

A wiry, towheaded child with bright blue eyes, dressed in sneakers and jeans and T-shirt, gazed out at him from the picture. For a minute Matt couldn't tear his eyes away.

He gave a confused shake of his head and handed the snapshot back to Cora. "It's me. Where'd you find it?" he asked, doing his best not to let on to Cora how truly shaken he was.

"In the window seat in a box of old pictures I was looking through last night," Cora said. "Tell me the truth, now. You thought it was Annie at first glance, didn't you?" she asked, clearly pleased with her little coup.

"Wrong, Cora. I knew it was me all along," he said, but his voice lacked conviction even to his own ears. "It's just the color of the hair and eyes. There are a lot of blond kids in the world. Honestly, Annie never entered my mind."

Cora eyed him skeptically. "Well, she did mine. The minute I saw the picture last night, I said to myself, 'Why there's Annie. What's she doing in that box?'"

*God, I've got to get out of here,* Matt thought. He had to get off by himself and sort things out. Marigold's note to Edra Hardy had opened his mind to a possibility that had never occurred to him before. And now here was this picture.

"Could I fix you some bacon and eggs, or some...?"

"Thanks just the same, Cora," Matt interrupted, thinking quickly. "I'm on my way to the marina to meet someone. I'll grab something to eat there. See you later."

With the lie in his ears, Matt crossed the kitchen and went out the back door. A minute later he was in the Taurus, speeding across the island to the marina, his mind on the letter that had raised such havoc with his sleep.

It had been written in pencil in what he recognized as Marigold's childish hand on a single rumpled sheet of lined tablet paper folded several times to fit a small envelope. The message was short:

Dear Edra,
Guess what! I had a baby! A baby girl born May 5th, 1985, and she looks just like a doll. She was born in Cheyenne, Wyoming. They're nice to me here. I think I'll name her Cheyenne. Sorry I haven't written, but there's not much to write about.

Love,
Your friend, Marigold

LANE WAS EXPLAINING the idiosyncrasies of one of the check-stand registers to a new clerk that morning when Roz stopped by the produce market.

"Got a minute to talk?" Roz asked. Her eyes told Lane it was a cry for help.

Before joining Roz in her office, Lane stopped by the bakery stall to ask Agnes Brandon to keep an eye on Annie and let Lane know at once if the man who'd created the disturbance a few days before appeared.

In the office Lane found her friend brooding over a cup of coffee at the counter.

"How goes the vacation?" Lane asked, guessing Roz had lain awake a good part of the night.

"Great," Roz answered brightly.

A typically upbeat Roz Kramer reply. Lane didn't believe it. She poured herself a cup of coffee, slid onto a bar stool at the counter and waited for her friend to tell her what was on her mind.

"Actually, not so great," Roz said after a minute, forcing a rueful grin. "Not great at all."

"Oh, Roz, I'm sorry."

"Damn it, Lane! For the first time in my life I've found a man who's like a dream come true," Roz said. "But we've got a problem."

"I'm not all that good at solving my own problems," Lane said, "but I'm a pretty good listener."

"I'm really in love with the guy. What's more, he's in love with me, and both of us want to get married."

"So?" Lane prompted.

"All I've thought of since I knew we were in love has been buying a house in some nice small town within commuting distance for Neal. I'm sick of my stupid career. I'd retire and have babies and join the PTA and the golf club and let out the suburban housewife that's been languishing inside me for years."

"Why, Roz, I'm amazed. I never dreamed.... More power to you, dear friend," Lane said. "So what's the problem?"

"The problem's what Neal sprang on me at the breakfast table this morning," Roz said acidly. "He's quit his firm."

It took Lane a moment to get the full picture. "You mean he's not going to practice law?"

"I mean he's not going to be earning all that money as a junior partner at Seymour and Lautze," Roz said. "He's quit the firm and intends to open a law office by himself. My God, Lane. It could be years—maybe never—before he can build enough of a practice to pay the rent on a decent office in Manhattan."

"Things could work out better than you think. Give it a little time," Lane said, trying to put conviction into her voice. She could see Roz wasn't listening.

"So while Neal starts over like a new kid fresh out of law school, I'll spend the best part of my life buying baubles for other women to wear just to keep us eating and to help pay Neal's office rent," Roz said. "There go the house in the suburbs and the babies and the golf club... and the... dream." On the last words, her voice broke.

Lane waited a moment, not sure what her friend wanted to hear, then realized Roz hadn't come for advice. She'd come for a listening ear.

"The ironic part is, he thinks he's doing it for me," Roz said as she got up to leave. "How can I tell the dear man I think he's locking me into a career I'm sick of for the rest of my natural life?"

SEEING ROZ OFF from the doorway of the office a few minutes later, Lane noticed Matt's monstrous old Chevy station wagon parked in the lot. With a skittery feeling in her heart, she turned her head to look for him and at once caught sight of Cora Meigs at one of the check stands, her basket loaded with fresh vegetables.

She couldn't visualize the gray-haired, grandmotherly woman behind the wheel of the cumbersome old car. Matt must surely be around somewhere. Her pulse quickened and she hurried to speak to Cora, then slowed to normal when Cora's first words were about finding the battery in her own car dead after Matt had left for the marina in his Taurus.

"It was either wait or drive the wagon," Cora said with a laugh. "It drives like a Mack truck, but I don't have much patience when it comes to waiting."

Cora left with her basket of produce and Lane turned to see Agnes Brandon hurrying toward her, a worried look on her face. A glance across the market at Annie's workbench told Lane the little girl was not there. She at once felt uneasy.

"Is Annie with you?" Agnes asked as she drew near.

"No, but I'm sure she's around someplace. When did you last see her?" Lane asked anxiously.

"She was there at her bench bunching radishes not over half an hour ago," Mrs. Brandon told her unhappily. "Then my helper tipped a gallon container of soft icing onto the floor and it got all over everything. I was so upset I forgot about Annie until we got the mess cleaned up. When I looked, she was gone."

"Have you checked around the market?"

"I came straight to you when I saw she was missing," Mrs. Brandon said, almost in tears. "Oh, Lane, if something's happened to her, it's all my fault."

"Let's don't start borrowing trouble, Agnes. Nothing's happened, and it's nobody's fault, so don't go blaming yourself," Lane said, realizing she wasn't making complete sense. Taking herself in hand, she said briskly, "Let's get organized before we start acting crazy. We'll put out a general alarm and go over the whole place."

A workman who had been unloading boxes of green beans from his truck behind the market came up with the only solid clue. He had run off a person who was loitering outside the rear of the market around midmorning. The workman had taken a good look at the man as he drove away in a maroon-colored van. His description left no doubt in Lane's mind that the intruder had been Wolf.

Debating what to do next, she rushed into her office to pick up the phone she could hear ringing persistently. She immediately recognized the pleasant, aging baritone of Colby Strawn on the other end of the line.

"Thought you might like to know that the detective we hired has found the Wolf's den," Colby told her. "He's rented a house in Quogue. The investigator's got a

stakeout on the place. They'll slap the restraining order
on him as soon as he shows up."

"We may be too late," Lane said, her voice filled with
despair. "Annie's missing."

IN THE EARLY AFTERNOON Matt, dripping bay water,
climbed over the side of the *Wanderjahr,* at anchor in
yesterday's sandy cove, and reached for a towel. He gave
his thick hair a vigorous rub, dried off and pulled on an
old pair of white cotton sweatpants and a shirt over his
naked body.

He hadn't come here to walk around on the floor of the
cove looking at marine life, he thought, slumping into a
striped canvas deck chair with a grunt of disgust. He had
come to finish what he thought he had resolved the day
after he bought back the sloop from Luke. To revisit the
half-forgotten summer that had belonged to Marigold
and his short, haunting relationship with her.

What he'd wanted most that day had been to put all the
emotional baggage associated with Marigold behind him.
Yet now he realized he'd left something unfinished. Everything had fit together, but there had been holes, as in
a puzzle that was not quite complete.

Getting to his feet, he moved his deck chair deeper into
the withdrawing shade and absently retrieved two cans of
soda water from a small cooler near the cockpit. Tipping his head, he drank one in a few gulps and took the
other can back to the deck chair.

Settling down again, he shut his eyes. Unbidden, his
thoughts turned to Lane and to the incredible hours of
love and disclosure that had been theirs the night before.
He saw her long, beautiful, moon-drenched body and felt
a pulse of desire. Shifting uneasily in his chair, he tried

to shut the door on his bewitching recollections and concentrate on the elusive puzzle of Marigold.

A minute later he jumped up and peeled off his clothes. In a shallow racing dive off the side of the boat, he skimmed into the steel-blue water below. In a fast, powerful crawl he headed out toward the buoy. Halfway there he turned and swam back.

Without bothering to towel off, he got back into the sweat clothes. Something Annie had said to him yesterday while he was showing her the tiller stuck in his mind.

"My real daddy showed Marigold how to sail his boat."

A missing piece or just another of Annie's fantasies?

Unlike Lane, he'd never seen any reason not to believe Wolf was Annie's father. According to Susan Craddock, Wolf was named as Annie's father on her birth certificate, but in the light of Marigold's letter to Edra, it seemed highly unlikely that he was.

No matter how many times he counted back nine months from May 5th, 1985, he came to his own blissful summer weeks of lovemaking with Marigold.

Stretched out prone on the deck, his head shielded from the sun by his arms, he closed his eyes again and let the pieces fall into place. Gradually the ambivalence that had tormented him since the early hour when he first read the letter disappeared. The picture Cora had shown him this morning pulled everything together.

Annie had been conceived on the *Wanderjahr* on the bunk in the cabin below, before Wolf ever entered the picture. At peace, his mind no longer questioning, he fell asleep.

ANNIE HAD BEEN GONE from the market nearly two hours, and Lane was becoming frantic. If only she could get hold of Matt. Right after she found out Annie was missing and called the police, she'd phoned the beach house, but no one had answered. She'd been trying at intervals ever since.

On the sidelines now, by unwilling default, she drifted in and out of her office, leaving tasks unfinished, sentences incomplete, her ears tuned always for the sound of the telephone.

News came first from Colby Strawn, whose opening words gave her new hope.

"Well, the stakeout worked," he said.

In her eagerness Lane couldn't wait for him to finish. "Is Annie all right?"

"When our investigator served the restraining order on Wolf, there was no sign of the little girl around the house or the van as far as he could see," Strawn told her. "Of course, he didn't have a search warrant, so we can't be sure."

"What do you have to do to get a search warrant?" Lane asked a little wildly, the stress of the ordeal beginning to tell.

"You'd have to be able to prove the man has the child imprisoned in the house or in his van. You don't even know for sure he's got her."

"No, but he's tried to take her more than once," she said defensively. "I'm certain he's mixed up in her disappearance. I don't need proof. I just know."

"This isn't the usual case of a father wanting custody of his own child for paternal reasons. Have you any idea what he's up to?" Colby asked.

"Not a clue, Colby," she said, anxiety making her voice come out edgy and thin. "Whatever he's up to, it means no good for Annie."

"We'll have the man tailed and put a watch on the house," Colby assured her. "Try not to worry. I'm sure everything will turn out all right."

As she stepped out of the office, the phone rang once more. She hurried back to pick it up.

"Fielding's Farm Market, Lane speaking."

"This is Cora Meigs, Lane. Before I say more, I've got Annie, so you can stop worrying."

Her words were so unexpected, for a moment Lane was afraid she'd misheard her.

"Cheyenne's with you?"

"When I got home she was in the back of the car under a pile of beach blankets and boat stuff of Matt's," Cora explained. "I'm sure you've been worried sick."

"Thank God." Lane's words came out on an exhaled breath. Choked with emotion, she needed a moment to compose herself before she could go on. "What in the world is she doing there?"

"Running away from Wolf, apparently. She says she caught a glimpse of him behind the market and was scared. She scooted out the front and saw Matt's old station wagon, so she hopped in and hid under the blankets, afraid even to peek out. I didn't know she was there until I got home just now."

"Cora, could you hold on a moment?" Lane interrupted, remembering the others waiting for news in the market. She put down the phone and hurried to the screen door. Surely Matt would have called instead of Cora if he were there, she thought.

"Annie's been found," she called out to the whole market. "She's okay."

Back at the phone, she apologized. "I'm sorry, Cora. Everybody's been going crazy around here since we discovered she was missing. I had to let them know she's been found."

"Of course you did," Cora agreed. "I'm sorry I was such a long time getting to you, but I didn't come straight home from the market. If I'd known Annie was with me, I'd have called while I was doing my errands."

A glance at the clock on the wall told Lane it had been more than two hours since she'd talked to Cora here at the market.

"Annie's been under a blanket in the back of Matt's station wagon all this time?" she said anxiously. "Is she all right?"

"She's fine," Cora reassured her. "Oh, a little overheated, I should think, and a little bedraggled, but no harm done. She's right here. I'll put her on the phone."

In delayed reaction as Cheyenne's voice came on, Lane's whole body became trembly with relief. In a small corner of her mind she wondered again if Matt was there.

"Hi, Lane." Annie's voice sounded tentative and thin.

Lane choked up. She hadn't realized how much she'd been holding back, how much she cared.

"Annie!" she burst out. After a moment she managed to go on almost normally. "Are you all right?"

"Yeah." There was a long pause. "It was hot under the blanket, Lane. I was real scared."

"I've been pretty scared myself, honey. I'm coming to get you right away. You can tell me all about it then," Lane said. Another silence. Lane asked, "Annie, are you there?"

"Yeah," Annie replied. After a second she said hesitantly, "Would it be all right if I stayed here awhile?"

Surprised and strangely hurt, Lane was at a loss for words. Then she got the picture. Annie was afraid.

Afraid to come back to the market, she thought sickly. *Oh, God, what am I going to do?*

"How about putting Cora back on the phone?"

On the line a moment later Cora Meigs said, "I heard. I'd love to have her. Why don't you just leave her here for the rest of the day? Give us a call when you're ready to close up this evening. By that time Matt will be back from the marina, and he can bring her home to you."

"I think she's afraid Wolf will come back to the market," Lane said reluctantly.

She wanted Annie here. She wanted to see for herself that the child was all right. She wanted to hug the little girl and assure her she didn't need to be afraid. But she knew in her heart that what Annie needed more than a hug was a solid sense of security the marketplace couldn't give her right now.

To Cora Meigs, Lane said at last, "I appreciate your offer, Cora, and if you really don't mind, maybe the best thing is to let her stay. Please tell Annie I'll see her tonight."

LANE BLAMED HERSELF for Annie's fright and subsequent disappearance. She shouldn't be trusted with the care of Annie. She shouldn't have been inside drinking coffee with Roz. She shouldn't have let Annie out of her sight. It only went to prove she was no good with children.

She tried to settle back into normal market routine, but the sound of guilt was still with her as she tried to put her mind to the open ledger on the desk. Gazing blindly at the figures before her, she asked herself if she had been negligent in her care of Annie. But when she tried to imagine more diligent measures a real mother might have taken in such a situation, she drew a blank.

Eventually she came to the conclusion that there was nothing wrong with her security measures. Analyzing, she began to smile.

She hadn't taken into consideration Annie's own streetwise penchant for taking care of herself. Wolf had never been any threat to her. All Annie would have had to do was alert Agnes or any one of the market people that Wolf was hanging around outside.

The solution was not to beef up security, but to reeducate Annie.

The events of the past few days had put Lane behind on her bookwork, and she gave the next hour to bringing accounts up to date. When the last figures had been entered, the final column totaled, she looked up to see the amiable face of Neal Roberts peering in at her through the screen door.

"Hi there, Neal," she called out in surprise. "What are you doing out there? Come on in." She got to her feet to open the door, but Roberts was already acknowledging her invitation by stepping inside.

"I brought you the guardianship papers to look over. Can you spare a minute?"

"Of course. But do sit down," Lane said.

"You can look at the papers anytime, Lane. If I've come at an awkward moment, it won't offend me to be told to get out," he said.

"Not at all. Stay and talk a minute," Lane replied. "Roz tells me you've left Seymour and Lautze and are planning to open your own law office in the city, so I'm curious. Why the city?"

Roberts looked at her intently for a moment, as if deciding what he was prepared to confide.

Finally he said, "There are two big reasons why the city. First, of course, is Roz. The second is, it shouldn't take too long to build a practice of my own there, because I've got lots of contacts. Money will be tight at first, but nobody will own my time and there'll always be some for Roz."

"Makes sense, but why couldn't you do the same thing in the suburbs—or for that matter, out here?"

"In Seahampton? I'd love it here, but there's no way I could make a living. I'm a stranger. It would take years before I could build up a practice," Neal said. "Furthermore, the town's too small to support another lawyer. It needs me like Mount Rushmore needs another face. And don't forget Roz."

"What *about* Roz?"

"If I practiced law someplace like Seahampton and she worked in the city, one of us would have a two-hour commute twice a day every day, or we'd spend the weekdays in our separate workplaces and see each other on weekends and holidays. Is that any way to run a marriage?"

"What if Roz quit her job?"

"Think about it, Lane," he said defensively. "Just because I'm marrying Roz doesn't give me the right to expect her to give up her career to accommodate mine. Can you imagine Roz, the consummate career person, moving out here to rusticate?"

Lane couldn't hold back her smile. "Have you ever discussed this with Roz?"

"What's to discuss? My God, Lane, what would she do with herself?"

"She could keep house," Lane said softly, "and have babies and join the PTA and become a member of a golf club."

There was a long moment of silence between them.

"Roz?" Roberts said. From the sound of his voice, she could tell the idea had never entered his mind.

"Roz?" he said again on a note of wonder.

"Roz."

"God, you must think I've been talking like a jackass."

"Don't feel bad. I never saw it myself until we had coffee together this morning."

Suddenly Roberts was on his feet. "I've got to go," he said, heading for the door. "Thanks, Lane. Thanks for everything."

"You might like to talk to my attorney—the one I told you was thinking about retiring," Lane called after him as he reached the door. "Get in touch with me if you're interested, after you talk to Roz."

## CHAPTER FOURTEEN

LANE WAS WATCHING for Matt and Annie from the big wooden swing on the porch that evening when Matt's old Nomad came into sight. A great feeling of relief flooded through her, and the next moment she was running down the steps, stepping over the low gate into the arms of the tall man and the small girl coming toward her.

For a moment they were a circle, then Matt stepped aside and let them both go, allowing Lane to hug Annie to her.

"I love you, Annie," she said. "You shouldn't have run away. I wouldn't have let Wolf get to you, honey."

The eyes, blue as forget-me-nots, looked back at Lane solemnly. Tears gathered and spilled over.

"He got to me that other day," Annie reminded her in a voice so alone it cut Lane like a knife.

"You run inside and start getting your things together, Annie," Matt said.

An alarm sounded in Lane's head.

The little girl's eyes focused unhappily on Lane. With a last look back, she scrambled over the low gate and ran up the path to the house.

"What do you mean 'start getting your things together'?" Lane asked in a level voice when Cheyenne was out of hearing.

"I meant I'm asking your permission to take Annie back home with me. Cora and I—"

"And if I say no?"

Matt reached out to touch Lane's face in a gesture of endearment, but she pushed his hand away.

"Be reasonable, Lane. It would only be—"

"You're saying she's not safe with me," she accused, bitterness creeping into her voice. "If Annie had stayed in the market where she belongs, there was no way Wolf could have touched her."

"Wolf had already accosted her at the market another time, don't forget," Matt pointed out. "You can't blame Annie for not feeling secure there anymore."

"Nobody was prepared for his coming that other time," Lane said. "But you can rest assured we're ready for him now," she added grimly.

"You may be right about your security, Lane, but you're going to have a hard time convincing Annie."

"I certainly hope you're wrong," she said, unable to keep anxiety out of her voice. "I'm going to do the best I can to reassure her, but if I can't, I can't. Knowing Annie, she will adjust."

From where they stood, Lane saw the light in Cheyenne's bedroom go on. She bent to open the gate, but as Matt moved to do it for her, she stepped past him and over. A moment later he was at her side.

They walked slowly on up the path and the steps to the porch, the controlled tension between them almost palpable. As if by tacit consent, they moved to the porch swing, still picking at the bones of their contention.

"Frankly, Lane," Matt said, "I'm not nearly as concerned about Annie's safety at the market as I am about the two of you alone at night in this big house miles away from police protection. It would be easy for Wolf to—"

"He wouldn't dare," Lane interrupted.

"Lane, listen to me. Please. This place is an open invitation. You're a good mile from your nearest neighbors. You keep all the windows open at night. You've said yourself you're pretty casual about security."

"I keep the doors locked," Lane protested with growing annoyance at Matt's intrusion into her own domain. "When I think I need help, I'll ask for it. I've had dealings with Wolf, and there's one thing I know. He's a coward. He's not about to do anything that'll get the police on him, like breaking and entering."

"That's pure speculation." Matt, too, was growing testy.

"We both know what you're getting at, Matt. You think you're going to take Cheyenne back to your house with you tonight," Lane said. "Well, you're not. This isn't the first time she's been scared. We've managed to work out her fears without any help before, and we'll do it again."

"I'm concerned about both of your safety, and I'd prefer to take the two of you home with me until Wolf is caged," Matt said. "It'll be no more trouble for you to get to the market from the beach house than from here, so don't try to argue that it'll interfere with your work. We've plenty of room, and Cora—"

"Stop right where you are, Matt Cheney," Lane cried, all but spitting fire. "Who gave you the right to turn my life upside down? If you think I'm going to let some small-time hood scare me out of my own home, you don't know me very well."

"Oh, I know you," Matt countered sardonically. "I know you well enough to wonder why I ever thought I could get you to come." He drew a deep breath and continued. "Well, I can't force you, but neither can you keep Annie here in the face of potential danger."

"This is Annie's home, too...."

"This is *not* Annie's home and never will be. Moving her to the beach house is just one more move along the way for Annie."

"What right have you...you...Johnny-come-lately, to think you can come here and take her away?"

"As much right as you have to keep her here," he said grimly. "You're not her mother. You're only borrowing her until you find someone to adopt her. Well, I've got news for you, darling. You can play mother to your heart's content, but I intend to see that Annie's safe from Wolf around the clock, every day of the week."

Lane glared at him in stunned disbelief. *Play mother?* Did he really believe that was what she was doing? Examining herself for the slightest truth in what he said, Lane knew he was wrong. If fostering Annie was "playing mother," it was play that called out every honorable, loving resource in her being and was as serious to her as anything in her life had ever been.

"That was a despicable thing to say," she said coldly. "If you think my taking care of Annie is an ego trip, last night's soul baring didn't accomplish much."

With a groan, Matt turned and pulled her, struggling, into his arms, pinning her arms to her sides. Burning with fury, she could do nothing but buck against him. After a moment she gave up, but he didn't relax his grip.

"You're right. Trivializing all you've done for Annie was a rotten thing to do," he said hoarsely. "It was pure frustration speaking."

He loosened his hold. Overriding her first furious impulse to pull away, Lane freed her arms but remained closely encircled by his. She felt a latent sympathy for what he was going through; she was feeling pretty frustrated herself.

"I'm sorry," he said. "God, Lane, please don't let's fight over this." Matt's voice sounded miserable. "I think we both know we're on the edge of something stupendous together if we can give ourselves time to figure out how to make it work."

"Well, I haven't exactly been Miss Congeniality, myself," she admitted after a minute. "I'm sorry, too." Lifting her face to his, she kissed him lightly on the lips in a gesture of . . . apology? Forgiveness? She wasn't sure which. When he made a move to prolong the embrace, she pulled away.

"Which doesn't mean I'm going to let you take Annie tonight," she said.

She felt his body stiffen.

Finally he said, "I suppose I could say, 'I'm stronger than you are' and storm the house and carry her off with me."

"I'm sure you could. Men are generally reckoned to be physically stronger than women."

She couldn't see his face now in the darkness. For a moment he didn't speak.

Then he said, "Oh, hell. Give me a break, Lane. I'm not comfortable with you and Annie out here alone," he said. "Maybe it's all right for you, though you may as well know I don't like it. But Annie's really afraid to stay. She's up there right now getting her stuff ready to go with me, and whether you like it or not, I'm not going to disappoint her."

"Since you feel so strongly about this, Matt, and for that matter, so do I, maybe the only thing to do is let Annie speak for herself," Lane said. "If she's ready to go with you I won't like it, but I promise I won't interfere. The same should go for you if she says she'd rather sleep in her own bed."

Silence stretched between them until finally Matt said, "You're on."

The house was dark inside. Lane turned on the light to the stairs and the two climbed up together to find themselves again facing total darkness at the top.

"What the devil...?" Matt muttered as Lane touched the switch that illuminated the upstairs hallway. One door was closed. There was no light showing beneath it.

"Isn't that Annie's bedroom?" Matt asked, puzzled.

Lane nodded. Softly she opened the door. The light shone in on the flower-sprigged room and fell on the small figure of Annie, sprawled across the bed in a tangle of sheets, sound asleep.

Quietly Lane closed the door and looked at Matt.

"You knew...." he accused.

"Not really. Well ... I did see her light go off a while ago," she admitted.

Matt glowered at her for a moment. Finally he said, "Where do you want me to sleep?"

Lane gaped. "What do you mean, where do I want you to sleep? As if I had a choice."

"You have a choice. I'm sleeping here. Would you care to show me to your guest room, or would you rather I slept with you?"

IN THE COLONIAL four-poster in the guest room, Matt stared into the darkness and imagined himself feeling his way down the unlit hallway to Lane's door. He imagined slipping into her bed and finding her welcoming; soft and warm and fully aroused. He moaned and rolled over.

A moment later he was wondering what she slept in, envisioning her in something white and filmy, hinting at the exciting curves beneath. He saw himself lifting aside the layers of veiling to find her silken body....

He swore softly and sat up, planting his feet on the floor. His body slumped. There was no way he would go to her uninvited, and there would be no invitation as long as they were at odds over Annie's safety.

With a resigned sigh, he left the bed and padded across the floor to the open window, and gazed down on the moon-washed lawn below. Her presence on the other side of the wall—so near and yet so inaccessible—played upon his senses. He might as well forget sleep. Her biting words pounded in his head.

*What right have you to think you can come here and take her away?* Would she have accepted his right to step in if he'd simply said, "I'm Annie's father"?

Why hadn't he told her?

Because she'd have believed he was making an outrageous last-ditch ploy to take Annie away with him?

He wouldn't have blamed her if she had. He would have found the statement hard to accept himself if he hadn't seen the snapshot. He remembered Cora once saying that Annie's hair was like his when he was a kid, but it hadn't meant anything at the time. Not until he'd seen the picture. It wasn't just the hair. It was the eyes...the high forehead...the grin. Now, every time he looked at her, the truth was in his heart. No more was she Lane's "orphan Annie." She was Annie, Matthew Cheney's little girl.

A night breeze lifted the sheer curtain at the window and brushed it across his face. He sneezed and moved away from the window. Crossing the room, he stretched out on the bed again. Staring into the darkness, he admitted the other reason he hadn't told Lane he was Annie's father.

The real reason, he knew in his heart, was not the fear that she might *not* believe him, but that she would. He was afraid she would want nothing further to do with him when she learned he had fathered a child out of wedlock. Not just any child. Annie.

Someday soon he'd have to tell her the truth. The truth—God help him—put him in a very bad light.

Bathed in a sudden cold sweat, he got up and went to the window again to gaze out with a sense of hopelessness. After a while he went to the bathroom and drank a glass of water before returning to the bed. The cycle of his sleeplessness started over.

LANE, WHO WAS HAVING her own problems getting to sleep, heard his pacing from her room next door. First the creak of one of the pre-revolutionary floorboards like the chirp of a cricket in the night, then silence and then the creak. She found that part of her was keenly attuned to his movements.

Gradually the feeling of grim victory that should have warmed her through the night went cool. What had she won? Peace of mind? Not exactly. Something petty, and at the expense of the pacing man next door.

Last night, with its overflow of understanding and passion, seemed light-years away.

At the renewed sound of the creaking floorboard, she sat up in bed and propped her head on her knees, listening. He was crossing to the window, she thought. Probably in the buff, thanks to his unexpected stay-over.

She pictured the long, lean body, the perfect congruity of its parts. A deep, sensual quiver started in the most intimate recess of her body.

Was it desire for her that made him pace?

She got to her feet and reached with trembling hands for the flowered silk kimono on the end of the bed. Not letting herself consider what she was about to do, she wrapped the soft robe around her and stepped quietly out into the hallway.

At the door of the guest room she hesitated, ready to turn back. She thought of him, virile and tender, awake and lonely, infinitely tempting. If nothing else, she must tell him she'd been unreasonable.

Boldly she tapped on the door and waited, her heart pounding so furiously she could feel the rise and fall of the silk that covered her breast.

"Lane?" From the sound of his voice, she knew he was not in bed, but near the window.

"May I come in?" she asked quietly.

"I'm undressed."

About to say, "It doesn't matter," she reconsidered. In her own eagerness, was she taking too much for granted?

She said instead, "You'll find a terry robe I keep for guests hanging on the bathroom door."

Wearing the robe, he opened the door a moment later and looked out at her from the darkened room.

"Well, this *is* a surprise," he said. "I'll turn on the light."

"Please don't," she said, brushing past him to walk to the window. "I...it's easier to say I'm sorry in the dark."

She turned and found him close behind her. She heaved a great sigh. "Today was two china plates scraped together...a fingernail-scratched-across-a-blackboard kind of day," she said flatly.

"A sharp crack on the crazy-bone kind of day?" Matt said, falling in line.

"Exactly. Oh, Matt, you *are* right," she said in a rush. "We shouldn't be quarreling about Annie. We both want whatever is best for her. Neither of us can be too far wrong. After all we've been through together, it hurt that Annie didn't trust me to protect her from Wolf."

He reached out and gently massaged her neck and shoulders through the silk of the kimono. She paused a moment, feeling her tension begin to fade.

"I might as well just say it," she blurted out. "It didn't help for you to show so little confidence in my ability to take care of Annie here, or even to take care of myself."

"You misread me, tigress," he said soothingly, his hands moving under the loose fabric as his fingers skillfully molded her flesh. "It's just that this is one hell of a big den for you and one small cub to defend."

"Well . . ." she said.

Relaxed now, she let him turn her with his hands so the full length of her back rested against him in the circle of his arms. She could feel his growing arousal against her buttocks and was overtaken by a sudden breathlessness. She wasn't sure how much longer she was going to want to talk, and there was more she needed to say. Reaching up, she turned his head with her hand.

"Wait, Matt. You're making me crazy. How would it be for you to take Annie home with you and Cora in the daytime and bring her back to stay at night until we know what we're going to do about Wolf?"

"Sounds good to me. You agree, though, that I'm going to spend my nights here at the farmhouse as long as there's a threat from Wolf."

"That's entirely up to you."

"Anything more?"

"I'm sorry I called you a Johnny-come-lately," she said. She couldn't resist adding, "But that's what you are. I still don't understand why you've suddenly decided to share the responsibilities of Annie with me."

But even as she finished she'd lost interest. She had eyes only for Matt as he discarded his robe and stood before her in the pale light of the moon. He untied the belt

of her kimono and slipped the silken garment over her
arms. Their bodies melding, they moved together to the
bed.

SLEEPWISE, it had been a short night, Lane thought
dreamily next morning as she sorted through a bin of dry
onions behind the market, tossing out bad ones. Long
after midnight she'd fallen asleep in Matt's arms, only to
leave them all too soon, before daybreak brought the
unpredictable awakening of Annie.

Hard as she'd struggled to keep Cheyenne from
spending her days with Matt and Cora, Lane had to admit it took a great load off her mind to have the little girl
safely away from the marketplace. For all her brave talk,
the dreadful possibility that Wolf might somehow manage to steal the child during a moment of mass inatten-
tion had tormented her far more than she was willing to
admit. With Annie under the joint observation of Matt
and Cora Meigs, Lane was free to give her mind fully to
whatever she was doing.

The whole place was beginning to show evidence of her
neglect, she thought guiltily, looking around as she discarded the last black, mold-encrusted onion and got to
her feet.

She pulled off the heavy work gloves she wore and
waved a greeting to Roz and Neal as they came out the
back entrance of the market into the loading area.

Turning the spoiled onions over to a workman to wheel
out to the compost heap, she led her visitors to the office, where a fresh pot of coffee was ready to pour.

"We came by to thank you for yesterday's favor," Neal
said as Lane headed for the coffeepot.

"You mean suggesting you go home and talk to Roz?"
Lane asked, smiling. "Right."

"We should have talked things out a long time ago instead of trying to do what we each mistakenly thought the other wanted," Roz said. "We needed someone to get us on the right track."

"Let's wait and be sure this track's not a dead-end street," Neal cautioned. "At the moment, I don't even know where to start looking for a location."

Lane took a sip of coffee. She wanted to send Neal to Colby Strawn but was afraid of building up Neal's hopes. Colby was a man of strong opinions. He didn't take to everybody. Suppose he didn't make Neal an offer?

"I believe I mentioned my attorney, Colby Strawn, had been talking about retiring," she said casually. "If you'd like to get his views on the life of a small-town lawyer, I'll be glad to give him a call and ask him if he can talk to you."

"I'd appreciate that, Lane."

"I'll see if he's in," Lane said. Picking up the phone, she dialed Colby's number and passed a minute of small talk with his secretary before the lawyer came on the line.

"Good morning, Lane," Colby's mellow voice greeted her. "I've been meaning to call you. The investigator we hired to stake out this Wolf fellow thinks he may have a criminal record. It might save you trouble in the long run to have that tracked down, even if it costs you a little more money."

"You're right, of course. Tell the detective I want him to find out everything he can about Wolf, especially why he's trying to get hold of Annie."

"I'll keep in touch."

"Thanks, Colby. That's not really what I called about, though. I have a friend here who's thinking of leaving his law firm in the city and relocating in a small-town area like Seahampton,'' Lane said. "You wouldn't have time to talk to him, would you?"

"Send him over around ten-thirty," Colby said good-humoredly. "I just had a cancellation. What's his name?"

"Neal Roberts."

"Fine. I'll be looking for him."

Lane put down the phone. "He'll see you in half an hour," she said. "It'll take you about ten minutes to get to his office from here. It's right downtown."

"That's nice," said Roz. "I'll shop the store windows while you talk to Mr. Strawn."

As they were about to leave, Lane remembered the guardianship papers she still hadn't received.

"By the way, Neal, about those papers . . . ?"

Roberts smacked the heel of his hand against his forehead. "Can you beat that! I came over here for the sole purpose of delivering those papers and never gave them to you."

Roz wandered out into the market, but Neal turned back and sat down on one of the stools at the counter and looked at Lane quizzically.

"Roz has prevailed upon me to ask you a question, Lane, at the risk of being told it's none of my business," he began. A serious, almost solemn note in his voice brought Lane to instant attention. "Instead of filing for guardianship, have you ever thought of adoption?"

The question, earthshaking, unexpected, crashed into the most secret chamber of her heart. My God, if he only knew! The thought had been haunting her for days.

"You mean *me* adopt Annie?" she asked faintly. In her ears the words sounded like a cry of pain.

"Why not? It's obvious to us both that you love the child deeply and that she's crazy about you," Roberts said seriously. "It could be the ideal solution to Annie's problems. She's too old for easy adoption otherwise."

Stunned, Lane could find no voice to reply.

When she didn't speak, Neal cleared his throat and said apologetically, "Forget I said anything, Lane. I'm sorry. I've got a nerve mucking around in your private affairs. Whatever your reasons for not wanting to adopt the little girl, I'm sure they are good ones. I shouldn't be questioning you this way. I hope I haven't offended you."

Lane put a detaining hand on his arm. "Of course not, Neal," she said warmly. "I consider the fact you asked the question a vote of confidence."

The man looked at her blankly. "I'm sorry. I don't..."

"The truth is, I've never really believed I've got the stuff to be a good mother," Lane said hesitantly. "I do want Annie with all my heart, Neal, but I've been afraid to let myself think about adopting her. I keep feeling she deserves better. Knowing you and Roz think I'd do okay gives me something to think about."

She realized her eyes were filling with tears. She turned her head to wipe them away with the back of her hand.

"Then you may not want to use these guardianship papers," Neal said after a moment. "I'll take them with me. You'll let me know?"

"I'll let you know," Lane said. "You'd better get out of here. Colby won't like it if you're late."

DRIVING HOME to the beach house that morning with Annie buckled into the front seat of the Taurus beside him, Matt decided he was like a juggler with too many balls in the air. Love for Lane, responsibility for Annie, newfound fatherhood, the threat of Wolf, the family firm. Oh, God! The family firm.

He felt suddenly smothered by guilt. Except to phone the office and go over a few matters with Cliff every morning, he'd hardly given a thought to the investment business all week.

"I'd a lot rather ride in the Nomad," Annie said plaintively, interrupting Matt's train of thought. She'd called the old wagon the Nomad ever since Matt had told her its factory name. The special pride with which she ran the word over her tongue amused him.

"I couldn't even get it to jump-start last night, remember?"

She gazed at him with solemn blue eyes. "Why don't you fix it?"

"I'm going to," Matt promised absently, his mind already back in his upstairs office.

"*Really* fix it, Matt?"

"Hmm? What do you mean, really? Don't I always get it to run?"

"Till it stops again," the child said disapprovingly. "I mean *really* fix it so it'll run all the time. You could paint it a real nice shiny color—like maybe yellow. Yeah. Yellow. And white on top. Wouldn't that be neat?"

Abandoning his guilt-ridden thoughts, Matt fell in with her dream. "Pretty neat," he agreed. "It could use new chrome strips around the sides and the bumper."

Annie gave a crow of satisfaction. "You going to do it yourself, Matt? Like you did before?"

"Why not? You want to help?"

"Let's start right now," Annie said eagerly as the car turned into the driveway to the back of the house.

Matt came crashing back to earth. What the devil was he thinking of? Annie or no Annie, he'd already goofed off more than he could afford.

"Not now, Annie. I've got to go to work."

The little girl slumped down in the seat, her face a study in disappointment. "You were just talkin'," she accused after a moment. "You're not going to do it."

Unexpectedly he thought of his father. He brought the car to the end of the driveway and came to a stop.

"I'll make a deal with you, Annie," he said at last. "You find something to do with Cora this morning while I get some work done. This afternoon you and I'll take a look under the hood and see what's wrong with the Nomad."

"I'd rather..."

"So would I, but I can't," Matt said cheerfully, ignoring her pouty lip. "I've got to work. We might as well both be good sports about it."

"Yellow? With a white top?" she said finally, a note of skepticism in her voice.

He reached over and gave her pigtail an affectionate tug.

"You drive a hard bargain, kid."

# CHAPTER FIFTEEN

LURED TO THE KITCHEN by the aromas of coffee and maple syrup, Lane came downstairs next morning, refreshed by nine hours' sleep. There she found Matt at the griddle and Cheyenne pressing freshly cut orange halves into the electric squeezer.

It boded well for the day to come, Lane thought; an assessment that proved uncannily accurate a short while after she got to the market. Matt arrived in his Taurus unexpectedly and Annie bounded out of the car prepared to stay.

"Hey, Lane, I'm here! You don't gotta do my jobs," the little girl announced. "Here I am, Angus," she called as he came through the back from the loading dock with a wheelbarrow piled high with carrots and beets and onions. She went running for her workbench, where the old farmer went to unload.

"Mind telling me why the sudden change of heart?" Lane asked Matt, who was coming toward her from the car, a wry smile on his face.

"It's not *my* change," Matt assured her. "I still don't think this is a great place for her to be when you people are all busy and Wolf's on the prowl."

"Then what's she doing here?" Lane asked.

"She's here because I just lost the damnedest argument I ever had in my life, and I'm not even sure what it was all about," Matt said, combing his fingers through his hair. "Among other things, you are her sister. Somehow she's letting her sister down. Something to do with your coming home tired last night. Seems to correlate with Marigold always being tired. I don't know what kind of magic you've worked on that kid, Lane, but she's all yours."

Lane's throat was suddenly choked. "I like that," she managed to say. Then, hoping to ease his mind, she assured him, "I won't let her out of my sight all day."

"Just mornings," Matt corrected. "We've got a deal. She comes here in the morning and does what she's supposed to do, and I come and get her around noon. She spends the rest of the day with me, until we meet back at the farm at night."

*She's all yours.* Lane looked across the marketplace at Annie, painstakingly counting out carrots and tying them into a bunch, and smiled. Maybe she had a knack for mothering after all.

The sound of the phone ringing in her office sent her hurrying to answer. She was pleased to hear Neal Roberts's voice at the other end of the line.

"Just called to tell you that I am, as of this morning, Colby Strawn's man. I'm calling right now from my new office."

"Oh, Neal, that's splendid. You two didn't waste any time, I must say," Lane said warmly. "Congratulations. May I have the honor of being your first client. I want to adopt Annie."

AFTER DROPPING ANNIE at the market, Matt returned to his office at home and spent the first half hour on the phone with Cliff Harris, checking on affairs at the Wall Street office and going over further changes in procedures.

If there was one thing he'd learned from this forced vacation, it was to appreciate Cliff's abilities, Matt thought as he hung up the phone. He'd always liked Cliff. Trusted him. Thought of him as a good man. It occurred to him that he'd been selling Cliff short. Harris was a lot more than just a "good man." He came close to being Matt's alter ego in matters of business.

Settling down to watch the early stock market returns on the computer screen, he was disconcerted to find his mind once again wandering to personal problems.

How long could he live in this fool's paradise with Lane without telling her about his relationship with Marigold? And Annie. How would she react? He realized he was afraid to find out.

After a while he pushed back his chair and walked to the window, staring at the dunes ahead of him and the sea beyond.

*Vacation?* Upheaval was a better name for it. Better to have followed the wisdom of the late Horace Cheney and stuck to his Wall Street desk all summer.

And missed learning what happiness was all about? No Lane . . . no Annie. His spirit rebelled. Life without Lane was too painful to contemplate, yet what the devil did he have to offer? The kind of marriage and family life his mother had endured?

Like the restless tide, his spirits ebbed and flowed until at last he left the window and headed out, seeking balm for his troubled soul. A short time later he was aboard the *Wanderjahr,* racing across the water before a capricious breeze that brought no answers but drove the questions from his mind while he grappled with the sails.

IT WAS THE OLD waiting-for-the-other-shoe-to-drop syndrome, Lane thought uneasily as she unloaded boxes of eggplant, crook-neck squash and bell peppers and arranged them on a table in a colorful display.

It was nearly a week and a half since the day Wolf had scared Cheyenne into hiding in Matt's old station wagon. Had the restraining order Colby had served convinced Wolf to stay away?

Meanwhile, she was presiding over a unique household. She found herself smiling. Hardly the traditional ménage à trois. Without consciously making it happen, she and Matt had slipped into a routine that had quickly taken the shape of a bona fide, well-functioning family: mother, father, child.

Like a proper family, they talked at the dinner table about the day just past. Still smiling, she thought of last night's progress report by Annie on the old station wagon she was "helping" Matt renovate. Lane liked to picture Matt under the car calling for a wrench and Annie handing it to him like a nurse attending a surgeon. The latest news was that the job was done. The Nomad was now getting a new coat of yellow paint with a white top.

Who did what in the household wasn't something they fussed about. Whoever got home first started dinner. In deference, she suspected, to her own long workday at the market, Matt usually managed to be at the farm when she arrived.

For her part, she came home loaded with the best of the market's daily offerings: watermelon and rosy-cheeked peaches for Annie, greengage plums and red raspberries for Matt, delectable baked goods from Agnes Brandon's bakery stall, fresh sweet corn.

By the time she got there, the kitchen would be richly fragrant with herbs and garlic and cooking smells, Matt in the midst of one of his culinary experiments and Annie singing a ballad in her sweet, sunny little voice as she set the table. Sometimes when he knew the words, Matt would be singing along with the little girl in the energetic, off-key baritone that made Lane smile.

As she reviewed the day's ritual, Lane's eyes grew dreamy. Her hand, holding a pepper, paused in midair as she envisioned the moment she waited for each day when Matt hooked a long arm around her and pulled her to him for a discreet welcoming kiss and a look replete with promise for later, after Annie was in bed and the lights were out.

The moment passed. Coming back to reality, she found a spot for the pepper in the display upon the table.

Last night as she'd lain in Matt's arms on the verge of sleep, she'd thought jubilantly, *So this is happiness!*

Now, in the stark light of day, she faced the facts. It was as if a piece of her life had been set off in time. One day soon she would be back in the life she'd known before Matt became its most important component. He would go back to his Wall Street office and emulate his late father. After a while he would sell the *Wanderjahr* again, and the Nomad wagon, resplendent in its new coat of yellow paint, would rust and crumble into ruins in the garage.

What else could she expect? Had he ever said a word that could lead her to think otherwise?

She'd vowed she'd never let herself be hurt again. Only this time it was *Matt,* and the love was real and the prospect of being hurt was more frightening than anything she'd ever known.

Turning her head to check again on Annie, she knew she was only going through the motions. If Wolf was going to show up again, he would have done it before now. It was something she should discuss with Matt, but suppose she convinced him the danger was over? Did she really want him to stop staying with them at night? As long as she could salve her conscience with the possibility Wolf would drop the other shoe, she knew in her heart she'd say nothing.

In late morning Lane was attaching price cards to the conglomeration of vegetables she'd finished setting up, when she caught a flash of color from the corner of her eye. She looked up to see the big two-door station wagon, white topped and resplendent in a brilliant coat of pearlescent yellow paint, turn into the marketplace with Matt at the wheel, looking vastly pleased with himself.

Every head in the market turned as the car came to a stop next to Lane's pickup in front of the office. Annie, who had finished her morning tasks and was helping Lane with the price cards, let out a hoot of delight and ran to meet Matt as he opened the door.

"We did it, we did it!" Annie babbled, hugging him around the legs until he picked her up and swung her high in the air.

"You bet we did, Annie girl."

By the time Lane reached the scene, several shoppers had left their marketing for a closer look. Matt had lifted the hood and was pointing out the intricacies of an immaculate engine, and Cheyenne was hopping up and down and telling one and all that she was Matt's helper.

After about the fifth time, a grinning Matt halted his demonstration to say, "Helper isn't the word. Call her my inspiration. If it weren't for Annie this noble Nomad would still be nothing but a rusty bucket waiting to be hauled to the junkyard."

Overwhelmed by his praise, Annie turned suddenly shy. Edging into the shelter of Lane's arm, she stared at the marvel, wide-eyed and solemn.

"It's bee-yoo-tee-ful," she said softly.

But when the audience had dispersed and the customers had gone back to their shopping, Cheyenne got her second wind. Lane could see that the child could hardly wait to get away for her first ride in the splendidly refurbished car.

"C'mon, Matt. Cora will be wondering what happened to us," Annie coaxed.

"Cora won't even notice we're missing," Matt said with a laugh. He turned to Lane. "My brother called a while ago from the city. He'll be out here pretty soon with his wife, Julia. Cora's fixing lunch. They've been in Costa Rica on an assignment and are taking off for Alaska as soon as they've done whatever they're here for in New York."

"When was the last time you saw Birch?" Lane asked.

"Almost a year ago." Matt's eyes clouded. "It's been a long time since Birch and I have had a good, uninterrupted talk. It doesn't look like we'll have one this time, either. They're going back to Manhattan tonight after dinner."

Lane immediately got the picture. After a moment's thought, she said, "Would Julia be offended if you and Birch went out on the *Wanderjahr* for the afternoon?"

"Julia? Definitely not. She'll probably spend the whole time she's here catching up with Cora," Matt said. "They're great friends. They probably have as much to say to each other as Birch and I."

"With all the catching up you and Cora will want to do, how about leaving Annie here with me?" Lane suggested.

She saw a momentary look of gratitude in Matt's eyes, but the little girl's lower lip began to droop.

"Then I won't get to ride in the Nomad," Annie wailed. Lane wondered which side Matt was about to take.

"You'll have plenty of time to ride in the Nomad, Annie," Matt said quietly. "We fixed it to last for a long time. If you come with me, you'll have to stay with Cora while I take Birch out sailing. Not much to do but listen to her and Julia talk about grown-up stuff."

"I could go out on the boat with you," Annie said.

"Not today, Annie."

She glared at him through her pale fringe of lashes. "You don't ever let me have any fun," she said with a pout.

Lane watched, amused, yet a bit uneasy, as the two pairs of blue eyes locked in confrontation. She'd seen this before and knew who would win.

"I don't?" Matt asked, unmoved. With a parting glare, Annie accepted the inevitable and said no more.

"Could you and Annie have dinner with us tonight?" Matt asked, turning to Lane. "I want Birch and Julia to meet you both. Cora sends a special invitation from the cook."

"Oh, Matt, we'd love to. Wouldn't we, Annie?" The injured look on Annie's face turned into a grudging smile. "What time? I can ask Angus to close up for me."

"About seven. I'll pick you up at the farm." To Annie, he said, "Run around to the other side and hop in."

Annie held back. "It's okay. I'll stay here and help Lane," she said in a martyred tone. "I can ride in the Nomad tonight."

"You can ride in it now if you'll get in. Cora asked me to drive out to the fish market and pick up some clams," Matt said. "I'll bring you back here on the way home."

WHEN SHE'D SUGGESTED Matt leave Annie at the market so he could have some uninterrupted time with his brother, Lane hadn't expected him to fall in with the idea so easily. However tempting her offer, she knew Matt would never have agreed had he still feared Annie was unsafe here. She had a sudden unsettling thought that Matt might not be staying at the farmhouse at night anymore.

The arrival of Mrs. Summers, the social worker who'd been doing the casework on Annie's adoption, served as a guilty reminder that she hadn't yet told Matt she'd put in her bid for parenthood.

The woman had been here before to talk to her and to Annie and had gone with them one morning to the farm to see Annie's home surroundings. Lane had found Mrs. Summers reserved, businesslike, not overly friendly. She always felt nervous during the interviews.

"I'm not here in regard to my work," the social worker said at once. "Your produce looked so inviting when I was here the other day, I came back to stock up."

"One of our neighbors brought in the first fresh tomatoes of the season this morning," Lane said. "I haven't tasted them yet, but they look very good."

"Thanks for telling me. My family loves tomatoes." Mrs. Summers picked up a market basket from a stack at the end of a counter. "Incidentally, I haven't told you yet, but in a case like Cheyenne's, where no one claims legal responsibility, the child is usually made a ward of the court and placed in a foster home until the adoption is approved."

For a sickened moment, Lane waited for her to go on.

"She seems to be doing too well to warrant disturbing her, though, so I've decided to leave her in your care, at least for the time being."

The few small words of encouragement sent Lane's morale soaring. All at once the niggling doubts that had plagued her were gone. What she was doing was right. She might even tell Matt what she was up to tonight when he took them home.

IT WAS MIDAFTERNOON. A gentle breeze filled the sails of the *Wanderjahr* far out in the bay. Matt and Birch tended the helm and sails automatically, the sailing incidental to the flow of their conversation.

"So, Birch, I've found my Julia," Matt said. "Unfortunately, unlike you, I don't know what the hell to do about it."

"Take the advice of your old bro'," Birch replied. "If you're sure she's your Julia, marry the woman. If she'll have you."

Matt grunted. "I'm not ready to talk about that one yet," he said. "Right now, I can't get past the recollection of what a lousy life our mother led as wife of the CEO of the family firm. As far as I can figure, it goes with the territory."

"Horace P. Cheney you're not," Birch said affectionately. "The firm is *your* territory now. Make the territory your style."

"And risk taking the business down the tube? Horace P. drove himself hard, but he ran a successful business," Matt said. "Since the board trusted me to take Dad's place, I don't see how I can give them any less than he gave."

Matt was suddenly aware that his brother, slouched nearby on the deck, a leg dangling into the cockpit, was eyeing him curiously.

"You always thought Dad was some kind of guru when it came to running the company," Birch said presently. "You really ought to start looking back on the old man in a different light."

"Like what?" Matt asked.

"You think he was a genius, Matt. Take it from me, he wasn't. There's more than one way to run a successful business. Dad's was a long way from being the best."

Matt looked at him, puzzled.

"Horace P. Cheney's easier to understand if you can look at him as just an ordinary man on a power trip who imagined he was the one person in the world who knew what it was all about," Birch told him. "He was a very wasteful executive, our father."

"Wasteful? I looked on him as tightfisted."

"About money, yes," Birch said. "About people, no. If he was a genius at anything, it was at hiring good staff. But then he squandered them ruthlessly. Let someone come up with an innovative idea, and Dad began to feel threatened. They didn't last long."

Matt fell into a brooding silence. After a while he asked, "How the hell do I keep the business from running my life, bro'?"

"Easy," Birch said. "Get the board to find themselves another CEO and kick you upstairs. Let them call you president of the company or chairman of the board, so you'll still be contributing to the firm. Then set your own pace."

For a minute Matt thought his brother was joking and laughed it off. "In case I decide I'm irreplaceable, let's hear some ideas for if I stay where I am."

"Learn to delegate authority. I really mean that, Matt. Don't try to do everything yourself. Take advantage of all the new technology to relieve the pressure on you and your staff. Do that and you could handle most of your work right here in Seahampton. You'd only have to be in Manhattan a day or two each week."

This time Matt listened thoughtfully, recognizing a lot of his own thinking in what Birch had just said. It was the keystone, pretty much, for the new procedural plan Cliff had been trying out for him while Matt was on vacation.

"Do you remember Cliff Harris?" he asked after a while.

"Of course I do," Birch said. "If you ever see him, give him my best."

"He's still with Cheney, McCrae."

Birch looked surprised and a bit troubled. "I just assumed he'd left. I hope you know what a good man you've got there."

"He's more than a good man," Matt said wholeheartedly. "He's been working with me on a new operation plan I'd been thinking about but probably wouldn't have had the guts to introduce without his moral support."

"The firm should have been grooming Cliff to be the next chief executive officer instead of me," Birch said regretfully. "I never wanted the job, but Cliff did and was too modest to say so. You weren't in the running when I left the company. You'd locked horns with Dad and were playing young-man-about-town to get even. I made the mistake of suggesting to Dad that he put Cliff in line for the next executive opening. That spelled the end for Cliff. He never went another step up the ladder. I don't know why he didn't quit."

"It wasn't for lack of better offers," Matt said musingly. "He told me once he was about to quit, but Dad got sick and he stayed on. Loyalty's only one of Cliff's many virtues."

For the rest of the afternoon, Birch's remarks about their father and the family firm, and his suggestions for running the business came and went along the periphery of Matt's consciousness. Conversation moved on to other subjects, but all the while Birch's words played like background music through Matt's mind—soothing, harmonic, inviting.

When the time drew near to head back to the marina, Matt had come to a decision. He was already on his way to a new way of life. A life that could include Lane, if she would accept it.

"You really think Cliff Harris would accept the position of CEO at Cheney, McCrae if it was offered?" he asked Birch.

Putting it into words, he felt a wonderful sense of release.

LATE THAT EVENING, after Birch and Julia had left for the city, Matt headed out the Montauk highway on the way home to the farmhouse. With Lane and Annie in the front seat of the Nomad beside him and a vision of a future for the three of them together, he was almost content. But the specter of telling Lane he was Cheyenne's father loomed large.

Driving through the warm, quiet darkness, Matt felt that happiness was almost within reach. Carefully, he planned his campaign. First he would tell Lane he loved her, how meaningless life would be without her. Then he would tell her about how he'd waited to ask her to marry him until he could be sure he wasn't offering her the kind of marriage his mother had endured.

Now came the hard part. He would say that before he asked the most important question he'd ever asked, there was a story she must hear, and he'd tell her about the summer with Marigold that had produced Annie.

"OOH, IT'S DARK," Annie said with a shiver as the Nomad turned into the driveway. "The house looks scary."

Matt came to the rescue with a flashlight out of the glove compartment. Tucking Annie between them, he and Lane whisked the little girl up the pathway and into the house before she had time to work up a good fright.

As Lane started upstairs with Annie, Matt said quietly, "Would you mind coming out on the porch when you're through? There's something I want to say to you."

With a nod and a quizzical smile, she left with Cheyenne, and Matt settled himself outside on the porch swing and resigned himself to patience. In a remarkably short time the screen door swung open, and he rose to meet her.

"Don't keep me in suspense," she said as she settled into his arms on the swing. "What is it you have to say?"

"I love you, Lane."

In the pale light through the window from inside he saw her eyes widen, as if in surprise. Surely she must have known, he thought.

For a moment she said nothing. Then she drew in a breath and let it out in a shy twinkle of a laugh. "Well . . . that was certainly worth coming downstairs for," she said. "Is that it?"

"No. As the ads say, there's more. Much, much more." Overcome for a moment with an attack of something akin to stage fright, he mustered his thoughts to begin the planned prologue to his marriage proposal.

Deeply earnest, determined to do it right, he tried to tell her how much he loved her, and when he ran out of words that came easily to his tongue, he told her that the family business—the reason he hadn't said all this before—no longer stood in his way.

As he started to explain why, her soft, full lips covered his mouth and silenced him. Reflexively, his own lips shaped into a kiss before he realized she was not kissing back. She was asking the kind of head-on question that was typically Lane. He saw his whole carefully planned agenda slipping away.

"Dear Matt, are you getting ready to ask me to marry you? Because if you are, there's something I guess I'd better tell you first." She hesitated as if unsure how to go on. "It's something you feel very strongly about... though I'm not sure I understand why." Her voice was breathless, and he heard the distinctive break that under other conditions drove him a little crazy.

"It's about... the adoption."

Matt looked at her in bewilderment. "Adoption?"

"I don't know why, but I somehow have a feeling you might not want to finish the proposal when I tell you that the adoption papers have been filed."

It was like coming up under an open cupboard door and catching his head on the corner. For a moment Matt felt dazed.

"My God, Lane! You can't do that," he said hoarsely.

In her eyes he saw a look of stubborn disbelief. "I don't know why not. I'm sorry you're not pleased, but it's something I have to do," she said, her voice a combination of disappointment and determination. "I'd hoped it wasn't going to come between us, Matt. There's nothing that can stop me from going through with the adoption."

"Oh, yes, there is. I happen to be Cheyenne's father," Matt said grimly.

In the half-light he saw her whole body shrink away from him. Her face looked suddenly drawn and pale, and he feared she was going to faint. Then he saw her begin to rally. She straightened and raised her chin. Though Matt braced himself, he was totally unprepared for the sudden contempt he saw in her eyes and for the outrage he heard in her accusing voice.

"How *could* you? Her mother was a *child*."

Dazedly he shook his head. *What in God's name was she talking about?*

"Where did you get such a strange idea?" he asked. "Marigold was twenty-one."

"She was sixteen, and don't try to tell me an old hand with women like you didn't notice," Lane said, her voice heavy with sarcasm.

With a sense of bewilderment, Matt rubbed one hand across his eyes and saw again the embodiment of contradictions that had been Marigold. Oh, God, could he have been so wrong?

"Lane, I swear..."

She stopped him. "Don't bother," she said curtly. "Edra knew her from the day she was born. It's hardly something Edra would lie about."

*But what about Marigold?* Clues he'd overlooked in the light of Marigold's world-weary pose and her revelation she wasn't a virgin long before he found it out for himself came back to haunt him. He understood for the first time her puzzling, naive illogic—childlike in one who was no longer a child; her wonder at simple pleasures that belied the role of maturity she'd so convincingly assumed. She'd said she was twenty-one, and he had believed her. It was as simple as that. A chill of fear settled around his heart, his mind filled suddenly with the unthinkable truth.

She hadn't even reached the age of consent the summer Annie was conceived. In Lane's eyes he had committed a felony!

If only he'd had a chance to tell her about his relationship with Marigold in the way he had planned, he might have been able to make her understand.

"It was a long time ago, Lane," he said, his hope vanishing. "All I can do is ask you to believe me. I didn't know—never suspected—she was . . . so young."

Silence closed in around them once more. Still she said nothing, but sat gazing out into the darkness looking utterly alone. Matt tried again.

"I love you, Lane," he said. He put his whole heart into the words. "I never knew love until I met you."

"How many women have you said that to? Besides Marigold," Lane said scathingly, turning her face to him, eyes ablaze.

"What I felt for Marigold has nothing to do with the love I feel for you. I want to marry you, Lane."

"Oh? You didn't care to marry the mother of your child?"

"That's not the way it was. . . ." He came to an abrupt halt. *Your child.* Her words crashed like cymbals in his head. He had to stop the adoption.

"Maybe we'd better not talk any more until tomorrow," he said, suddenly terribly tired. "Which doesn't mean I've given up. I love you and want you to marry me."

"How can you expect me to think about love or marriage after what you've just told me, Matt?" she said, a sound of desperation in her voice. "How can I know how I feel about you anymore? How can I know how I feel about anything?"

Her profile was silhouetted against the pale ribbon of light from the window, the firm set of her jaw and slightly lifted chin a clue to her state of mind. He felt himself sinking into a morass of hopelessness.

"About Cheyenne, Lane," he said. "You understand, of course, that I intend to keep her. Tell those people she's not up for adoption."

She turned her head and looked at him with cold surprise. "You plan to sleep at your place tonight?" she asked.

"You know that as long as Wolf's on the loose, I intend to sleep here." Seeing she was overwrought and thinking to save her more trauma, he said gently, "If you'll tell me the name of the people who've applied for the adoption, I'll take care of having it withdrawn and save you—"

But Lane jumped to her feet and pressed her hands to her ears. "Don't!" she cried fiercely. "Please. I can't bear any more." In the next second Matt was beside her, reaching to take her in his arms, but she pushed him away.

"Leave me alone," she said through gritted teeth. Matt dropped his arms.

"Don't you understand?" she said in a controlled voice. "I'm the one who is adopting Annie. If you try to take her away from me, we'll settle it in court."

## CHAPTER SIXTEEN

ON ONE SIDE of the telephone booth was a barber shop and on the other a variety store. Wolf stepped in, leaving the door open when he found the cubicle hot as hell inside. He lifted the receiver and was about to dial when he noticed people walking near the booth. The last thing he needed was to have someone overhear him talking to Hugo.

He put back the receiver and walked out on the street. Looking up and down for another phone booth, he swore when he found none.

Damn it, he had to talk to Hugo. Hugo was the one who'd got him into this inheritance mess. He wasn't going to take it anymore.

Still swearing under his breath, Wolf stepped back into the booth and pulled the door shut against eavesdroppers. By the time he had Hugo on the line in Manhattan, it was close to a hundred degrees Fahrenheit in the cubicle. Perspiration was dotting his forehead and face and beginning to trickle down his neck.

The moment he heard Hugo's voice on the phone he began to yell, cursing him to the full extent of his vocabulary.

"Goddamn you, Hugo! Why didn't you tell me the Fielding broad could have me served with a restraining order? It says here I'll be in trouble with the law if I try to get near the kid."

"Oh, hell," Hugo grunted. "I thought I told you to keep a low profile."

"You told me to cozy up to the kid. I can't do that without someone seeing me. She's got like the Secret Service around her, twenty-four hours a day."

"You mean the kid's got a bodyguard?"

"I mean there's no way I can get near her at the market with every jerk on the woman's payroll watching her like a hawk," Wolf said resentfully. "Besides, the kid's only there in the mornings. A guy by the name of Cheney comes and gets her at noon. He takes her out to a house on the dunes and he and some old woman ride herd on her the rest of the day. Then it's out to the farmhouse where the kid lives with the Fielding dame. The guy stays there all night."

"A man, you say?" Hugo sounded more interested.

"I called you to say I quit."

It was as if Hugo hadn't heard him. "And the woman. They won't let the rightful father get near his own child, right? Hmm. Get the picture," he said, and Wolf knew the pseudolawyer was coming up with an idea he didn't want to hear.

"Stuff it, Hugo!" Wolf yelled into the phone. The sweat was soaking through his shirt and the phone booth was turning into a steam room. "You're setting me up for the slammer."

"Shut up, Wolf. I can't think when you yell."

"Don't bother thinking. I'm through. This phone booth is like a teakettle. I'm going to hang up."

"You might as well. The way you're hollering, you can go out on the street and talk to me. Simmer down,"

Hugo said. "What the hell are you doing in a phone booth? Don't you have a telephone at your house?"

"And get listed with the phone company? Not on your life," Wolf said darkly, quieter now but ready to catch fire again.

"Get yourself an unlisted number."

"The hell with that. The cops would put a tap on the line."

"You're paranoid, Wolf. Shut up and listen," said Hugo. "I've figured out what we're going to do."

"I said stuff it." Wolf's voice was rising again.

"And I said shut up. We stand to split close to five million dollars between us, take away what we have to give to the kid."

What did he mean, "split"?

"If we're going to split the money, I want a hell of a lot more than any lousy half of it," Wolf said sullenly. "*You* aren't taking the risk. The risks are all mine."

"There won't be any risk," Hugo said soothingly. "You've got proof you're the kid's father. That's all you need. I'll take care of the rest. We're going to let the law go to work for us."

"I don't know.... You're not the one that's going to be in trouble if it hits the fan," Wolf muttered. "With a prior on the record they could put me away for ten years. I'm not going to go on with it, Hugo. Goddamn it, I'm getting out of this phone booth before I cook."

"Stay right where you are. You'll be cooked before I get through with you if you try to back out on me now. I'll have the narcs on you before you can get out of town."

"You wouldn't do that, Hugo."

"The hell I wouldn't. Now shut up and listen to me," Hugo ordered again. "I'll be out there at your house by four this afternoon, and you better be there or you'll regret it. Now get the hell out of that phone booth before they have to ladle you up with a spoon."

## CHAPTER SEVENTEEN

NEXT MORNING, in the last moments of sleep, Lane fought her awakening. Something ugly was waiting for her once she gave in to full consciousness, something she wanted desperately to avoid.

Her mind numbed by the shock of what Matt had told her, she had gone to bed the night before and fallen asleep at once. It was as if she had boxed the sordidness away in some dark corner of her mind, to be taken out and sorrowed over later.

Now the day came crashing in upon her. The sleep of escape had left her unrested. She lay open eyed, gazing blindly at the ceiling, piecing together a bare-bones scenario from what she'd learned, first from Edra, and now from Matt. Matt had seduced a helpless, love-hungry sixteen-year-old girl and left her without looking back. Left her, pregnant with his child, to the dubious mercies of the first scoundrel who came along. Left her to be abused by Wolf and die unmourned, except for Annie, eight years later.

What he'd done was despicable, a voice within her cried out.

And another voice said, *It was a long time ago. He was young.*

No one is that young, the first voice said.

And the second moaned his name and whispered, *God help me. I love him.*

How can you love a man who behaved like a beast?

*That was eight years ago, another Matt Cheney. The Matt I love would never do anything so contemptible.*

And so the dialogue went until the creak of the floorboards in the next room told her Matt was up.

She rolled over and scrambled out of bed and into the shower to prove...what? That she was not hors de combat after the blow he'd struck last night.

Dressed in her standard workday clothes—blue jeans and a cotton shirt—she came down the stairs on her way to the kitchen. Not ready yet to meet Matt head-on, not sure that she would ever be, she stopped midway as his and Annie's voices drifted up to her from below. They were arguing over the breakfast menu. Annie was putting up a vigorous argument for pancakes; Matt holding out, rather listlessly, Lane thought, for hot oat bran.

"Lane says I'm making you too many pancakes," he said. "Oat bran's better for you as a steady diet."

"Yech. Oat bran's yucky," she heard Annie say. "Lemme get the griddle out. If you're already started on pancakes when Lane gets here, she's not gonna make you stop."

"I wouldn't bank on it. You'd better ask her first," he said as Lane came on downstairs and into the kitchen.

So I'm the wicked stepmother, Lane thought touchily. Aloud she said in her best voice of good cheer, "Isn't anybody going to say good-morning?"

Matt gave her an uncomfortable smile and an uneasy "good morning." Annie darted to give her a hug saying in one breath, "G'mornin'-Lane-can-Matt-make-pancakes?"

"You and Matt settle that between you. I have to get to the market early. I'll have a cup of coffee over there,'

Lane said. Before either could get a word out, she was out the door and on her way.

SHE WAS IN HER OFFICE an hour later when Annie came to the screen door and announced her arrival, turning to wave to Matt, whom Lane could see at the wheel of the Nomad in the parking lot. Usually, when he delivered Annie in the morning he came in. Lane was not surprised today to see the car drive away when he had satisfied himself that she was there to receive the child.

Instead of skipping on her way to the workbench after she'd checked in with Lane, Annie moved to the counter near the desk where Lane was working and hoisted herself onto one of the stools.

Pushing aside the invoices she was checking, Lane turned to give Cheyenne a quizzical look, disturbed by the troubled expression in the child's eyes.

"Got something on your mind, sweetie?"

"Matt's mad at me," Annie said.

"What about, for goodness' sake?" Lane said a little crossly. "You two didn't get in a row over the pancakes after I left, did you?"

"We didn't even talk pancakes," Annie said in an aggrieved tone. "I would have ate the yucky oat bran, but he made pancakes."

"Doesn't sound like mad to me," Lane said a little impatiently, annoyed at Matt for letting his own unhappiness upset Annie. "What was it he said that made you think he was?"

"He didn't say anything. He didn't say crazy stuff, or argue with me like he does, or tell me I'm a neat kid ... or ... anything," the child said.

"Good heavens, Cheyenne, that's no reason to think he's mad at you," she said, her growing anger at Matt giving an edge to her voice. Couldn't he have put up a better show for his own child?

Yet it hurt Lane somehow to have Annie mistake Matt's breakfast-time quiet for displeasure, and she came to Matt's defense.

"You can't expect everybody to feel chatty all the time, Annie," Lane said. "You mustn't think that when a person isn't talking as much as usual they're angry with you."

Annie gazed at Lane solemnly, but made no move to go.

"I've got work to do, Cheyenne, and if I'm not mistaken, so do you," Lane said, uncertain how to handle the situation. Annie reached down from the stool with her feet until they touched the floor. The child's eyes were pools of unspilled tears.

"You're mad at me, too. Why are you and Matt mad at me, Lane?"

Lane slipped from her chair and in one swift movement caught the little girl in her arms, holding her so she looked directly into her troubled eyes.

"Dear little girl, I give you my solemn word I am not mad at you, and neither is Matt," Lane said, her heart so full of emotion she had trouble with the words. "I can't speak for Matt on many things, but on that I can. I love you, Annie. I can't think of anything you'd be apt to do that could make me truly angry."

"Well, you're both mad at somebody," Annie said stubbornly. "If you're not mad at me, you must be mad at Matt. And Matt's mad at you. And...oh, *Lane*..." The child's voice was rising in a wail. Burying her face in Lane's bosom, she began to cry, sobbing as she tried to talk. "I can't stand for you to be mad at each other. I don't want Matt to go away."

Lane lifted the crying child and carried her to the couch, where she snuggled her into her lap. Resting her cheek on the silken head, Lane let her own held-back tears wash over the pale gold hair. She cried first for Annie and then for Marigold. And finally for herself and Matt.

When Cheyenne's sobs turned at last into spasmodic hiccups and eased off, Lane set the child on her feet. She dried the heart-shaped face and perky little nose with tissues from a box on the counter. When she'd blown her own nose, she tipped up Annie's face so their eyes met.

"Annie, love, Matt and I both owe you an apology for letting adult problems get us out of sync with you," she said earnestly. "Sometimes grown-ups can be more childish than children."

"ELAINE FIELDING?"

Busy setting up a display of homemade jams and jellies from the kitchen of a local farm wife late that morning, Lane turned her head at the sound of her name. "Yes?" she said.

Behind her stood a man in a seersucker suit. In his hand he held out papers for her to take.

"These are for you," he said. Passing the papers to her, he walked away. Lane glanced down at what she'd been given. The papers had an official look that told her this was no advertising flyer. She took a closer look and drew in a quick breath as her eyes caught Matt's name and her own and the words *Summons and Complaint*.

Reaching the signature at the end, she was immobilized for a moment by a growing feeling of apprehension. Then she bent and pushed the boxes of jars under the table and headed for her office.

Her first thought was to call Matt, but when she reached the phone, she quashed her instinct and dialed the number of Colby Strawn's law office instead. Then she asked for Neal Roberts. In a matter of seconds she heard the lawyer's pleasant voice.

"Good morning, Lane. How's everything?"

"I'm not sure," Lane said, her throat tight with anxiety. "A man just walked in here and handed me some legal papers. A Summons and Complaint. I think I'm going to need you. Frankly, I'm nervous."

"I'm sorry, Lane. Process servers tend to do that to a person," Roberts said. "How about telling me what the complaint says, and we can talk about it."

"It accuses Matt Cheney and me, in effect, of conspiring to deprive Wolf of his parental rights to the custody and control of Cheyenne," Lane told him, striving to keep her voice steady. She heard a muted whistle from Neal at the other end of the line.

"What's Cheney's connection with Cheyenne?" the lawyer asked.

Bracing herself, Lane replied, "He believes himself to be Annie's natural father. I just found out about that last night. His proof is all circumstantial, but I'm sure he is, even though Wolf Wilding is named as the father on her birth certificate. Wolf seems to have a copy of it."

"We can always get another copy if we need one," Roberts said. "Do you still plan to go through with your adoption of Annie?"

"Absolutely," Lane said.

"Fine. Now, back to Matt Cheney. Have you talked to him since the papers were served?"

Lane shook her head and said with a weak attempt at a laugh, "I thought I should discuss it with my lawyer first."

"Before we go into this any further, maybe you'd better call Cheney and suggest he discuss the matter with his attorney, if he hasn't already," Roberts said. "Call me back as soon as you've talked to him, and we'll take it from there. Oh, and if you don't mind, I'll ask Colby to sit in with us when you come. He has a keen mind and a lot of horse sense. He also knows everybody from Sag Harbor to Montauk on a first-name basis, which might come in handy."

"Please do. You know how I feel about Colby."

When she'd hung up, Lane left her desk and went to check on Annie from the office window. She smiled when she saw the child at her customary place talking with Angus. It occurred to her that such vigilance was probably no longer necessary, now that Wolf had started legal proceedings to get Annie.

She returned to the desk and forced herself to pick up the phone and punch out Matt's number. After the second ring the phone was answered by Cora, a worried note in her voice.

"I think he's on his way to see you, Lane," she said. "Somebody came and served him with some legal papers that he said have something to do with you and Annie. He tried to get you on the phone, but your line was busy, so he took off. He should be there pretty soon."

Lane put down the phone and rested her head for a moment on her arms, bracing herself for the imminent meeting with Matt. She was simply not ready yet for a major discussion with Matt about anything. Her feelings about him were too mixed up. How could you love a man and not love him at the same time?

Outside she heard a trill of laughter and Annie's excited little voice and then Matt's. In the next second Annie came bursting in the door, eyes shining.

"Matt's here, Lane. Here's Matt," she bubbled, and mouthed silently, "He's not mad."

"Hello, Lane," he said.

Lane rose to meet them. "Would you excuse us a moment, Matt?" she said, striving, for Annie's sake, to keep her voice from sounding restrained. "I need to talk to Annie a second."

Without demur, Matt backed out and left the woman and the little girl alone.

"What we were talking about this morning, Annie," Lane said, her arm still around Annie's shoulders. "A prob..." She stopped and began again. "Something has come up that Matt and I need to discuss together...alone, just like you and I need to talk alone sometimes. I just don't want you to get the idea ever again that anyone's mad at you, Annie. Okay?"

"You mean you want me to get out?"

"Yes, please," Lane said.

"Matt's not mad at me, either," Annie said musingly. "Maybe you and Matt *oughta* talk. Want me to tell him to come in?"

*Out of the mouths of babes,* thought Lane. She said aloud, "Please do."

A minute after Annie scampered away Matt returned, looking not so much uncomfortable now as bemused.

"Did you tell Annie to get out so we could talk? No? If it was her own idea, she's one very wise little kid," he said. "Last night—"

"What about this Summons and Complaint?" Lane interrupted.

Matt combed his fingers through his hair in a gesture of frustration and sighed. "I'd hoped they hadn't gotten to you yet," he said. "I thought... Oh, hell. Never mind.

The complaint is what we should be talking about, I guess."

"Won't you sit down?" Lane asked, motioning toward a chair as she perched herself on one of the stools at the counter.

"The conflict is really only between this Wolf Wilding and me, of course," Matt said as if he hadn't heard her. "There's no reason for you to be mixed up in it. As soon as I can get it established legally that I am Cheyenne's natural father there should be no problem getting you removed from the complaint."

"You have no right to do that," Lane said indignantly. "Until it's decided otherwise, I'm just as much Annie's parent as either one of you. I won't be counted out."

Matt looked at her broodingly, but he didn't argue. He said instead, "There's no point in doing anything until we've both talked to a lawyer."

"I already have. He said I should suggest you get in touch with your lawyer if you haven't already."

"I'm thinking I might find an attorney out here," Matt said. "Mine is a partner in the Manhattan firm that does Cheney, McCrae's legal work. I doubt that he's had any experience with family practice."

Lane considered a moment, not sure it would be wise to suggest he talk to her lawyers. In the end she gave him a brief background sketch of Colby Strawn and Neal Roberts.

"I'm sure Colby could recommend some other local attorney if you want to go talk to him about it," she said in conclusion.

"Is there any reason Colby and Roberts can't handle my part of the case?" Matt asked.

Again Lane hesitated. "Not if there isn't a conflict of interest, but I'm not sure there isn't. If the court declares you Cheyenne's father, that should certainly get rid of Wolf, but it won't get rid of me."

Matt's jaw set in a hard line. "Let's cross that bridge when we come to it. Right now, the only person we're fighting is Wolf Wilding. Neither of us wants Wolf to get custody of Annie. Doesn't it make sense to go after him together?"

Lane wondered unhappily if she would ever again feel good about togetherness of any kind with Matt. The pure blue eyes, so nearly the color of Annie's, bored down on her with the same tenacity. In the end she gave in and placed a call to Neal Roberts.

"It won't do any harm to talk to him about it," she said reluctantly. "If he says no, maybe Colby can refer you to someone else."

She stayed on the line while Neal conferred with Colby, who said he'd be there during the lunch hour if they could come right away.

In spite of her anxiety, Lane laughed. "I have so many lunch-hour appointments at Colby's office, the town's going to think we're having an affair. But what about you? Maybe you'd prefer to eat lunch like other people?"

"No problem," Neal replied. "Colby keeps a fridge full of deli stuff. No one's going to starve."

Off the phone again, Lane explained the impromptu appointment to Matt.

"What about Annie?" he said. "Have we time to take her over to Cora?"

"No, we have not," Lane said with asperity. "Even if we had the time, there's no need for it. Think about it. If there's anything good about this court order, it's that

Annie doesn't have to be watched over like a mobster's daughter. This sets her free."

"Free?" Matt repeated blankly. Then, with a noticeable lack of enthusiasm, he said, "You're right. There's no reason for Wolf to try to snatch Annie now that he's decided to put the law to work for him."

*He doesn't look very happy about it,* Lane thought, and knew they were both thinking the same thing. There was no longer any reason for Matt to spend his nights at the farmhouse. She felt a wrench at her heart and a deep sadness that the intermezzo was over.

As they left the office together, Lane walked ahead, turning into the marketplace. "I'll be right with you, Matt," she said. "I want to let Annie know I'll be gone and ask Angus and Agnes Brandon to look after the place until I get back."

"CIRCUMSTANTIAL EVIDENCE may carry you most of the way, Matt, but against documents that include the birth certificate, you're going to need some solid proof," Colby Strawn said. "In the end, the judge will no doubt order a DNA analysis of the three of you—Wolf and you and the little girl. That's the genetic test that can pinpoint the parentage of a child from samples of blood."

Matt, sitting by Lane across the conference table from Roberts and Strawn, grinned wryly.

"You're afraid I won't pass?" He went on seriously, "Strangely enough, it's one of the few things about all this I don't worry about. It's not just the circumstances and the dates and the actual physical resemblance between us that makes me so sure. It's a gut feeling that Annie is my child. It's just something I know is true."

"I'd still feel more comfortable going before the judge with solid DNA proof in my pocket. I don't like surprises," Colby said. "I can arrange for the local hospital lab to take blood samples and have a friend who operates a forensic lab in New Jersey run a DNA for us. We'll have the results back by the time we need them."

It was a moment before Matt spoke. "Don't think I haven't thought about this. Short of using force, I see only two ways to get a blood sample from a seven-year-old girl: lie to her or tell her a truth she's too young to understand. I'll be damned if I'll be a party to either."

"Suit yourself, but I'd prefer proof in my pocket," Colby said grumpily. He gripped the arms of his chair and hoisted himself to his feet. "If you change your mind, let me know and I'll make the lab arrangements."

"The advance testing would make your attorneys feel easier," Neal Roberts interjected. "It's quite likely that when we get to court the judge will order the tests anyhow, so what do you gain?"

But Matt refused to budge. "I don't need lab tests to tell me I'm Annie's father," he said as he took his cue from Colby and rose to leave. "Time enough to start worrying about testing when the judge orders it done."

As the two attorneys saw Matt and Lane to the door, Roberts said curiously, "I'll bet Colby hasn't had many cases where both litigants seeking custody were single males, have you, Colby?"

"Not as far as I can recall," Colby said. "It's too bad you're not married, Matt. If you were married, you'd stand a better chance of gaining custody of the child, even when another man's name is on the birth certificate. You may as well face it. When it's two single men fighting over a minor child, the one on the birth certificate's got the edge."

THE RIDE BACK to the market was quiet. Once again, Lane found herself wondering what was on Matt's mind. Was he thinking about Colby's final remarks or about the dilemma of a blood test from Annie?

When he told her he was Annie's father, it had never occurred to her to doubt it was true. After the initial shock wore off, her first reaction was to wonder why she'd never noticed the strong resemblance between Annie and Matt before. She still didn't doubt the truth of it, but Colby was right. There would be an inner security in having the proof. Yet how could she fault Matt for refusing to manipulate Annie?

As Matt turned the Taurus into the parking lot at the market, Lane broke the silence that had sat uneasily between them throughout the ride. "You can leave Annie here for the afternoon. It's all right now," she ventured.

"It may be all right with you, but Annie will have my ears if I go back on my promise to take her sailing," Matt said, smiling slightly. "She's finally talked Cora into going with us this afternoon. Cora's never been on the water and would just as soon keep it that way, but it wouldn't sit well with Annie if I let her down."

Lane held back for a moment. A part of her wanted simply to walk away, but a stronger force prevailed.

Not certain she was going to say the words until she heard them in her own ears, she said, "Bring Annie to the house when you get back from sailing. I'll get there first and fix us something to eat."

Without waiting for an answer, she stepped out of the car and called, "Don't get out. Annie'll be with you in a moment."

WHEN ANNIE WANTED to eat outside under the dogwood tree and watch the sunset that night, Lane rejected the too-poignant reminder of the first night she and Matt made love. But when the little girl persisted Lane gave in.

On the surface it was the kind of easy, playful evening the three had often spent together during recent weeks, but there was an undercurrent of tension. The joking and good-humored teasing was between Matt and Annie or Annie and Lane, never between Matt and Lane.

Since one of the few rules of the house was that the cook didn't do the dishes, Matt and Annie did the cleaning up. Lane waited in the front porch swing, where they joined her shortly.

With Matt's foot providing the necessary power, they swung lazily back and forth. In the stillness, Annie began to sing. When her seemingly endless cache of songs appeared to be running low, Lane sent her, protesting, upstairs to take a bath and go to bed.

"You'll come up and tuck me in pretty soon?" Annie asked anxiously as she left them, and Lane assured her they would.

Once again an uneasy silence settled over them. The moon was dark. Lane was grateful that the light that reached them through the front parlor window was low and filtered through soft voile curtains. There was something she had to say to Matt, something she could never bring herself to say in full light. Like a kid jumping into icy waters, she sucked in her breath and took the plunge.

"Please don't misread what I'm about to say, Matt. I still haven't gotten used to what you told me last night. Maybe I never will," she said. "The truth is, I get chills at the thought that if we don't do everything there is to be done to prevent it, Wolf could get custody of Annie."

She saw the dispirited slump of Matt's shoulders and steadied herself to continue. "You heard what Colby

Strawn said this morning about the advantage a married man has over a single one in a child custody case?"

She saw him turn his head suddenly to look at her. She regretted, now, the lack of light that hid his expression.

When he didn't speak, she called up all her mettle and plunged ahead. "Don't you think it would be a good idea for us to get married?"

## CHAPTER EIGHTEEN

THE AIR WAS CHARGED with electricity. Waiting, Lane was hardly aware she held her breath. The last thing she expected when Matt spoke was the cold, disbelieving contempt she heard in his voice.

"How can you talk about marriage? Nothing has changed since last night."

"Wait a minute, Matt," she said, striving for a reasonable tone. "Last night has nothing to do with this. This is about Annie."

"But I'm still the same man," he said bitingly. "The man you scorned as little better than a rapist less than twenty-four hours ago."

"That's not..." she began, but stopped before she could say "true." *Wasn't that pretty much how she had felt?* She began again. "For Annie's sake..."

He was on his feet, a tower of frustration and fury. "In that case, you and I sure as hell don't have the same concept of what a marriage is all about," he said.

He crossed the porch and slammed through the door. She heard the muffled thud of his footsteps as he mounted the stairs.

A fresh breeze had come up. The night had turned unexpectedly cool, but Lane lacked the spirit to move. Hugging her bare arms around her for comfort as much as for warmth, she curled her legs under her and huddled despondently in one corner of the wooden swing.

Would she have suggested marriage to Matt if she had really looked on him as a rapist? Something in her rebelled at the thought. Not even for Annie.

A memory of Roz at sixteen, looking five years older than she actually was and the envy of other teenagers competing for the attention of college men, rose unexpectedly in Lane's mind.

Suppose Matt had really believed Marigold was twenty-one? Suppose...

If only she had given herself time to think last night instead of blurting out an accusation. If only she'd had the good sense to say something like, "Excuse me. I've got a headache," and gone to bed.

Now any hope of evening the odds for Matt's custody battle was lost.

As the first fingers of dawn colored the sky next morning, Lane rose after a long night of shallow and broken sleep. Tying her kimono, she slipped downstairs to the kitchen and had just finished loading the coffee-maker when the sound of a muffled step in the hallway brought her head around.

Matt was standing in the doorway, dressed for the day. His face looked drawn, his eyes bleak.

"If you're still willing to make your valiant sacrifice, it would be petty of me to let pride stand in the way," he said, his words tainted with bitterness. "It is, after all, for Annie. If you can meet me at the clerk's office around ten o'clock, we can get the marriage license."

He turned to go. Lane stared after him, speechless.

She found her voice. "Matt? Where are you going? I just put on the coffee."

"I'm going back to the house," he said. "I'll have coffee with Cora."

THE WEDDING TOOK PLACE at seven o'clock two eve-
nings later in the study of retired village judge Carlos
Segal, a lifelong friend of Lane's late Uncle Charlie. Cora
and Angus were witnesses. An ecstatic, albeit somewhat
critical observer was Annie, who let it be known to anyone who would listen that it wasn't her idea of a wedding. When she got married she would wear a long white
dress with a veil and a train that swished out behind her
and all the flowers she could carry.

Lane had bought a long-waisted dress of shell-pink
handkerchief linen for the occasion, mainly to mollify
Annie, she told herself. She was somehow not surprised
when a slim florist's box was delivered to her office containing two white roses, just beginning to open, their
petals blushed with crimson. Matt, too, must have ac-
ceded to pressure, she thought. The enclosed card, however, was something of a letdown: "Cora assures me it's
not a wedding without flowers."

The ceremony itself was brief and straightforward.
*Dispassionate* was the word that came to Lane's mind.
When Matt repeated, "With this ring I thee wed," and
slipped a heavy plain gold band on the third finger of her
left hand, his eyes looked down at her without expression. She wondered if her own revealed the pain that was
in her heart.

A wedding without emotion. She wondered what
would happen now that the time had come for them to
kiss.

Out of the sudden silence Annie's voice sang out sweet
and clear in a ballad Lane had never heard before. "We
were always meant to be/ together;/ whether/ time or
tide or circumstance/ allow."

All the emotion she had thought missing flooded up
inside Lane, blocking out sight and sound. She strove to

hold back the sob she was mortally afraid was about to roll out. Dear God, she couldn't bear it. Through a mist of tears her eyes involuntarily sought Matt's, and she saw that his, too, were dewed. He took her hand and held it through the last words of Annie's song. "And now we are together/ forever/ together."

"You may kiss the bride," said Judge Segal. There was a moment's hesitation before Matt bent his head and their lips met in a self-conscious kiss.

They went back to the farmhouse, and Cora and Angus and Judge and Mrs. Segal followed for a wedding toast. There they found Roz and Neal and Colby waiting to surprise them in a house festooned with ribbons and flowers. There were caterers to serve champagne and a sumptuous buffet from a table centered with an elaborate wedding cake.

Still not fully recovered from the emotions Annie's sweet, sentimental singing had evoked, Lane was afraid for a few minutes she was going to have to retreat upstairs and compose herself before she could cope with any more twangs on her heartstrings. Whether or not he sensed her fragile state, Matt stayed with her. When Annie sandwiched herself between them to make sure it was understood they were a threesome, Lane began to feel more amused than maudlin.

"You didn't think you were going to pull this off without a celebration?" Roz asked as she embraced Lane. "Now introduce me to Matt. I'm the only person in the house who has yet to meet the bridegroom."

After the introduction Roz confessed that she'd been "gaga" over him as a teenager when he used to come to the Seahampton Marina. Matt accepted the gratuitous pleasantry with a dismissive grin.

Then, somewhat to Lane's surprise, he said, "If you used to hang out at the marina you may have known Cheyenne's mother, Marigold."

Annie gazed up at Roz with big, solemn eyes.

"Not really," Roz said, "though I used to envy her from afar. I loved the way she sang and played the guitar, but I would have felt cheeky trying to speak to her. I was tongue-tied in the presence of anyone but other teenagers at that point in my life."

Her words lent further credence to Matt's assertion that he had never guessed that Marigold was a minor, and Lane regretted that she'd never thought to question Roz about Annie's mother.

"DO I HAVE TO TAKE a bath?" Annie asked with a cavernous yawn as she stood on the porch with Lane and Matt, seeing the last of the guests on their way. Her organdy dress, the color of her eyes, was limp and bedraggled and she was all but asleep on her feet. Lane exchanged a look with Matt, who declined to intervene.

"It's a special night," the child wheedled.

Lane looked again at Matt, but now his eyes were turned away. He bent to hoist Annie up on his shoulders.

"Hop on, snooks. I'll piggyback you up to bed."

"And no bath tonight," Lane said. "I'll come and undo all those slippery little buttons for you and help you into your nightgown."

In the bathroom Lane helped Annie out of her wrinkled "wedding dress" and stood by while she washed teeth and face. Going back into Annie's bedroom, she found Matt, looking oversize and uncomfortable in a flower-sprigged rocking chair, waiting for their return.

When the little girl was in bed, Lane dropped to the floor beside her and smoothed her hand gently over the satiny cheeks and hair. "Thank you for your lovely song, Annie," she said, raising her eyes to include Matt, who had come to stand beside her. "We will remember it forever. It's a new one to me."

"It was Marigold's song. She made it up," Annie said. "I didn't ever want to sing it before."

"You couldn't have given us a more beautiful present," Lane said. Her heart so overflowing with emotion it ached, she kissed Cheyenne good-night and rose, turning to leave as Matt folded his long body to touch his lips to the child's.

What comes next? Lane wondered as she closed the door behind them and they walked away from the room together. Already she could feel the distance between them widening once more.

At the door to the master bedroom she hesitated. It was their wedding night. Would he come in? Looking up, she saw the memory of their ugly confrontation clouding his eyes and had her answer. She didn't wait for the rejection she knew lay there.

"Good night, Matt," she said.

"Good night," he said stiffly, and walked on to the guest room, closing the door behind him.

WITH THE COURT APPEARANCE bearing down on them, time went into high gear. Matt, whose vacation period would be over before the date of the trial, left for the city to lay the groundwork for withdrawing as chief executive officer of the company. Neal Roberts flew to San Francisco to talk to Susan Craddock about her encounter with Wolf.

Afraid that Matt would ask her not to, Lane seized the chance afforded by his absence to call Colby Strawn and suggest he make arrangements for DNA tests for Annie and Matt.

"How did you get around Matt's objections?" Colby asked curiously.

"I haven't told him yet," Lane admitted.

"Now wait a minute, Lane. How do you expect to do this without Matt's consent?"

"We'll have Annie's blood test done first, while he's in the city. Matt won't have any reason not to consent when he's presented with a fait accompli."

"I can't be a party to that," Colby said flatly. "He refused to risk traumatizing the child, and much as I'd like to have proof of a DNA match, I have no choice but to respect his wishes."

"But I have a way to handle the blood test that will do that and won't upset Annie, either. In fact, I'm sure she'll go for it," Lane said.

"You're on your own, Lane. You'll have to do it without me."

"I promise you I won't lie to her, Colby. I'm going to tell her the truth from a different angle than Matt sees it," Lane argued. "Cheyenne's no hothouse flower. She's tough and resilient and wonderfully bright. Finding out after it's over that Matt is her father will be the best thing that ever happened to her."

"What if he's not?"

"He is," Lane assured him. "But whatever happens, I promise you she won't be traumatized."

"I . . . I don't know about this, Lane."

"Trust me, Colby," Lane said. "I'll call you back."

Cradling the phone, she gazed absently through the window at the bustling market outside her office door.

She could see Annie practicing tricky footwork with her jump rope under the apple tree. Leaving her desk, Lane called to her. "Can you come here a minute, sweetie?"

Annie came bouncing through the door and plopped herself on the couch. She looked up with a question in her eyes.

"How would you feel if I told you there might be a way we can prove Wolf is not your father?" Lane asked.

Cheyenne sat up straight, her eyes brightening at once. "I'd sure be glad," she said soberly.

"Someone at the hospital lab would have to take a sample of your blood," Lane said. She wanted to make sure the little girl understood what was in store for her.

"You mean with a big long needle?" Annie asked, screwing up her face.

"Right. It hurts some when they stick the needle in. I'd be lying if I told you it didn't," Lane said. "And there is always a possibility that when it's over the test may not have proved what we want to know."

Annie looked suddenly rebellious. "You mean it might prove Wolf *is* my father? I won't take the yucky old test."

"No, I don't mean that," Lane said emphatically. "If the test doesn't tell us Wolf is *not* your father, it won't tell us anything useful at all."

Annie slumped back on the porch. "Okay. How soon can we do it, Lane?"

"I'll call Mr. Strawn and find out when it can be arranged. Run on out and play, honey. I'll let you know."

With Colby on the phone, Lane said, "Thank God my instincts are still in good working order. Annie is eager to have the blood test, Colby, just as I thought she would be."

"Before I call the lab, you're going to have to tell me what you said to the child," Strawn said, his tone still disapproving.

"I asked her if she'd be interested in giving a blood sample that *might* prove that Wolf's not her father," Lane told him. "She wants to have the test done just as soon as it can be arranged."

There was a silence on the phone. Then Colby said, "Well, I'll be jiggered. I don't see any harm in that. I'll make the arrangements and call you back."

A few minutes later, the lawyer told her, "You can bring her in anytime this afternoon. I've only got one thing to say. I hope your husband doesn't fire us both when he gets back from the city."

"So do I," Lane said with a strained laugh as she hung up. Then she realized it was the first time she'd heard Matt called "your husband." She felt a thrill of wonder.

*"Husband,"* she said softly. What a lovely word. But the echo of Colby's final words levered her back to reality. Matt was already carrying a load of resentment toward her as high as a haystack. By having the blood tests set up for him and Annie, was she piling on the final straw?

BUCKLED IN next to Lane in the front seat of the pickup as they came back from the lab that afternoon, Cheyenne plucked thoughtfully at the bandage the technician had placed in the crook of her arm.

"It didn't hurt much, did it?" Lane asked.

Annie darted her an injured look. "It did, too."

"But you didn't cry."

Annie shot her another injured look. "Only little kids cry."

Assuming Annie's peckish responses meant she didn't want to talk about it, Lane lapsed into silence. They were nearly back to the market when Annie scooted around within the confines of her seat belt and looked up at Lane.

"When Matt took me and Cora sailing the other day, he said he used to know Marigold a long time ago before I was born, when she was young?" she said, making a question out of the statement.

"That's what I've been told," Lane said a bit uneasily.

Again there was silence. Finally Annie said wistfully, "Do you think maybe Matt could be my secret daddy?"

The question came so unexpectedly Lane was lost. When she didn't respond, Annie reached over and touched her arm. "Could he be, Lane? Maybe? My secret daddy?" she persisted.

"Nothing's impossible, honey," Lane said at last. But the inquisition was not over.

After another stillness, Annie said hopefully, "You think that blood they got outa me could tell somebody that Matt's my...?" She stopped, as if afraid to say the word.

*Oh, boy, does this little girl ever dig deep,* Lane thought. She was glad to be turning out of highway traffic into the market so she could be forgiven a delayed answer.

She pulled to a stop in her usual space, unbuckled her seat belt and reached to help Annie out of hers. Free, Annie still didn't move, obviously deep in thought.

"I s'pose they'd need some of Matt's blood, too," she said finally. "Huh, Lane? When he gets back I'm gonna ask him—"

With a sense of helplessness, Lane brought her to a stop. "Not so fast, Annie. Wouldn't it be better to wait and let him think of it himself?"

Annie furrowed her brow. Finally she said with a resigned sigh, "Okay, but I'm not gonna wait a long time."

MATT ARRIVED back from the city shortly before dark the following evening, a full day earlier than Lane had expected. She went to the car to greet him, and for a moment something in his face gave her a glimmer of hope, but a second later it was gone.

For an uncomfortable moment neither spoke. Then both started at once and stopped.

"How did things go in the city?" Lane asked politely when it appeared he was giving her the right-of-way. She fell into step beside him as he started up the pathway toward the house.

"Fine, thanks," Matt said and hesitated. Then, as if relieved to be on solid ground, he began to elaborate. The reorganization of the family firm was proceeding even better than he'd dared hope. There would be no opposition to making Cliff Harris the chief executive officer, and there was unanimous agreement to creating a position that would let Matt work wherever he liked.

She might have been able to share his satisfaction had he given any sign he considered her a part of the plan. It was as if their wedding had never happened. Nor had it, in any true sense, she thought with a shadow of bitterness. She had a feeling that already the two of them had grown too far apart for the breach to ever be healed.

Side by side they stepped up on the porch, Lane bracing herself to tell him about the blood tests. Why hadn't she waited and let things take their course? She herself had never doubted that Matt was Annie's father. Was it because, knowing Neal and Colby *did*, she hoped they would argue Matt's case with more conviction if they had proof?

As they were about to go in, a car entered the driveway and pulled up in front of the house. Matt turned to Lane with a questioning look.

"Geraldine," Lane explained as Annie hopped out and the car drove away. "Annie went to play at her house, and they asked her to stay for supper."

"Matt!" Annie yelled, and came pell-mell up the pathway to fling herself into his arms.

"What have you been doing with yourself while I've been gone, young lady?" Matt asked as he lifted her up for a hug.

"Oh, nothin'," Annie said, self-conscious at the direct question. Recovering, she went on in a singsong voice, "Playing with Geraldine. Bunching carrots and stuff. And...hey, Matt!" Her eyes were suddenly bright with excitement. "Guess what? Maybe pretty soon I can prove to people that Wolf's not my father. Huh, Lane?"

The look on Matt's face was like a vise closing on Lane's heart.

"Did Lane make you have a blood test?" he asked in a chillingly controlled voice.

A sick feeling rose in Lane's throat.

Annie looked up with troubled eyes at Matt and then at Lane. "No. Lane didn't *make* me. She told me it would hurt, but I didn't care. I'd do lots worser things than that to prove Wolf's not my father."

Her words were like a battle cry to Lane. She bent to drop a kiss on the little girl's head, aware of Matt's eyes burning a hole in her back.

"It's late, sweetie," she said. "Run on up to your room now and get ready for bed. We'll come up for a good-night hug."

Annie's eyes moved from Lane to Matt and then back. Lane expected her to protest, but her mouth opened instead into a huge yawn.

With only a shade of reluctance, she turned to go inside. "I'll call you when I'm in bed."

Lane watched the little girl cross the front porch and go into the house. Then, with her eyes still averted from Matt, she said, "I suppose now you're angry with me for interfering. Well, you may as well know I'm pretty out of sorts with you, too."

"Mind if I ask why?"

"Because you know as well as I do how ashamed Annie is that people think she's Wolf's child. Without a sample of Wolf's blood—which we're not about to get—testing your blood is the only way we can prove she's *not*."

She turned in time to see a look of stunned comprehension sweep over his face, but she refused to ease up. "Your refusal doesn't make sense. Annie's been dealing with grown-up truths all her life, a lot of them pretty ugly. What do you think you're protecting her from? The truth you have to tell her isn't ugly."

After a long pause Matt said in a troubled voice, "No. Whatever else it may have been, it wasn't ugly, but is Annie old enough to understand that?"

"The only ugliness is the shadow of Wolf that hangs over her. You're the one person who can free her from that. How can you refuse?"

He drew a deep breath. When he spoke, his voice betrayed his inner turmoil. "I never looked at it like that before. I've been so focused on proving that Annie's my child it never occurred to me it might be a lot more important to her to know Wolf's *not* her father."

"That's not true, Matt," Lane protested, dismayed at the conclusion he'd drawn from her words. "Nothing in the world could mean as much to Cheyenne as knowing you're her father."

"Nonsense," he said harshly. "I have no reason to think the idea has ever entered her mind."

"But I have. You underestimate our Annie's 'smarts,' Matt," Lane said wryly. "Hardly a day goes by that she doesn't try to con me into speculating on the possibility that you might be her 'secret daddy.'"

"She does?" Matt said incredulously. "Since when?"

Lane hesitated, reluctant to say more. "I'm afraid I started the wheels turning with the blood test," she confessed. "Ever since, the question has kept popping up. She wanted to know if she told you it only hurt a little did I think she could get you to take the test, too. The fact is, Matt, like it or not, she's primed to talk you into having that blood test."

"Oh, my God."

"Damn it, Matt, Annie has a right to know who her father is. It's not fair to keep her on pins and needles."

"Lane..."

He placed his hand on her cheek and turned her face up to him. She heard a note in his voice that made her meet his eyes with a wave of relief.

"You're not mad?"

"Mad? Not at you. At myself for never having realized until now that Annie's spent her whole life adjusting to adult screwups without coming unglued. If I had, I might not have been so set against telling her what the blood tests are all about. Thank God I married a woman with the good sense to know when it was time to step in."

He lowered his head, and his lips met hers in a long, tender kiss. Lane offered no resistance when his strong hands shaped themselves around her buttocks and pulled her to him. She lifted her arms and slipped them around his neck, closing the space between them, reveling in the feel of his body through the thin layers of summer clothing.

"Wait, Matt," she said breathlessly when their lips parted. "I won't rest easy until you forgive me for accusing you falsely. I do believe that Marigold led you to believe she was older. The Matt Cheney I love would not have had an affair with a sixteen-year-old girl. Deep in my heart, I think I knew that all along." She paused for breath, then went on, suddenly shy. "You do know I love you, Matt?"

"Enough to stay married to me?"

Before Lane could answer, Annie called down to them from the head of the stairs inside. "Are you guys coming or not?"

Their eyes met as they stared at each other helplessly. For a stolen moment longer, they kissed.

"Hey, Lane," Annie called again. "Did you hear me?"

With regret they moved apart. "Coming," Lane answered.

Inside, Annie waited for them in her nightgown at the top of the stairs. Matt swung her up in his arms and carried her into her room, tumbling her into bed. Beside him, Lane dropped to her knees at the bedside for the ritual good-night kiss. Annie reached a hand up for Matt and tugged until he sat on the bed beside her to form a circle of three.

Annie began to sing. "We were always meant to be/ together/ whether..." She stopped and looked at Lane and Matt in surprise. "You know what I betcha? She didn't know it, but Marigold wrote that song for us."

With a sigh of satisfaction, she dropped back on her bed and rested her head on her pillow before she picked up the song again in a dreamy voice that drifted in and out of silence as drowsiness encroached.

"Whether time or tide...let us be...In our hearts...forever...together."

When her eyes closed and her voice was still, they slipped quietly out of the room. As Lane closed the door behind them, tears spilled over and rolled down her cheeks. She brushed them away with the back of her hand and looked up to find Matt gazing down at her, his blue eyes, so like Annie's, filled with compassion.

Too overcome with emotion to speak, they started down the hall toward the two rooms they'd occupied since their marriage. Nearing the master bedroom, Matt laid a detaining hand on Lane's shoulder and brought her to a stop.

"You never answered my question," he reminded her.

"Do I love you enough to stay married? The truth is..." But she couldn't go on. Hesitating, she struggled to control feelings that swelled within her, making it hard to speak.

"I never believed I had room in my heart for all the love I feel for you, Matt," she said at last, her voice breaking in spite of herself.

Then, in that wonderful off-key baritone she loved, Matt began to sing, "We were always meant to be/ together," but the words drifted into silence.

"Your place or mine, Bride?" he asked.

A laugh of sheer joy bubbled up past the lump in Lane's throat. *"Ours."*

She moved to throw open her bedroom door to welcome him in. As the door swung wide, Matt caught her up in his arms and carried her across the threshold.

## CHAPTER NINETEEN

THE REPORT from the blood tests still hadn't arrived when they met at Colby Strawn's office the morning of the hearing. Colby left instructions for the courier to deliver the dispatch to him at the courthouse when it arrived. When Lane entered the courtroom with Matt and the two attorneys a short time later, she felt as if they were going into battle unarmed. She had given her lawyers Marigold's letter to Edra, but it was hardly proof of Matt's paternity.

The sight of Wolf at the plaintiff's table, looking for all the world like a respectable family man, sent her spirits plummeting. Until that moment she hadn't realized how much she'd been counting on Wolf's disreputable appearance to work in Matt's favor.

As Wolf sat in the witness chair later and told his version of the Annie story to Judge Stanyan, Lane could hardly believe he was the same crude, unkempt bullyboy who had twice accosted her. She fumed in silence as Wolf described himself as a loving parent whose cherished only child had been taken away, brainwashed and turned against her own father. He implied that his little girl had been made off with by uncaring outsiders for their own underhanded purposes.

Would the judge believe Wolf's self-portrait of a newly widowed father too grief stricken by the death of his wife to realize what was happening until his child was lost to him? If her memory of the wild man who had come after her with a knife weren't so vivid, she might have been able to evaluate him objectively. Did he really sound almost convincing? She couldn't deny that he looked and sounded decent enough.

Freshly shaved, his hair carefully styled, Wolf could pass for a middle-class Main Street citizen. Dressed in a good off-the-rack gray worsted suit, white shirt and diagonally striped navy-and-red tie, he looked almost benign. What frightened Lane most was that he even sounded the part of the person he pretended to be. Dear God, suppose he could pull it off?

She didn't have to look far to see who was responsible for the make-over—Hugo Maxwell, the gimlet-eyed attorney steering Wolf through a succession of carefully phrased questions.

Next to her at the witness table Matt sat tight-lipped. There was a sustained fury in his eyes that turned the blue to ice as the witness answered the questions put to him with an air of humble sincerity. Only when Matt's eyes met hers did the coldness in them melt for a moment.

At the defense table with Lane and Matt, Neal Roberts and Colby Strawn took notes while Lane kept turning an anxious eye to the door, willing a courier to appear with the DNA report. When the questioning ended, Judge Stanyan granted permission for the defense to cross-examine, and Roberts left the table to confront Wolf.

"Mr. Wilding, were you and your late wife living together at the time of her death?" Roberts asked.

Wolf's eyes sought his lawyer, uneasily. Maxwell jumped to his feet. "Your Honor, the question is irrelevant."

"In the light of Mr. Wilding's testimony implying a close family relationship, I think not, Mr. Maxwell," Judge Stanyan said. "The witness will answer the question."

Maxwell sat down, but Wolf's eyes still stared at him helplessly. The lawyer gave Wolf a look that plainly said Wolf was on his own. For a few seconds Wolf appeared to have lost his power of speech.

Finally the judge ordered sharply, "Answer the question."

"What . . . what do you want me to say?"

"I'd advise you to tell the truth, Mr. Wilding. Anything else is perjury, punishable by fine or imprisonment or both. Answer the question."

Wolf obeyed, reluctantly. "No," he said weakly with a pleading look at his attorney, who didn't appear pleased.

Roberts continued, "How long, prior to your wife's death, had it been since you'd seen your wife and child?"

There was a long pause.

"Three years," Wolf said finally. Maxwell glowered.

From his seat in the witness box, Wolf blurted out, low-voiced, "Goddamn it, Hugo . . ."

The judge banged his gavel. "Mr. Wilding, another outburst such as that and I shall find you in contempt of court. This is a domestic court, and although the procedure is somewhat less formal than Superior Court, this hearing will be conducted with proper respect. Any offender will be held accountable. You may proceed, Mr. Roberts."

At the defense table Lane's eyes met Matt's again. She saw in them a new look of hope that matched her own. But she also saw the lingering tension and remembered that even if Wolf destroyed his own eligibility as a suitable father, Matt was not home free. There was still the question of his own paternity to be resolved.

If Matt produced proof he was Annie's natural father, wouldn't the judge almost have to grant custody to him? Without the DNA report, their best hope was that Wolf would destroy himself on the witness stand. Otherwise, they were done for. All Matt had going for him at the moment was their marriage. At least *single* wouldn't be a factor.

If Wolf blew it, but by some quirk of fate the judge still chose not to grant custody of Annie to Matt, would Lane be allowed to adopt her? Would they let his wife give Annie, through their marriage, the father the judge had already denied her?

Finding small comfort in the bizarre scenario, Lane focused her attention back on Roberts as he continued to cross-examine Wolf. Gradually she began to take heart. Under Roberts's skillful questioning, Wolf unwittingly continued to destroy the artfully constructed persona his own lawyer had fashioned.

By the time Roberts was finished with him, glimpses of the sullen bully had begun to appear through Wolf's unctuous veneer.

When Roberts had returned to his seat, Judge Stanyan proceeded to question Wolf about the documents Hugo had submitted in evidence early in the hearing. Under the judge's evenhanded questioning, Wolf gradually eased back into the ingratiating manner that had served him earlier.

*And still no courier.*

The judge questioned Wolf at length, primarily about dates of his marriage and of the birth of Cheyenne, about where the events had taken place, and about the death of his wife. He listened to Wolf's explanation that his wife had used her "professional" name on the marriage certificate to protect her family from unwelcome publicity. This specious testimony strengthened Lane's long-held theory that Wolf had not known who Marigold really was until after she was dead.

Through with his own questioning, Judge Stanyan adjourned the hearing for lunch. The defense would present its case when court reconvened at one o'clock.

Motioning Wolf to follow, a grim-faced Hugo made for the door.

A SHORT TIME LATER, as she was about to emerge from the ladies' room, Lane heard a low, angry voice speaking in the hall. It sounded like Wolf's attorney, Hugo Maxwell. Disregarding her own counsel to Annie about eavesdropping, Lane stayed her steps.

"... screw up every time I don't put the words in your mouth," Hugo was saying. "And another thing, if you're going to lie, goddamn it, lie to the judge. Don't lie to me. You let me think Goldie was still with you when she died."

The voices grew fainter, and Lane peeked into the hallway. The two men were walking away.

About to emerge, she noticed that the pair had been stopped by a third man, who was partially screened by the other two. She watched curiously. Maxwell's back was to her, his head bent as he scribbled on a clipboard and handed it to the third man. He accepted an envelope in return and began to tear it open.

As the third man walked away, she recognized the short-sleeved summer uniform of a familiar messenger service. The courier? She started swiftly down the hall, bent on intercepting the man on his way out.

Bypassing Maxwell, now engrossed in the contents of the envelope, and Wolf, whose glazed eyes passed over her without recognition, she caught the man as he reached to press the down button of the elevator.

Keeping her voice low, she said, "I beg your pardon. That letter you just delivered, was it by any chance addressed to Colby Strawn?"

"Yeah, I lucked out. I stopped those guys to ask where I could find Strawn and one of them turned out to be him."

"I hate to be the one to disenchant you," Lane said, "but neither of those men is Colby Strawn."

"What?"

"The one over there reading Colby's mail is a lawyer named Maxwell. He has a case against Mr. Strawn in court today," Lane told him. "The other is Maxwell's client."

The courier eyed her uncertainly. "What do you want me to do about it?" he asked.

"Get it back. It's not his to read," she said.

The man hesitated, then turned and walked over to the two men, Lane following close behind.

"Hey, you! Give me back that letter," the courier demanded. "Unless you can prove you're Colby Strawn."

Maxwell looked up from the paper and for the first time seemed clearly aware that he and Wolf were not alone. He stood motionless as recognition dawned in his eyes. Savagely, he thrust the paper into the hands of the courier.

"Take the damn thing. It's no good to me." In a blaze of anger he turned, and for a moment Lane thought he was going to hit Wolf with one of his clenched fists.

"You son of a bitch," he snarled. "I should have known you lied. You're not the kid's father." In the next breath, he made for the stairs and was gone.

"Hugo? Hey! Where you going?" Wolf yelled, but the attorney didn't stop. Swearing bitterly, Wolf took off after him.

Folding the document back into the envelope, the courier said in a disgruntled voice, "I still don't know where to find the guy it's for."

"He's meeting my husband and me for lunch in a few minutes. I'd be glad to take it for you," Lane offered eagerly.

The courier hesitated, tempted, then shook his head. "Naw. I'd better not."

"Then leave it at the judge's office," Lane said. "The clerk will sign for it and see that Mr. Strawn gets it when court reconvenes this afternoon."

WHEN JUDGE STANYAN entered the hearing room for the afternoon, Wolf sat alone at the plaintiff's table, nervously watching the door. At the defense table sat Matt and Lane, Roberts and Strawn.

The judge tapped his gavel for attention. "Mr. Wilding, where is your attorney, Mr. Maxwell?"

"He didn't say where he was going. He's supposed to be here," Wolf said, his agitation apparent.

A minute ticked by. The judge summoned the bailiff.

"Go out there and see if you can find what's become of Mr. Maxwell and tell him to get in here," he ordered and marched back to his chambers, robe flying.

A long minute of silence was broken by the sound of a siren and an ambulance racing down some nearby street. A clerk from the court's office entered to summon Colby Strawn to the telephone. The clock ticked on.

Lane watched Wolf at the table across the room with a kind of fascination. The transformation that had caused her apprehension that morning seemed gradually to be reversing itself. The gray worsted suit somehow seemed not to fit him so well. There was a spot of catsup on his shirtfront. The collar and tie were awry. A faint shadow of a beard now gave his face an unwashed, brutish look. His eyes, which turned repeatedly toward the door, had taken on a look of growing unease.

Suddenly, out of the silence, Wolf spoke up. Lane at first thought he was talking aloud to himself. Then she realized he was addressing one or another of those seated at the defense table.

"Don't think I'm not wise to your game," Wolf said darkly, his eyes fixing finally on Matt. "You went and looked up old man Fairchild's will. You know Annie's going to get half his estate by right of—" he looked around, as if for help from the missing Hugo "—whatever. You want to get yourself made guardian of the kid so you can get your hands on all that bread."

"So *that's* why he wants custody of Annie," Lane said quietly to Matt and Neal. "I never thought of that. I just assumed that since Mr. Fairchild died without ever knowing Marigold had had a child, there'd be nothing in it for Annie."

Matt looked none too happy at the development. Turning to Roberts, he said, "If Judge Stanyan decides I am Cheyenne's father, you'll have to arrange to put the inheritance in a trust where nobody can touch it until she's old enough to take the responsibility for it herself."

Wolf, who had slumped in his chair after his outburst, suddenly jumped to his feet and started for the courtroom door, muttering something about going to look for

Hugo. He slammed out, banging the door behind him, just as Colby came back through the other door, looking immensely pleased.

With a glance around the courtroom, where only Lane and Matt and Neal Roberts remained, Colby eased himself into his seat at the defense table.

"Did you pick up the DNA report while you were in the office?" Lane asked anxiously.

Drawing the envelope from an inside pocket, Colby handed it to Matt to examine. "Congratulations," he said. "You are a father."

The return of the bailiff, signaling the judge's imminent arrival, steered Colby in another direction.

"There's more good news, but I've got to talk fast," he said. "The phone call was from Mike Kuhn, the investigator we hired to check out Wilding. Wolf's got a criminal record, all right. He's been in prison on a narcotics conviction and he's out on parole. He's been reporting regularly to his parole officer, but now there's a warrant for his arrest from California. Our Susan Craddock has finally mustered enough gumption to file a complaint against him for robbery, threatened assault with a deadly weapon, etc., etc."

"Well, bully for Susan," Lane said.

"Mike tells me there will be officers to pick him up on parole violation when he walks out of the courthouse," Colby added.

"Apart from keeping all of us in a state of turmoil and going after Lane with a switchblade, what's he done to violate his parole?" Matt asked acidly.

With a shiver Lane thought, *Oh, yes. The knife.* She hadn't thought of it since she'd turned it over to the local police.

"The knife should come in handy if they ever get him back to California," Colby said. "Right now the narcotics people are interested in him. And he's traveled outside his parole area several times. That alone is enough to send him back to prison."

He broke off as Judge Stanyan entered and took his place at the bench, scowling down on the court, his eyes flashing the fire of a short-tempered man as the bailiff approached the bench.

"Your Honor, they're both gone," the bailiff said.

Raising his eyes to scan the courtroom, the judge apparently noticed for the first time that Wolf, too, was missing.

"There were two officers waiting outside for Wilding, and they took him away, Your Honor." The bailiff continued, "Maxwell is not anywhere on the premises. It's hard to say when he'll be back."

"It's unlikely we'll see him again," the judge said. "I just had a computer check run on him. He's not licensed to practice law. It's reasonable to assume he got cold feet."

Turning back to the three remaining litigants, he said snappishly, "Let us proceed.

"In the matter of the paternity petition filed by Mr. Roberts on behalf of Mr. Cheney..." he began. He paused, his expression softening. "Perhaps we can facilitate the process by dispensing with some of the strictures. I believe we can accomplish what we're here for by an informal dialogue between Mr. Cheney and myself, if that is agreeable to Mr. Cheney's attorneys."

Roberts looked at Colby. Colby nodded, and when Matt signaled his agreement, Colby hoisted himself out of his chair to address Judge Stanyan.

"Your Honor, I have here the results of blood tests from samples taken from Mr. Cheney and the child, Cheyenne, which I should like to submit to the court."

Accepting the document from Colby, the judge took some time to study it carefully before turning his attention to Matt.

"This DNA report leaves no doubt that you are the child's natural father, Mr. Cheney," he said. "However, since the tests were performed by laboratories not under this court's certification, I shall have to ask you to repeat the testing at a court-approved laboratory at your earliest convenience."

"Yes, Your Honor," Matt said.

"I shall want to have a talk with Cheyenne after I have talked with her father," the judge continued. "I see she is not in the courtroom. Can you get her here within the hour?"

"I'm sure I can. She's with an old family friend a few miles away, Your Honor," Matt replied. "We'll have to arrange to have her brought here."

"Mrs. Cheney, you may be excused to go get the child," the judge said, turning toward Lane.

Lane would have given almost anything to hear the exchange between Matt and the judge, but she couldn't see herself protesting to the testy man on the bench. Rising slowly to her feet, she cast a helpless glance at Matt, but his attention was fixed on the judge.

"Now, Mr. Cheney, please tell me in your own words about the background of your paternity," Judge Stanan began. "Tell me what you can about you and the mother at the time the child was conceived...."

They were the last words Lane heard him say as she closed the courtroom door behind her and set out to get Annie.

EAGER TO GET BACK to the hearing room, Lane kept a heavy foot on the gas pedal and chafed against the summer tourist traffic as she cruised along the highway in Matt's Taurus. She was missing the opportunity of a lifetime to hear the whole true story of Matt's relationship with Marigold.

*All I ever wanted to know and will always be afraid to ask,* she thought wryly. But as she reached the crossroad that obliged her to slow down for the right-angle turn that pointed her toward Matt's house, her thinking changed direction, as well.

In her heart she knew that Matt must be going through hell back there in the hearing room, telling a total stranger all the secrets of that summer, answering every probing question, no matter how intimate.

What satisfaction had she imagined to get out of hearing Matt's disclosures about a personal and private passage from his past? Looking at it from Matt's viewpoint, she felt ashamed.

ANNIE AND CORA had just come back to the house from a picnic on the beach when Lane arrived. Annie looked a trifle wind tossed and pink in spite of an enormous straw hat that sheltered her from the sun.

"Shouldn't you take her home and get her a little more dressed up?" Cora asked anxiously when Lane had explained her mission.

Lane surveyed the child critically for a moment and shook her head.

"This is our Annie, the way she really is," Lane said "We'll give her a quick brushup to get rid of the sand and then we'll be on our way."

The day in court had been explained to Cheyenne in vague terms centering on their wish to be free from

Wolf's harassment, and Annie had accepted that. Now, as Lane got into the car for the return trip, it was all she could do to keep from telling the little girl that Matt was her father. A sense of fair play told her it was not her news to tell. That, and an almost superstitious fear of planting in Annie a seed of hope before the fact was unequivocally confirmed by the court.

But there was still something she could safely tell Annie that would bring joy to the child's heart.

"I have good news for you, Annie," she said as she turned the car onto the highway. "We know now for sure that Wolf is not your father. The report on your blood test came this morning."

For a moment Annie was still. Then she let out a great, trembling sigh. "That's one of the goodest things anyone ever told me, Lane," she said soberly. Scooting down in her seat, she retreated into a thoughtful silence.

After a while she said, "Could I get something like maybe a license or a credit card I could carry around and show people so they'll know it's true? Can I have another name?"

"Name? I thought you liked Cheyenne," said Lane.

"Not Cheyenne," Annie said. "The other one. The one I never say."

"Oh. I see," Lane said helplessly. "We'll have to wait and see about that."

They rode the rest of the way in silence until they reached the parking lot behind the courthouse. When the car came to a stop, Annie put aside her inner communion to ask a purely pragmatic question. "What's the judge going to say to me, Lane?"

"I don't know, Cheyenne," Lane said truthfully. "He'll probably ask you about how we live and what we do and how you feel about Matt and me. Things like that, I imagine.''

"What do you want me to tell him, Lane?" Annie asked anxiously, clearly willing to throw herself on a sword for them.

"Just tell him the truth, love. Whatever feels right to you."

MATT AND THE TWO attorneys were still sitting at the defense table when Lane and Annie came into the hearing room. The judge had withdrawn to his chambers. The clerk went to summon him as they came in.

Annie walked up the aisle of the courtroom to where Matt was sitting. He reached to pull her to him and place a kiss on the top of her blond head. The stress of the ordeal he'd just been through lay like a shadow across his face as he rose and pulled Lane and Annie into his arms.

Lane looked up to see that Judge Stanyan had emerged from his chambers and was heading straight for Annie. She nudged Matt with her foot.

Cheyenne gazed wide-eyed at the judge as he crossed the courtroom and stood looking down on her.

"How do you do, young lady?" he said. "You must be Cheyenne." Lane heard an unexpected kindliness in the gravel of his voice.

"Yes, I am," Annie replied formally. "I guess you're the judge. The way you're dressed you look like a king, kinda."

To Lane's astonishment and relief, she saw a smile play across Stanyan's austere features.

Turning to the two attorneys, he said, "Cheyenne and I are going to visit a while in my chambers. If you gentlemen have more pressing matters elsewhere, you may consider the proceedings adjourned. We will meet in my chambers tomorrow at eleven and finalize the matter." He turned to the spellbound child. "Now, Cheyenne, if you will come with me, please?"

Annie hesitated and looked to Lane and Matt questioningly. When they nodded assent, she walked trustingly away with the judge.

"Thank you, gentlemen," Matt said to the departing attorneys. "We'll be talking to you again tomorrow."

"Before I leave, what about the adoption, Lane? Do you want me to have it dismissed?" Roberts asked.

The adoption had been on Lane's mind, but uncertain how Matt would react if she brought up the subject, she'd said nothing. When she was slow to answer, Matt spoke up.

"Unless Lane has other thoughts, I suggest you follow through on the adoption," he said. "It's only right that Annie should have a bona fide mother as well as a father."

Oblivious to her surroundings, Lane caught Matt around the neck and gave him a heartfelt kiss.

ALONE in the courtroom, Lane and Matt waited nervously for the judge to deliver their child. Waiting, they began to plan for the future—something they had never dared do before. At the top of their list were questions such as where they should live. Both had a fondness for the roomy old farmhouse. Both wanted to keep the beach house for vacationing and for Cora. Having proved to himself that business and domesticity functioned poorly under the same roof, Matt decided to rent office space in the village to carry on his responsibilities for Cheney, McCrae.

As time moved on they lapsed into a moment of silence, exploring thoughts that took shape in their minds.

"You told me once that you hoped someday to buy your aunt's share in the farm," Matt ventured after a while. "Do you think she's ready to sell?"

Lane darted him a curious glance. "Yes, if only to keep her son happy. Howard won't rest easy until his mother's money is in T-bonds, but it'll be a few years yet before I can afford to buy her out. My big worry is that in the meantime Howard may find her a buyer who wants to farm, and I'll be saddled with a partner who has other ideas on how to run a farm like ours."

"Would I do?"

"You?" She laughed. "You don't know the first thing about running either a farm or a produce market."

"Exactly. You'd never have to worry that I'd try to muscle in. Or have you some objection to your partner being your spouse instead of your aunt?"

The thought that Matt would consider investing in her struggling venture had never entered Lane's mind.

"You can't be serious!" But she saw in his eyes that he was. Her own eyes misted, and she felt a puff of solemn pride. *He believed in her.*

"I think it would be perfect," she said, her voice breaking in a trill of emotion. "Welcome aboard."

"God, how I wish I hadn't wasted so much time getting here," Matt said after a moment.

Reaching for his hand, Lane pressed it against her cheek.

"Dear Matt, if you're sorry about the Marigold part don't be. Without Marigold, we would have no Annie."

TIME PASSED. At last the door to the judge's chambers opened and the judge came out. Tall, white haired, craggy of face, his formidable presence almost obscured the small towheaded figure who marched sturdily at his side. Her back as straight as a grape stake, she walked with a new dignity, pacing herself to the man's stride by taking two steps to his one. Lane felt a breath of fear at the gravity in the heart-shaped face.

With Matt she rose and stepped away from the table to await the little girl and the imposing man as they crossed the judicial platform and stepped down to the courtroom floor like marchers in a ceremonial drill.

Where was their scrappy little hop-skip-and-a-jump Annie? What had the judge said to Cheyenne that had robbed her of her ebullience? Lane glanced away to see Matt's reaction. When she looked again, she realized how wrong her first assessment had been. Annie's eyes were as bright as two new stars, and she looked as if she were about to burst with excitement.

The judge paused and lowered his head to say something to the child. Lane saw her look up at him uncertainly, then turn her eyes to Lane and Matt. She hesitated and looked at the judge again with hopeful, questioning eyes. Laying a hand on her shoulder, he sent the little girl scurrying across the courtroom to Lane and Matt. In a valiant effort to hug them both at the same time, she threw herself upon them. Giving up, she wrapped both arms around Lane's waist.

"I *belong*." The muffled word came from somewhere around Lane's midriff where Annie had buried her head.

With one hand still gripping Lane's, Annie reached to slip her other hand into Matt's. "He said, 'Your father and mother are waiting for you.' *My father and mother. He meant you.*" Annie hesitated, then asked cautiously, "Is that okay?"

*Say yes. Say yes,* the blue eyes pleaded. It was a look Lane had seen in Annie's eyes before, but never had it held such poignancy. Lane longed to reassure the child, but her voice broke and the words couldn't get out past the lump in her throat. Matt spoke for them both.

"Welcome home, Annie," he said. "It's more than okay. It's the best. We've been waiting for you all your life."

Judge Stanyan, watching from nearby, came forward to extend a hand to Lane and Matt.

"Whatever you're doing must be all right," he said. "She's a wonderful little girl. The three of you will make a fine family."

Lane's eyes met Matt's. She saw in them a reflection of her own dream of family—the kind of together family she had longed for all her life, the kind neither she nor Matt nor Annie had ever known. It was theirs now, their dream, to take and make come true.

For a moment their eyes shared the question, knew the answer, made a vow.

In the solemnity of commitment they were aware only of each other until the voice of the judge intruded.

"It's been a pleasure making your acquaintance, Cheyenne Cheney," Judge Stanyan was saying. Taking her small hand in his large one, he shook it gravely before he turned and walked away to his chambers.

Saucer-eyed, Annie watched him go. When the door closed behind him she looked up at Lane and Matt and heaved a sigh of satisfaction that seemed to come from all the way down in her toes.

"Cheney," she said softly. "Cheyenne Cheney. Wow. That's a pretty neat name."

# HARLEQUIN SUPERROMANCE®

## A PLACE IN HER HEART...

Somewhere deep in the heart of every grown woman is the little girl she used to be....

In September, October and November 1992, the world of childhood and the world of love collide in six very special romance titles. Follow these six special heroines as they discover the sometimes heart-wrenching, always heartwarming joy of being a Big Sister.

Written by six of your favorite Superromance authors, these compelling and emotionally satisfying romantic stories will earn a place in your heart!

SEPTEMBER 1992

#514   NOTHING BUT TROUBLE—Sandra James
#515   ONE TO ONE—Marisa Carroll

OCTOBER 1992

#518   OUT ON A LIMB—Sally Bradford
#519   STAR SONG—Sandra Canfield

NOVEMBER 1992

#522   JUST BETWEEN US—Debbi Bedford
#523   MAKE-BELIEVE—Emma Merritt

## AVAILABLE WHEREVER
## HARLEQUIN SUPERROMANCE
## BOOKS ARE SOLD

*Harlequin Superromance*®

## Come to where the West is still wild in a summer trilogy by Margot Dalton

**Sunflower** (#502—June 1992)
Robin Baldwin becomes the half owner of a prize
rodeo horse. But to take possession, she has to travel
the rodeo circuit with cowboy Matt Adams, living
with him in *very* close quarters!

**Tumbleweed** (#508—July 1992)
Until she met Scott Freeman, Lyle Callander was about
as likely to settle in one spot as tumbleweed in a
windstorm. But who *is* Scott? He's more than the
simple photographer he claims to be . . . much more.

**Juniper** (#511—August 1992)
Devil-may-care Buck Buchanan can ride a bucking
bronco or a Brahma bull. But can he win Claire
Tremaine, a woman who sets his heart on fire but
keeps her own as cold as ice?

**"I just finished reading *Under Prairie Skies* by
Margo Dalton and had to hide my tears from my
children. I loved it!"**      —A reader

# JAYNE ANN KRENTZ

A two-part epic tale from one of today's most popular romance novelists!

## Dreams
### Parts One & Two

*The warrior died at her feet, his blood running out of the cave entrance and mingling with the waterfall. With his last breath he cursed the woman— told her that her spirit would remain chained in the cave forever until a child was created and born there....*

So goes the ancient legend of the Chained Lady and the curse that bound her throughout the ages—until destiny brought Diana Prentice and Colby Savager together under the influence of forces beyond their understanding. Suddenly they were both haunted by dreams that linked past and present, while their waking hours were filled with danger. Only when Colby, Diana's modern-day warrior, learned to love, could those dark forces be vanquished. Only then could Diana set the Chained Lady free....

# WELCOME TO

**The quintessential small town, where everyone knows everybody else!**

Finally, books that capture the pleasure of tuning in to your favorite TV show!

## GREAT READING...GREAT SAVINGS...AND A FABULOUS FREE GIFT!

Each book set in Tyler is a self-contained love story; together, the twelve novels stitch the fabric of the community. The covers honor the old American tradition of quilting; each cover depicts a patch of the large Tyler quilt.

With Tyler you can receive a fabulous gift, ABSOLUTELY FREE, by collecting proofs-of-purchase found in each Tyler book. And use our special Tyler coupons to save on your next TYLER book purchase.

Join your friends at Tyler for the seventh book, ARROWPOINT by Suzanne Ellison, available in September.

*Rumors fly about the death at the old lodge! What happens when Renata Meyer finds an ancient Indian sitting cross-legged on her lawn?*